STARSH
MAGE

A DARKER
MAGIC

BOOK TEN
OF THE STARSHIP'S MAGE SERIES

All rights reserved. For information about permission to reproduce selections from this book, contact the publisher at info@faolanspen.com or Faolan's Pen Publishing Inc., 22 King St. S, Suite 300, Waterloo, Ontario N2J 1N8, Canada.

This is a work of fiction. All the characters and events portrayed in this book are fictional, and any resemblance to any persons living or dead is purely coincidental.

This edition published in 2021 by:
Faolan's Pen Publishing Inc.
22 King St. S, Suite 300
Waterloo, Ontario
N2J 1N8 Canada

ISBN-13: 978-1-989674-14-7 (print)

A record of this book is available from Library and Archives Canada.

Printed in the United States of America
1 2 3 4 5 6 7 8 9 10
First edition
First printing: March 2021

Illustration © 2021 Jeff Brown Graphics
Faolan's Pen Publishing logo is a trademark of Faolan's Pen Publishing Inc.
Read more books from Glynn Stewart at faolanspen.com

STARSHIP'S
MAGE

A DARKER
MAGIC

BOOK TEN
OF THE STARSHIP'S MAGE SERIES

GLYNN STEWART

FAOLAN'S PEN
PUBLISHING
faolanspen.com

CHAPTER 1

THE MOUNTAIN deserved the capitals. If nothing else, Olympus Mons remained one of the largest mountains in the Solar System, its peak rising well above Mars's magically terraformed atmosphere. Beyond that, though, its slopes were girdled with a city of millions of souls, the bureaucrats, administrators and leaders who managed both the Kingdom of Mars and the Protectorate of the Mage-Queen of Mars.

Over a hundred inhabited planets hailed to the Mage-Queen of Mars and the Mountain she ruled from. Those millions of administrators supported hundreds of thousands *more* who lived inside the Mountain itself, in hundreds of kilometers of rune-encrusted tunnels and century-old geothermal power generator equipment.

Mage-Lieutenant Commander Roslyn Chambers had never even entered the regular tunnels, let alone the more heavily secured chambers and caverns higher up the slopes where the Royal Family lived. But her ship was in orbit, undergoing a minor refit, and her long-standing relationship with the Prince-Regent had resulted in an invitation many officers of the Royal Martian Navy would kill for.

"Afternoon, Lieutenant Commander Chambers," the red-armored Royal Guard reviewing the invite told her. "You're expected, of course."

The veteran Combat Mage, one of the elite who protected the Mage-Queen herself, grinned down at her from his exosuit battle armor. The armor's helmet was slung over the man's shoulder, a sign of the trust he was showing the black-uniformed blonde Mage.

"You wouldn't have made it *nearly* this far if you weren't," he concluded. "He's waiting for you, but be warned: he's a tad distracted right now. This *is* a social invite."

"I wasn't sure," Roslyn admitted. "Guard-Captain...Romanov, is it?"

"Denis Romanov, yes," the dark-haired Guard confirmed. He was maybe ten years older than Roslyn's own early twenties and attractive—in an intimidating way. "I head the Prince-Regent's security. And like I said, Commander, he's waiting for you. Just be ready for babies and kittens."

That was all the warning Roslyn got before Romanov tapped a command. The armored hatch slid aside to reveal the mountainside office of the Prince-Regent of Mars, His Excellency Damien Montgomery.

Even after repeated encounters over the last six years and continued communication, Roslyn was still shocked by how short Montgomery was. She was far from a tall woman, but she towered over his hundred and fifty centimeters.

She had *enough* warning, as it turned out, to spot a black kitten barely bigger than her hand making a dash for the door. She couldn't have caught it with her hands—but Roslyn Chambers was a fully trained Jump and Combat Mage of the Royal Martian Navy.

Catching a hundred-and-fifty-gram kitten with magic and lifting the animal to her shoulder was easy enough—and earned her a chuckle from the room's main occupant.

An occupant who, she now realized, had been prevented from containing the kitten by the baby he was holding on his lap. The small, dark-haired man's hands were covered in gloves to hide an old injury, but he was still able to keep an arm wrapped around his daughter.

"I'm not sure that getting kittens for babies who barely crawl is a great plan," the second-in-line to the throne in the Mountain told Roslyn. "But I was overruled."

"He's getting used to it," the other adult occupant of the room observed with a chuckle of her own.

Roslyn registered the baby on the other woman's knee first—and *then* registered who the slimly gorgeous twenty-year-old redhead had to be.

"Your Majesty!" she gasped, dropping to one knee in front of Kiera Michelle Alexander, the Mage-Queen of Mars.

"This is a social occasion," the Queen told her sharply. "Get the fuck up."

The Mage obeyed swiftly, the kitten somehow managing to maintain its balance and purr into her ear.

"When a junior officer of the Mage-Queen's Navy gets an invite to dinner with the Prince-Regent, she doesn't *assume* it's actually social," she admitted.

"Told you," Montgomery muttered. "You haven't met my daughters, have you, Roslyn?"

"I've seen pictures," Roslyn replied. She looked at the two chubby girls and wished she was good enough with babies to tell them apart. "Jessica and Samantha, yes?"

"*Princesses* Jessica and Samantha McLaughlin," Alexander added, but a chuckle undermined any heat to her correction.

"Grab a chair, Roslyn," Montgomery instructed. "Watch out; there is another kitten around here somewhere. Persephone was grooming Charon last I saw him—and you've met Nyx."

The office held a massive desk against one wall, but there was a large open space for meetings and similar as well. That space had a section of transmuted transparent metal forming a wall, allowing them to look out over the city.

It had been the Mage-King's office before. Now it was the Prince-Regent's—and in another year, it would be the Mage-*Queen's* office when she ascended the throne in her own right.

Roslyn pulled a chair onto the rug, realizing there were just the three adults in the room.

"No Admiral McLaughlin?" she asked.

"Grace is about three-quarters of the way back to Sherwood right now," Montgomery told her. "She can only spend so much time here— she almost missed the girls' *birth*, which seems like it would have created some interesting complaints later on!"

Grace McLaughlin was Montgomery's partner and the mother of the twin girls. Roslyn had expected her for a social event—and *not* the Queen, which made her suspicious.

"So, there are guards at the door and we're in one of the most secure offices in the Protectorate," she said slowly. "I'm not seeing tea or dinner anywhere yet, and the only people in the room are the rulers of the Protectorate, a pair of babies and me.

"Why do I think this is not just a social invitation?"

"Told you," Montgomery repeated, making a vague gesture toward the Queen. "I didn't end up recruiting her for illegal special ops as a seventeen-year-old because she was stupid."

That recruitment had allowed Roslyn to get into the Royal Martian Navy *despite* a teenage conviction for vandalism and grand theft auto. Helping out the Hands of the Mage-King—specially authorized troubleshooters like Montgomery had been then—covered for a lot of sins.

"There will be a dinner in about an hour, yes," Alexander said quietly. "And it will be a purely social event with a number of other people, many of whom lack the clearances present in this room.

"Despite your junior rank, you're one of the few people in the Protectorate fully cleared on the Rune Wrights," the Queen noted. "That means we can tap you for the problem that has come up without having to brief someone *else*."

Roslyn inhaled sharply, then forced herself to relax and pet the kitten still purring on her shoulder. She'd served as Flag Lieutenant to the Mage-Queen's aunt, the current Crown Princess, Mage-Admiral Jane Alexander.

Like the Mage-Queen and Damien Montgomery, Jane Alexander was a Rune Wright: one of the rare Mages who could *see* magic as well as wield it. It gave them many unique gifts, but most important was the ability to create Runes of Power and augment their own strength far beyond any other Mage.

"I would prefer not to be pulled from *Song of the Huntress*," Roslyn admitted. "But I am yours to command. That is my duty."

She was the tactical officer on the destroyer *Song of the Huntress*. She'd held that role for two years, since being promoted to Lieutenant Commander after saving Jane Alexander's life.

"We won't be moving you from *Huntress*," Montgomery told her. "We've made arrangements for *Huntress* to be assigned where we need you. Mage-Captain Daalman will be receiving her new orders tomorrow."

"I see," Rolsyn said. "What do you need of me?"

"First, we need to brief you on one of the bits of ugliness about the Republic we *haven't* talked about," Alexander said grimly. "We've been open about a lot of what was going on with Project Prometheus and Dr. Samuel Finley, but we've kept some secrets still."

Roslyn stopped petting the kitten, earning her a disgruntled squeak as she looked down at the floor. The Republic had been a group of worlds that had seceded from the Protectorate to "escape from the domination of the Mages."

Since the Mages were the key to interstellar travel, they'd needed a new solution. Their answer had been Project Prometheus: where thousands of Mages had been murdered and their brains used as the core for a pseudo-technological jump drive.

And Dr. Samuel Finley had been the architect of that project.

"Finley is dead, isn't he?" she asked carefully. Nyx batted at her ear and she pulled the kitten back into her lap.

"Oh, he's dead," Damien said grimly. "I saw one of our ex-Republic agent allies put two through his skull myself. What we *haven't* told anyone is that he was a Rune Wright."

Roslyn nodded slowly. She still wasn't petting the kitten, and with one final disgruntled mew, the animal jumped back onto the floor and set off in pursuit of her sibling.

"I see potential problems there, I suppose," she allowed. "But he *is* dead, so..."

"We've been digging through the Republic's files for two years," Alexander noted. "But even a mere three years of a mostly functional governmental, military and research infrastructure produces a *lot* of files.

"We focused on Project Prometheus and some of the related research projects early on. But there were a few detached projects that we didn't identify until recently."

"The Martian Interstellar Security Service now believes that Finley was running a network of covert labs that the Republic wasn't fully aware of," Montgomery said. "He was basically defrauding the Republic to pay for it, so it was well concealed even in their files."

"I didn't meet him," Roslyn said slowly, "but given what he publicly got up to for the Republic, that seems...dangerous."

"We agree," the Mage-Queen told her. "*Song of the Huntress* is being sent to the Sorprendidas System. It's a Fringe star system that only saw stealth scouts from our side in the war. They weren't really involved in anything, though Sorprendidan personnel served in the Republic Interstellar Navy."

"MISS sent several agents to investigate the data we had on the lab," Montgomery told her. "All of them have stopped reporting in. They wouldn't have had Link access, so it's possible they just lost access to their communication networks, but we..." He shook his head. "We're assuming they're KIA.

"Your job is to find them if you can, find whatever breadcrumbs they left behind if you can't. Locate the lab, assess the threat level and *neutralize* it if the threat is unacceptable."

"Damien wanted to read in all of *Huntress*'s senior officers," Alexander noted. "MISS wanted to keep the whole thing under wraps— and the Rune Wright factor argues in their favor.

"You will be authorized to brief Captain Daalman if you feel it necessary, but you will also carry a Warrant of Our Voice," the Mage-Queen said firmly. "If necessary, you will use that Voice to assume command of all Protectorate resources in the system to do what you deem fit.

"We do not believe the laboratory will present that much of a threat, but...we do know that at least two of Finley's Mages are there. Those people are war criminals, Lieutenant Commander Chambers. They must be brought to justice."

"And the irony inherent in that the worst criminals of the war are *Mages* is not lost on us," Montgomery said, his tone grim. "It leaves us with no choice but to see them caught and punished, otherwise the promises we made to *end* the war become hollow at best."

A Warrant. Roslyn shivered. A Warrant of the Mage-Queen's Voice meant that Roslyn would speak with the Mage-Queen's full authority for the duration and scope of her mission.

"That is...a lot," she said quietly. "Are we sure this lab requires it?"

"No," Montgomery allowed. "But four MISS agents are missing or dead. The system has turned into a black hole for our operatives—and we owe it to them to find out what's going on.

"And we owe it to everyone Samuel Finley and his people killed to make sure that his *assistants* are brought to justice. That is your primary mission. But, given the potential threat inherent in a Rune Wright's secret projects...we want you to be ready for anything."

"I am an officer of the Royal Martian Navy," Roslyn said. "I serve at Your Majesty's will. I'm not sure I'm the best choice for this, but I will do what I can."

"I think you're a perfect choice for this," Alexander told her. "You have Montgomery's complete trust and mine. Find our missing people, Commander. And find the bastards who betrayed their blood for money and power."

"As you wish, Your Majesty."

CHAPTER 2

SONG OF THE HUNTRESS was basically a brand-new ship. The new *Bard of Winter*-class destroyers had been designed during the war against the Republic of Faith and Reason and laid down afterward, as the Protectorate had realized the many weaknesses of its warship design.

The UnArcana Rebellions had been the first actual war the Protectorate had ever fought, after all. The *Bards of Winter* had been the second of the new "escort" destroyer classes built, designed from the keel out to carry the new generations of missiles and even more of the RMN's rapid-fire laser anti-missile turrets.

Roslyn was junior enough that the new design didn't look *completely* off to her, but she'd served on enough ships to be extremely used to the standard design of a Martian warship: a massive spacegoing pyramid, built to maximize engine area and point all of the weaponry forward.

Her shuttle took her around the destroyer, allowing her to examine the ship from the outside and smile at its odd-seeming appearance. The *Bard*-class ships had the same hundred-meter square-based pyramid as the older destroyers, but they now had an inverted skirt made up of the bottom twenty meters of a second pyramid. They gave up some of the massive surface area of the base of the pyramid but expanded the volume of the ship and provided mountings for more than the most basic weapons pointing behind the ship.

The Royal Martian Navy had learned that sometimes, even *they* had to run away.

"We're on final approach, sir," the pilot informed her. "Clearance from the landing bay. Captain Daalman says, 'Welcome home.'"

Roslyn smiled and nodded her acknowledgement of the courtesy. Like her examination of the ship she'd lived on for twelve months, it helped distract her from the buzzing hive of bees in her stomach.

There were another two dozen people on the shuttle, the last of *Huntress*'s crew returning from liberty, but Roslyn's attention was focused on the small bag of personal items at her feet. Buried in the middle of that bag, wrapped in a black silk negligee she didn't expect to use—retail therapy was still reassuring and very few people were going to poke at the tactical officer's lingerie—was a plain manila envelope containing a standard datachip and a sheet of archaic parchment.

Both bore the crowned-mountain seal of the Protectorate, and both said the same thing: for the duration of their mission to Sorprendidas, Mage-Lieutenant Commander Roslyn Chambers spoke with the Voice of the Mage-Queen of Mars.

That was stunning. Roslyn knew that she was a protégée of both the Prince-Regent and the Crown Princess, for a number of reasons and in a number of ways, but to carry a Royal Warrant was a far heavier weight than she was ready for.

But she was an officer of the Mage-Queen of Mars. She would do what she was called to do. What terrified her was *why* she carried the Warrant. Secret labs run by rogue Mages, built by the *Rune Wright* psychopath who'd created the Republic's Prometheus Interface?

That was taking some digesting, even before she tried to accept that *she* had been tasked to deal with it—and to keep it secret.

All of that was a messy set of problems that kept her trying and failing to distract herself. There wasn't much she could do about any of it until they reached Sorprendidas.

When Roslyn spotted the dark-eyed blond man standing by the off-loading ramp, she initially glanced around to see if there were new officers among the other passengers of her shuttle. The only other officer was a Lieutenant from Engineering she already knew, so the executive officer wasn't meeting a new arrival.

"Mage-Commander Kristofferson," she greeted the XO. He beat her to saluting by half a second. That was one of the oddities of her position: after two years, she was no longer one of the ten youngest Lieutenant Commanders in the Fleet—she was now the *twelfth*-youngest—but she was also one of seven living holders of the Mage-Queen's Ruby Medal of Valor.

That meant she'd been awarded the Medal *twice*—once for rising to act as tactical officer of a destroyer on her cadet cruise, and once for rescuing the Crown Princess Mage-Admiral Alexander from Republic captivity.

"Mage-Lieutenant Commander Chambers," Yaakov Kristofferson returned her greeting. "Welcome home. How was your leave?"

"Mars has friends but no family," Roslyn said after a moment's thought. "Even assuming they keep coming, I'm not sure I'll *ever* get used to social invites to the Mountain."

Her boss laughed.

"Kvetch, kvetch," he told her. "Not many people saved the life of the Mage-Queen's aunt. I imagine you're popular around here."

Roslyn stepped out of the way of the other passengers and shook her head at Kristofferson.

"I vaguely understand it," she conceded. "Anything come up while I was gone?"

The XO wouldn't have taken time out of his day to meet the tactical officer without a reason.

"Yes," he conceded. "Real tsuris."

She glared at him. Nobody *else* on the ship spoke Yiddish that she was aware of. Roslyn could fumble her way through Mandarin Chinese if she had to, but she only really spoke English.

"We had a problem with the missile launcher software," he said more grimly. "They had to completely wipe and reboot everything, and now you have a brand-new tactical operations system."

Roslyn winced. That was...not great. It wouldn't be the end of the world—at this point, she and her people spoke fluent warship, and there were only so many ways to set up a TOS, but switching without planning for it was a pain.

"Thanks for the heads-up," she told him. "I presume MarShips sent us training documents for the new mess?"

"We are the seventh lucky prototypers for version seventy-eight," Kristofferson told her. "That means the documentation is fragmentary at best and part of your job will be to build the software techs' tutorials into something the Navy can use."

"I see," Roslyn said. "It sounds like I need to get back to work ASAP."

The Martian Department of Ship Design was usually better than that, but she guessed *someone* had to write the tutorials MarShips usually sent out with software updates.

"Sorry, I know it's always better to ease back into things after two weeks' leave," Kristofferson told her. "But they sold Captain Daalman on it being the fastest way to get our missile launchers back and, well, the skipper wasn't impressed with losing our main offensive firepower."

"I get it," Roslyn said. If Mage-Captain Laura Daalman had signed off on the changeover, she didn't even get to complain much. Unlike prior generations of Royal Martian Navy warships, *Song of the Huntress* might have a Link quantum-entanglement communicator...but her Captain was still very much her master after God.

"Lieutenant Jordan will be back tomorrow," the XO noted. "Lieutenant Samuels *should* have been back this morning, but she was in a groundcar accident on the way to the spaceport."

"Is she okay?" Roslyn asked. "Why am I only hearing now?"

Mage-Lieutenants Semele Jordan and Kirtida Samuels were her two subordinate officers. Both did double duty as Jump Mages and had the same mixed ethnicity as Roslyn and Kristofferson.

"You were already on the shuttle when we got the update," Kristofferson told her. "This was the first opportunity I had to tell you. She got hit with some bad whiplash and is undergoing soft-tissue treatment in Curiosity City. She should be back aboard in three days."

Roslyn sighed and nodded her thanks. She'd check in on Samuels anyway. While the XO had overall responsibility for everyone aboard the ship, Roslyn was responsible for her tactical department.

"Your Chiefs have already had a first crack at the software, so while I refuse to micromanage, I *will* tell you to check in with them," he concluded. "If you need anything—help, access to the MarShips techs who coded the damn thing, *anything*—let me know.

"Last rumor I heard had us shipping in five days at most," Kristofferson warned. "We want to make damn sure the tactical team is at least able to fire the guns by then."

"Unless MarShips has done something *spectacular*, I'm confident my people can fire the guns right now," Roslyn replied. "But we'll be better, given time. Five days will be plenty."

Her own briefing from the Queen and Prince-Regent suggested they might not even have five days—but Roslyn hoped she was going to have the three to get her junior officer back!

CHAPTER 3

"MARSHIPS HAS DONE worse by us," Chief Slavka Westcott noted as she and Roslyn looked over the new operating system. Roslyn had a practice copy of the software projected to her office wallscreen, to make sure they didn't accidentally fire off gigaton missiles in Mars orbit.

Roslyn was the destroyer's first tactical officer, a keel-plate owner like most of the rest of *Huntress*'s current crew. In thirteen months, she'd done as much to personalize the space as she felt she could. There were framed photos on the wall of her parents, flanked by several pieces of abstract three-dimensional art.

Someday, Roslyn would have time to learn how to make that art herself. For now, she just bought pieces made by two of the girls she'd gone to prison with.

The tactical operating system main display at least made more sense on first glance than the abstract art. There were rows of icons for the destroyer's three main weapon systems: Phoenix IX antimatter-drive missiles, ten-gigawatt battle lasers, and five hundred-megawatt RFLAM turrets.

Roslyn could even see how the display would adjust for larger warships that carried the Samurai bombardment missiles. There was more on the main screen than on the prior version of the software, where she'd had to drill down to see details on the individual weapons systems.

Of course, limiting the people handling a particular system to seeing what they were responsible for had been an intended feature.

"It seems reasonable on the surface," Roslyn said, poking an icon to drop down into the rear-facing missile battery. Four of *Huntress*'s launchers surrounded her engines, giving her a shot at a pursuer. The other sixteen of her missile launchers, plus all twelve battle lasers, pointed forward.

The software gave her ammunition counts and status reports, but it took her more than a few seconds to find the targeting systems.

"Okay, I see where I give targeting commands." She shook her head. "This isn't bad, but why did they change it?"

"Because they're software geeks, sir," Westcott said with a chuckle. She was a pale-skinned blonde, older and lighter-skinned than her boss. "If it isn't broken, you haven't optimized it enough yet."

Roslyn snorted.

"All right. Is this going to be a problem for anyone?"

"We'll walk people through it. The tutorials...exist," Westcott said. "There's only really you and maybe the XO and skipper who need to know the mass-targeting interface, though I poked at it to see if I could help you learn it."

"Prepare for the worst, Chief," Roslyn told her. "I want both Lieutenants and all three of you Chiefs fully trained on the top-tier interface alongside me. People *die*, Chief Westcott. This ship needs to fight even if that happens."

Westcott nodded, her face unreadable.

"I see your point, sir," she conceded. "But...we aren't at war anymore. Pirates can't hurt *Huntress*."

"We lost an average of two-point-three destroyers a year to hostile action prior to the war, Chief," Roslyn reminded her subordinate. "We now know *some* of that was Legatus backstabbing us, but we *also* know that there are rogue Legatan warships turned pirate out there still, too.

"We might not be expecting to go into battle on a dreadnought's flanks this week, but we need to be prepared to engage peer or superior combatants. You've heard the speech, Slavka. Do I need to echo Captain Daalman on this?"

"No," the Chief said. "Not arguing, sir. Just...pointing out. The galaxy's changed a lot in two years. We're the only ones out here again."

Roslyn concealed the shadow that passed over her at the Chief's words. Almost every former Republic system had voted to rejoin the Protectorate. Having spent time with some of the Republic's former leadership—as a prisoner they were trying to convert, to be fair—she had to wonder how much of that had been fear of what Mars would do.

Once, they had been the UnArcana Worlds, where the practice of magic was banned. Then they had been the Republic of Faith and Reason and had waged active war against Mars and the Protectorate.

Now, officially, those worlds were just...ordinary worlds of the Protectorate. There were no laws against magic there now—though the new Constitution of the Protectorate had removed some of the special status of Mages that the UnArcana Worlds had opposed.

"That's what we say, at least," she murmured. "Orders will be coming, Chief. Once Mage-Lieutenant Jordan returns, we'll sit down and go through the entire software suite as a group and see if we can improve MarShips's tutorials.

"Then we can *test* those tutorials on Mage-Lieutenant Samuels," she concluded with a grin. "After three days laid up for soft-tissue regen, she'll be *desperate* for a challenge, I think."

Roslyn was in her office late that evening, digging through the inevitable paperwork from having been on leave for two weeks—with both of her juniors joining her for the second of those weeks.

The knock on her door was a surprise, if for no other reason than that the door had an admittance chime and people generally didn't knock.

"Come in," she ordered.

The door slid open to reveal the lanky form of Mage-Captain Laura Daalman grinning down at her.

"Welcome back aboard, Commander Chambers," Daalman said, leaning against the frame of the door. "Do you plan on working all night or are you going to eat at some point?"

"Still catching up, skipper," Roslyn replied. "Lots of work."

"There always is. We're in orbit of the capital of our Protectorate, under the protective envelope of an entire squadron of capital ships and more defensive fortresses than I can count," the Mage-Captain said drily. "If there's ever a day or a place to not worry *too* much about the work, this would be one."

"I suppose so, sir," Roslyn conceded.

"I mean, to be fair, I only just shut things down myself," Daalman told her. "Officers' dinner in the Captain's mess in five minutes, Chambers. Walk with me?"

"Yes, sir," she agreed. She took one final quick glance over the file she was reviewing—a request from Chief Atkins to swap fifty of their oldest missiles with freshly serviced weapons from Mars's magazines—and decided it would wait for morning.

She closed down the work station, flashing the remaining files to her wrist-comp, and rose to join Daalman as the Captain chuckled at her.

"Conscientious as always, I see," the older woman said. "Still convinced you only got the promotion from nepotism?"

"Favoritism, sir," Roslyn conceded as she fell into step beside Daalman. "Nepotism would imply I was somehow related to Mage-Admiral Alexander."

"A fair correction, I suppose," Daalman replied. "I suggest you consider the math, though."

"The math, sir?" she asked.

"You were promoted to Lieutenant at the age of nineteen, skipping direct from Cadet and missing two and a half years of your Academy training," the Mage-Captain reminded her. "You were promoted to Lieutenant Commander after eighteen months, which is *not*, actually, particularly unusual.

"Adding that missing two and a half years to your age would make you, what, twenty-six?"

"Roughly, sir," Roslyn said slowly.

"Twenty-six, Commander Chambers, is the exact median age of our Mage-Lieutenant Commanders. You see? You are hardly underage or underqualified for your position, even ignoring the Ruby Medal of Valor."

Roslyn shook her head.

"I'm not sure most of our comrades see it that way, sir," she admitted.

"That is because our comrades look at you and see an adorable blonde thing," Daalman said bluntly. "With the exception of the ones who get stuck on your boobs. Thankfully, the RMN is mostly better than that."

Daalman had a good twenty centimeters on Roslyn, giving her the main impression of lankiness, but she was built such that she'd almost certainly *also* encountered that problem of Roslyn's.

"It's easy for others to forget that you have almost three years' more experience than your age suggests," the Mage-Captain told her. "I try not to. You definitely shouldn't. Understand, Lieutenant Commander?"

"I think so, sir," Roslyn admitted. "Hopefully, it will be...less so as I get older?"

"Almost certainly," Daalman agreed. "It helps that a *lot* of people got accelerated promotions when the RMN expanded for the war—and I haven't seen anything from on high suggesting we're going to be drawing down fleet strength anytime soon, either."

"Any idea why, sir?" Roslyn asked. "I have to admit, I've wondered. As one of my Chiefs said today...we're the only ones out here."

They'd arrived at the door to the Captain's mess and Daalman chuckled.

"If you have any clues from your friends on the Mountain, let me know," the Captain instructed. "For now, I have no idea...but I do have orders, hence officers' dinner.

"After you, Lieutenant Commander."

CHAPTER 4

IT WAS NOT, at least, the full officer's dinner that would put all of the destroyer's twenty-six commissioned officers in one space. As Roslyn made her way to a seat at the long table in the Captain's mess, she realized it was technically a *senior* officers' dinner—everyone there was a department head, which made Roslyn the youngest officer by two years.

A time frame, she noted, that was *less* than the amount of Academy time she'd lost. Now that Captain Daalman had pointed it out, she'd have to check—but it was quite possible she had more time-in-grade than Lieutenant Commander Jamshed Abiodun, the destroyer's logistics officer.

She didn't think that was the case with the other three officers around the table. Lieutenant Commander Nikoleta Franklin, the chief engineer, was the oldest of the ship's five department heads at thirty. Mage-Lieutenant Commander Eva Lehr, their navigator, was only two years behind her. Lieutenant Commander Ignác Frost, the coms officer, was halfway between Abiodun and Lehr.

"Officers," Daalman greeted them all. "I apologize for the late notice and I'm glad everyone made it here in time. Mage-Commander Lehr has the watch, which leaves her eating a sandwich on the bridge, but the rest of us get *slightly* better food than that.

"Steward Washington will be here momentarily with the dinners, and we will refrain from *discussion* until dessert, but I do have our new orders and wanted to share them with you all."

That had everyone's attention and Daalman nodded approvingly.

"Abiodun, you're going to have your work cut out for you for a few days," she told the logistics officer. "We are shipping out in seventy-two hours—and the only reason it's seventy-two and not twenty-four is because Lieutenant Samuels is in a Mars-side hospital.

"Command decided that waiting for us to have our full Jump Mage complement was going to get us to our destination faster," she continued.

The math made sense to Roslyn. With the Captain, the XO, the three tactical department officers and Lieutenant Commander Lehr, they had six Jump Mages aboard. Each could teleport the starship a full light-year roughly once every eight hours.

With Samuels aboard, they could travel twenty-four light-years a day. Without the sixth Mage, they were jumping twenty times each day. It would extend the time to get to Sorprendidas, on the edge of Protectorate space, from five days to six. Waiting two days to save one made sense, especially when *not* having that Mage and watch-standing officer would give *Huntress*'s crew multiple other problems.

"That destination is deep in former Republic space," Daalman continued. "We are on a standard patrol and show-the-flag run to the Sorprendidas System, where we will relieve the *Honor*-class destroyer *Unrelenting Pursuit of Justice* as the system's primary RMN presence.

"The tour is expected to last three months. Because we have a Link and *Unrelenting Pursuit* does not, we make a far better tripwire than she does." Daalman beamed beatifically at her crew. "We will be responsible for assisting the local sublight security forces in providing search-and-rescue and general security in the system, with a limited patrol radius of the standard jump zones around the area.

"Our patrols will be kept to a minimum because our main purpose in Sorprendidas is to be *seen*," she noted. "I will hammer this point into you a dozen times before we arrive; and I expect you to hammer it into your subordinates: we will be the single largest symbol of the Protectorate in the system.

"We must be on our best behavior and in our most generous mood. Our job is to remind the people of the benefits and value of Her Majesty's protection. Any and all opportunities to help or otherwise make a good impression are to be seized immediately."

"We're not going to make them love us," Franklin said grimly. "The Repubs—"

"The Republic no longer exists," Daalman said sharply. "These people are citizens of the Protectorate of the Mage-Queen of Mars. They have elected Senators and Members of Parliament here in Sol. They are not our enemies and I will *not* tolerate my senior officers, *especially*, regarding them as such.

"Or using derogatory nicknames born out of a war that ended over two years ago," the Captain concluded. "Am I understood, everyone?"

Nods and quiet murmurs answered her.

"I hate to do the parade-ground bullshit," Daalman told them, "but I did *not* hear you. I said, *is that understood?*"

"Sir, yes, sir!" Roslyn joined the other Lieutenant Commanders in chorusing, hiding a grin as she did it.

"The people of the former UnArcana Worlds have a thousand reasons to distrust a destroyer of the Royal Martian Navy," Daalman told them. "I trust *Unrelenting Pursuit's* crew to have ground down some of those fears—and we will continue to grind down those fears, until for every reason they have to distrust us, they have a dozen positive memories of what the RMN has done for them."

As if to cap off the speech—and quite possibly in response to a concealed signal—the door to the mess slid open and Steward Washington emerged with an assistant and several trays of steaming pasta.

"Dinner is served," the Steward told them all. "I ask that you refrain from more work discussion until you have at least *tasted* my cannelloni, please?"

"What do we know about Sorprendidas?" Frost asked as the desserts were brought in and the already-stuffed officers looked at the cheesecake with trepidation.

"Fringe World, settled sixty-two years ago," Kristofferson replied, the XO clearly having been expecting the question. "Original founding group was a Spanish Catholic diaspora effort. They're *not* technically a theocracy, but the planetary Cardinal has *always* been elected Governor."

"Does anyone even run against them?" Abiodun asked. "I've seen that kind of mess before."

"Surprisingly, yes," Kristofferson said. "Like most colonies, Sorprendidas hasn't *stayed* as monocultural as it was planned. It's young enough that the population are still mostly Spanish and Spanish-descended Catholics, but that still leaves a few million people who are neither Spanish-speaking nor Catholic.

"Despite the Cardinal-Governors being both religious and secular fig-ures—and generally *very* anti-Mage—the actual culture of the place is ex-tremely welcoming and accepting, according to the reports we have," the XO continued. "As an UnArcana World, they followed Legatus into the Secession and became a member of the Republic of Faith and Reason."

"And managed to avoid every single actual conflict of the war," Mage-Captain Daalman told them. "Records show that there was an MISS scout ship that swept the system while we were looking for the Hyacinth Accelerator Ring, but that was the only time anyone from the Protectorate was there.

"We've posted a destroyer in the system since the end of the war, with the support of the current Cardinal-Governor. No problems, no trouble."

She shook her head.

"It's a show-the-flag task, people. We're not expecting trouble."

Roslyn felt a chill run down her spine, which she concealed by taking a bite of the excellent cheesecake. From the nature of her secret mission, there was more going on at Sorprendidas than anyone thought.

Martian Interstellar Security Service agents didn't generally just *van-ish*, after all.

"We're looking at twenty-five million people on two continents," Kristofferson told them. "There are three more continents that are habit-able but less pleasant than the two they've settled, and some of the usual asteroid extraction infrastructure.

"They've got an asteroid belt for raw materials and a gas giant for fuel and a generally warm and pleasant inhabitable planet." He shrugged. "Give them another fifty years and they'll have levered themselves into MidWorld status without much external help."

The Fringe Worlds were generally self-sufficient for food and had a couple of local industries but needed to trade for most technological systems. MidWorlds were complete industrialized economies, with moderate sources of wealth and usually their own defensive security fleets.

The Core Worlds were the first dozen colonies. No one had yet decided on criteria for a MidWorld to become a Core World.

"Do they have any local defenses?" Roslyn asked. She hadn't had time to look that up since being briefed by the Prince-Regent and Mage-Queen.

"The Republic set up a prefabricated gunship base in orbit with thirty gunships," the XO replied. "Like most of the in-system defenses set up by the Republic, Sorprendidas kept them. Enough to cause us trouble, I suppose."

"I'll make some notes and prep some exercises," Roslyn replied. "We should be able to handle thirty gunships—even if mostly by running away until they run out of missiles."

Several of her colleagues chuckled. There was no one there who hadn't served in the war, and they all remembered the strengths and weaknesses of the Republic Interstellar Navy's sublight parasite warships. They carried a lot of launchers for their mass—and very few missiles for those launchers.

"That wouldn't be fun for them," Franklin said. "Squish-squish."

Song of the Huntress, like the rest of the RMN, used magic for gravity. RIN warships had needed to either spin or accelerate to achieve similar sensations of "down"—and the gunships were too small for any kind of spin. Roslyn had seen the inside of several after the war, and they were designed for short-term operations with acceleration tanks and suits to allow them to withstand high thrust.

"We don't plan on fighting the locals," Daalman headed the engineer off drily. "Those gunships are more likely to be backing us up than fighting us."

"I'll prep some exercises for that, too, then," Roslyn said cheerfully. "I don't think many of us have practice thinking about how to *use* ex-RIN gunships."

"Agreed. We should work on that," *Huntress*'s Captain said. "We may have scrapped every carrier they built, but there are still a *lot* of gunships running around."

The gunships, after all, hadn't been built using people's *brains* as their main engine.

CHAPTER 5

WHEN SAMUELS finally reported aboard, Roslyn found herself in the same position as Kristofferson had been on her own return. She was standing behind the safety barrier as the shuttle slowed to a halt—and felt the vibration as the megaton-and-a-half-plus starship's main engines came to life.

Mage-Captain Daalman had already made it clear they wouldn't be hanging around once the Mage-Lieutenant was aboard. There were a few others reporting in late for a few reasons, but their sixth Jump Mage was the only person they were going to hold up the entire destroyer for.

Kirtida Samuels saluted crisply as soon as she spotted Roslyn. The Lieutenant was a dark-skinned woman with naturally copper-red hair that contrasted sharply with the rest of her features. Like most Mages by Blood, born from the descendants of the brutal eugenics program that had created the modern Mage, her genetics were...complicated.

"Welcome back, Lieutenant," Roslyn greeted her subordinate. "How are you feeling?"

"I *feel* fine," Samuels said. "I've felt fine for at least a day, but apparently they're really careful around soft-tissue injury." She shrugged. "I'm not allowed to work out for a minimum of a week—other than the specific exercises they gave me—and I have to follow up weekly with the ship's doctor for two months."

"Sounds like a plan," Roslyn said. "Check in with medbay as soon as you get a chance and schedule those. If at all possible, I'd prefer we not have to shift your watch schedule—but we'll do what it takes to make sure you get the care you need."

"I'm pretty sure I'm fine," the younger woman said with a chuckle. "But I'll follow orders, sir. Yours and the doctors'."

"Good Lieutenant," Roslyn said, gesturing for Samuels to follow her. "There's a briefing packet prepped for you on our mission. Jordan is fully up to speed—she's on watch with Captain Daalman right now—so she can fill you in if you have questions."

"Of course, sir," Samuels accepted. "The Chiefs will fill me in on the rest, I'm sure."

"They do that," the tactical officer agreed. "Now, you should also have got an update on the new TOS? We get to guinea-pig for the entire RMN."

"Lucky us," Samuels noted. "Any problems, sir?"

"Nothing major, but watch your controls for the first few days. Nothing is *quite* what you expect it to be."

"Of course, sir."

"Tactical chiefs and officers' meeting after the jump," Roslyn concluded. "That'll give you a couple of hours to get squared away. We'll learn what you need to catch up on quickly."

"I'm just glad to be out of the hospital, sir," Samuels admitted. "And doing *anything.*"

"Oh, you are going to *regret* that," Roslyn said with a wicked grin.

The bridge of any Martian warship was also the simulacrum chamber. Civilian ships often split the two, leaving the Mage jumping the ship with a private sanctum at the center of the starship—but a civilian ship's simulacrum could only augment the jump spell.

A warship's unrestricted amplifier could augment any spell the Mages aboard cast, giving it a deadly weapon at shorter ranges. Combined with the general tendency of the ship's commander to be a Mage and the need to save cubage and mass alike on the armored warships, the two were combined.

That left the bridge as a spherical space at *Song of the Huntress's* exact center, roughly six meters across in each dimension. Every wall of the sphere was covered in high-fidelity screens that showed everything around the ship in perfect detail.

Positioned through the spherical bridge were the stations for the bridge crew, each a small platform with computer consoles a small step away from another platform. At the very center of the bridge was the simulacrum itself, a ninety-centimeter-long model of the hundred-and-twenty-meter-long starship.

Even at that, the magic of the amplifier matrix had been changed since the last ships Roslyn had served aboard. Those had all been exactly a one-hundredth-scale model, resulting in five-meter-long simulacra aboard cruisers and even larger on battleships.

Roslyn watched in silence as a dozen metrics on her screens slowly reduced. A warship *could* jump from close to a planet, but it was uncomfortable and rather dangerous. Normally, they would get a full light-minute clear of the planet—which was an easier task on a warship with magical gravity and ten gravities of acceleration than on a civilian ship.

"We are sufficiently clear for a safe jump," Mage-Lieutenant Commander Lehr reported.

"Thank you, Lehr," Mage-Captain Daalman replied.

The Captain was seated in front of the simulacrum and surrounded by a smaller set of screens. All of those screens were folded away now, giving the Mage a near-perfect view of the rune-encrusted screens that surrounded them all.

"Record for the log, please," Daalman continued calmly. "We are jumping...now."

She laid her hands—with the same silver runes inlaid on the palms as Roslyn and the rest of the Jump Mages had—on the simulacrum.

Years of practice on the Captain's part made the whole affair far smoother than Roslyn dared hope *her* jumps would ever become. One moment, Daalman was placing her hands on the simulacrum; the next, a surge of disorientation washed over Roslyn and all of her screens were reporting different data.

"First jump complete," Daalman said loudly, her voice tired. Jumping took a *lot* out of a Mage. "Lehr, you're up next in ninety minutes. Let's keep this show moving."

Even with six Mages aboard, it was going to be a long trip.

CHAPTER 6

THE TUTORIAL for the command portion of the new tactical operating system ended, leaving Roslyn and her subordinates looking at the wallscreen in her office with mixed levels of distaste.

"I don't think I ever realized how much credit we needed to give the first crews to test out this kind of software," Chief Westcott finally said. "I'm used to us receiving really complete and detailed tutorials that emphasize what we need to know."

"This is not that," Lieutenant Samuels agreed, the dark redhead looking at the now-frozen display with a shake of her head. "This is…"

"The basic tutorial on functionality prepared by the techs who wrote the software," Roslyn finished for her. "They know what we need for the actual *programs* and work with active-duty officers to get to this stage, but the final tutorials and instructions have to be prepared by people using the system in the real world."

She tapped a command, wiping away the tutorial video and replacing it with the practice version of the tactical operating system, the same main screen she'd gone over with Westcott when they began their plan for this.

"The six of us need to write and record those tutorials," Roslyn continued, gesturing at the two junior officers and three Chief Petty Officers in the room with her. "And unfortunately for the Chiefs, all three of us officers are on the Jump Mage rotation, which means we're going to be shattered even when we're awake for the rest of the trip."

If they'd been expecting serious trouble, Roslyn would have argued to keep at least one of the ship's six Mages on a longer cycle than the others. Currently, everyone would jump the ship on an eight-hour cycle. That meant that they'd been asleep at least half the time and at less than their best the rest of the time.

"I hate to undermine the myth that the Chiefs don't actually *need* officers, but that's going to be a pain," Westcott conceded. "We'll make it happen. We're the RMN."

"The protectors of Her Majesty's Protectorate," Roslyn agreed. "I know we're going to drop a lot of this on you three, but we all will be here, I promise. The XO and the skipper are aware of what's going on too, so Kristofferson is available for backup when needed."

"What about the skipper?" Samuels asked.

"My plan is to test our final tutorials on her," Roslyn replied. "Captain Daalman is familiar with more iterations of the TOS than any of us except Chief Westcott. She'll make a good first audience for the tutorials we put together—and so long as one of us is available to run the command interface, it doesn't threaten the ship if she's a bit rusty."

No one was expecting trouble on this trip, but it was always wise to prepare for *some* trouble. Even ignoring Roslyn's secret orders, she knew the ship needed to be ready for action at any moment.

"So, let's go through this practice setup, shall we?" she asked. "Section by section."

She studied the iconography for a moment, then shrugged and tapped a command. One group of icons, currently colored amber, zoomed in and took up the entire wallscreen, more data appearing as the icons expanded.

"Someone want to read off what this is telling us?" Roslyn suggested. "Jordan?"

Mage-Lieutenant Jordan coughed and studied the screen.

"We're looking at the offensive laser suite," the pale blonde officer with the watery blue eyes noted. "Batteries Alpha, Bravo, Charlie, Delta." She gestured at each section as she indicated them. "Each section has four ten-gigawatt battle lasers, and the color-coding is warning us that the capacitors are only at one-third charge.

"Oh." She paused with a questioning tone as she looked at the notations. "*That's* handy. It's showing the current capacitor charge rate and how many shots until we're dry with current levels and charge rates."

Jordan chuckled.

"That is, if anyone didn't know it already, *one*."

Roslyn joined in the general amusement at that. At battle stations, with the fusion reactors at full, the lasers would be charging fast enough to offset the Book's set rate of fire for the weapons. With the capacitors charged, they could double that rate of fire for a *very* small number of shots.

"All right, everyone comfortable with the laser screens?" she asked.

"I need to play for a bit in the practice software, but I think most of the detail pages haven't changed much," Samuels noted. She held primary responsibility for the lasers and the teams who handled them.

"Good. So, next is…"

Roslyn swapped to another screen and looked at it for several long seconds.

"Okay, what *am* I looking at?" she finally asked. "I don't recognize half of this iconography, and I'm reasonably sure I know all of our weapons."

"Bombardment, I think," Westcott said slowly. "That's the standard impactor icon, but I'm not sure what the other four are."

"Did we miss a memo?" Roslyn asked aloud, and one of the other Chiefs coughed. "Chief Trevis?"

Chief Janez Trevis was the juniormost of her three Chiefs, but he held the vague title of *Weaponeer*. He'd come up through the ranks as a missile operator and was responsible for coordinating with Logistics to make sure they had all of the weapons they needed.

"You might have missed it, yes," the tanned man told her. "We received the new Talon Tens during our layover. They're modular weapons, with multiple warhead options."

He gestured at the screen.

"So, we can adjust the number of projectiles from five to ten and switch the warheads on each projectile."

Roslyn studied the TOS display and nodded slowly. Now she knew what she was looking for, she saw the section of the report that told her that *Song of the Huntress* actually carried both the new Talon Ten and the older—but still new, introduced in the war—Talon Nine.

The Talon Nine was a nine-warhead MIRVed precision kinetic impactor, capable of taking out anything from an armored bunker to a city depending on dispersal and velocity.

The Talon Ten options were...complicated.

"Okay," Roslyn conceded. "I'm *guessing* these new icons as cluster, penetrator, airburst, explosive and..."

The last icon looked like a crossed-out network transmission symbol.

"Electromagnetic pulse, sir," Trevis confirmed. "We retained the standard impactor, but we gained two options for small and mid-size antimatter warheads for area destruction, as well as three specialty munitions.

"We now have an anti-vehicle munition that turns a single impactor into forty-four smart anti-vehicle missiles, an anti-bunker munition that is significantly denser and capable of penetrating up to four kilometers of stone, and an electromagnetic pulse warhead to disable enemy electronics."

"I'm reasonably sure any enemy we'd run into would have hardened electronics," Westcott pointed out. "What's the point of an EMP warhead?"

"Depends on the enemy, I suppose," Trevis replied. "We used to deal with a lot of terrorists, after all. Knocking out all electronics for a few hundred square kilometers might be necessary there.

"Plus, well, keep overloading it and even *our* electronics can shut down."

"We can turn them back on if they do," Roslyn countered. "But that can provide a few moments of critical vulnerability."

She shrugged.

"It's useful to have options, at least. Though god knows I have no desire to *ever* fire a planetary impactor!"

There was a chorus of agreement. Even in the war, the RMN had done everything in their power to avoid having to use their ground-attack munitions. Even the most basic mode of the new Talon Tens could easily destroy a city—and if Roslyn was reading the data correctly, *Huntress* now had the ability to deliver ten one-hundred-megaton warheads with near-perfect precision from a single missile.

That wasn't killing cities. That was killing *continents*.

CHAPTER 7

"JUMP COMPLETE," Roslyn reported, wavering slightly as the exhaustion washed over her. "Welcome to the Sorprendidas System, everyone."

"Take your seat, Lieutenant Commander," Daalman ordered gently. Roslyn was still on watch, though the expectations were always low for a post-jump watch.

Chief Westcott was already at her station, pulling the default information the Captain would want now that they'd arrived at their destination. Roslyn dropped heavily into her seat next to the NCO and tapped a command to mirror the Chief's screen.

"What are we seeing, Tactical?" Daalman asked.

"Chief?" Roslyn said, clearly passing the question to Westcott to make sure the NCO got credit. She *could* read the analysis Westcott was doing off the screen in front of her, but that would be rude as far as she was concerned.

"Geography is as expected," Westcott reported crisply. "Two balls of burnt rock, a habitable planet named Sorprendidas, two balls of *frozen* rock, an asteroid belt and two outer gas giants.

"Scans show *Unrelenting Pursuit of Justice* is in Sorprendidas orbit," she continued. "Flagging space installations throughout the system, but nothing materially off from the reports we received prior to our arrival.

"Thank you, Chief Westcott," Daalman said. "Chief Zaman? Fire up the Link and inform Command that we have arrived."

Unrelenting Pursuit of Justice was a pre-war design that lacked anything resembling faster-than-light communication. Before the war with the Republic, the only form of interstellar communication available to humanity had been the Runic Transceiver Arrays, large and complex magical installations that only transmitted the voice of a Mage.

But the Republic had developed the long-sought holy grail of quantum-entanglement communicators under the unassuming name of "the Link." Now replicated by the engineers of the Protectorate—some of them the same engineers who'd designed it for the Republic—it was being installed in all new RMN ships.

Refitting older ships took time, and old destroyers were at the bottom of the priority list. Roslyn figured a ship like *Unrelenting Pursuit* was likely to be scrapped before she received an FTL communicator.

"Once we've called home, let's get messages fired off to Cardinal-Governor Guerra and Mage-Captain Mac Gille Fhaolain," Daalman continued, the Gaelic name coming far more smoothly off her tongue than Roslyn figured *she* could manage.

"The locals know we're coming, but there's only one Link on the whole planet and it's Republic-built," the Captain noted. "Regular radio, please."

The RMN might be comfortable enough with the Links *they'd* built and the Republic might be dead...but they were *not* going to connect their FTL communication network with the one the Republic had built.

There were interfaces used to integrate the old Republic network with the new civilian network, but small as the risk was, the RMN had chosen not to take it.

"Command confirms our arrival," Zaman noted. His boss, Lieutenant Commander Frost, was off-duty, leaving the noncom as the senior coms person on deck. "Sending standard greetings to Cardinal Guerra and Mage-Captain Mac Gille Fhaolain."

"And now we wait," Daalman murmured. "Lieutenant Ambrogi?"

The shaven-headed officer at the navigation console turned their head to face the Captain.

"Sir?"

"Do you have a course for Sorprendidas?"

"Yes, sir," the junior navigator confirmed. "ETA three hours, eleven minutes."

"All right. Make it so, Lieutenant," Daalman ordered. "Let's go meet the locals."

With Daalman holding down the watch and a clear lack of threats in the Sorprendidas System, Roslyn was able to retreat to her office after an hour or so. It was helpful, in her admittedly biased opinion, that all of her superiors were *also* Jump Mages and understood exactly how wiped she was after jumping.

Even with the exhaustion from jumping, a Mage could still only actually *sleep* for eight to ten hours a day, so they ended up doing work in a manner best described with the ancient aphorism of "puttering."

Amidst the paperwork she was going through for her own department, she pulled together the information she had on the missing MISS agents. Four had gone into Sorprendidas in the last nine months. Two men, one woman, one genderqueer.

The genderqueer agent, she at least knew what had happened to. Against a background of three other agents ceasing to report, the car accident was suspicious as hell. Isi Yuan had been hit by a drunk driver and died before they'd even reached the hospital.

They'd been following up on the research done by Pallavi Rose. Rose had been on Sorprendidas since before the war, a long-term surveillance asset. She'd been the one to identify Dr. Finley when information on the Rune Wright had gone out to every agent to track his movements.

Rose had flagged Finley as having repeatedly visited the planet and had even identified several businesses he'd been working with. Only part of that list had managed to make it back to Mars before Rose had stopped reporting.

Yuan's investigation had been intended, at least partially, to find out what had happened to Rose.

Timur Spiker had left Tau Ceti barely twenty-four hours after the MISS office there had learned of Yuan's death. By the time he'd arrived, at least, the Link on Sorprendidas had been interfaced with the civilian Link network in the Protectorate so he could send *some* reports.

Not many though, Roslyn saw. There was only so much access a covert agent could get to an expensive and still heavily-controlled communication device.

Spiker had sent in three reports in four weeks and then gone silent. A fourth agent had already been dispatched to support him, though Angus Killough had arrived to find himself alone. The initial report Roslyn had from him sounded shaky.

Killough had been more careful with his reports than Spiker, sending them in once a month after his arrival report. They'd gone through an encrypted drop box in the civilian network, buried in the corporate reports of several different Tau Ceti-based corporations that probably didn't even know they were being used for MISS coms.

His last report had been five weeks earlier. More MISS assets were supposed to be deployed, per the notes she had from the Prince-Regent. None were expected to be in the system for another few weeks, at least, but they would make covert contact with her once they did.

Roslyn sighed and shook her head.

"They're all dead," she muttered grimly. "Someone is killing our people."

She probably shouldn't be talking to herself about this, but she was tired. Sighing, she shook her head and pulled up another document. This one gave her a list of virtual classified sites running on Sorprendidas and specific messages that would be posted as emergency alerts.

It would take some finagling to get archives from those sites, but even from half a light-minute out, Roslyn could access the planetary datanet. She told her computer to pull those classifieds and grabbed herself a coffee as they downloaded.

She wasn't entirely surprised that there were no calls for help concealed in the ads she pulled. Whatever was going on on this planet, somebody had made *very* sure that all of the MISS agents who'd gone in to investigate it were dead.

That meant Roslyn needed to talk to people—because she was feeling far from suicidal, and that meant she was investigating with Marines.

CHAPTER 8

"YOU ASKED TO see me, Lieutenant Commander?" Daalman asked as Roslyn entered the Captain's office.

Daalman had made more of an imprint on her office in the months they'd been aboard than Roslyn had. *Song of the Huntress*'s commissioning seal of a bow with a music note hanging above it was emblazoned on the wall behind her desk. Simple plastic bookshelves marked one wall, filled with an assorted array of nonfiction, reports and novels.

Pride of place on the wall that had avoided bookshelves was a massive picture of a family of five in front of a gorgeous estate house in the countryside somewhere. It took Roslyn a moment to recognize Mage-Captain Laura Daalman in the brilliantly smiling mother in the oil painting.

"Yes, sir," Roslyn admitted. She hesitated, standing by the chair in front of Daalman's standard-issue metal-and-plastic desk.

"Sit down, Chambers," the Captain ordered. "Is this where I get to find out what the Prince-Regent put in your ear while you were having dinner with him?"

Roslyn took the seat, trying not to wince at the accuracy of her commander's guess.

"How did you..." She trailed off helplessly, feeling *very* young.

"I figured the odds were sixty-forty that the Prince-Regent had wanted you for more than a social dinner," Daalman noted. "And then you ask for a private meeting, which throws the odds to at least seventy-thirty.

"I'm guessing you have secret orders under the Mountain's seal that you're authorized to brief me on as you need assistance," she continued. "I won't pretend I *like* that, but I can work with it—and it makes sense to me that the Prince-Regent would lean on a young protégée like you.

"Tell me, did he introduce you to the Queen?"

Roslyn blinked. Now she was *completely* out of her depth.

"Yes?" she admitted.

"I figured," Daalman said. "Kiera Alexander desperately needs a core cadre of officers and officials within spitting distance of her own age. Hell, Chambers, I'm almost as young to be a Mage-Captain as you are to be a Lieutenant Commander, and I'm over *twice* Her Majesty's age.

"I've never met Montgomery, but from talking to people who have, I suspect he is very aware of the Mage-Queen's lack of friends and allies of her own age group. I approve, strongly, of him helping her make those connections."

"I hadn't thought of it that way," Roslyn admitted. "She's...impressive. Clever, compassionate...but I had *one* dinner with her, sir."

Daalman gestured at the painting of her with her husband and three children.

"And at one point, I'd had one dinner with Roger," she pointed out. "Friendships have to start somewhere. Now, however."

She leaned on her desk and studied Roslyn.

"I have impressed with my acuity and intuition, but you had a reason for scheduling this meeting, and it wasn't for me to horrify you with what being the Prince-Regent's protégée entails.

"What kind of mission have they saddled you with?"

Roslyn sighed.

"I'm to brief you as you need to know, sir," she admitted. "That suggests against fully reading you in. But...I've been tasked to follow up on an investigation MISS was handling. *Their* agents have gone missing, so I need to catch up on what I can.

"That means I'll need some time on the planet, away from the ship. But given that multiple MISS operatives are missing, presumed dead...I was hoping to borrow some Marines."

"This is the ass end of fucking nowhere," Daalman said bluntly. "Which I'm guessing is a great place to hide something. I'll write the orders authorizing you to borrow a shuttle and travel to the surface as you need, but I have a requirement for lending you Marines, Lieutenant Commander. One I'm not going to budge on, no matter what your orders are."

"Yes, sir?"

"If you're taking Marines with you into this kind of mess, you brief them," the Mage-Captain told her. "You can leave *me* with as little as I need to know, but the Marines at your back need to know everything. They can't judge the risks otherwise—and you can trust Martian Marines to keep their mouths shut, too."

"My orders say *need to know*, sir," Roslyn noted. "I think that covers briefing my immediate escort."

"Good." Daalman waved her hand over her desk, activating a touchscreen interface linked to her wrist-comp. "I'll touch base with Major Dickens and see which of his squads he'll want to assign. He doesn't need to know as much as I do, but he needs to know *something*."

The Mage-Captain smiled coolly.

"Like I said, Chambers, I don't *like* my officers having secret orders," she reminded the junior woman. "But I understand the need and I understand the officer in question being you. You didn't pick up multiple ranks of the Medal of Valor by being useless."

"Sir," Roslyn acknowledged.

"The Major will advise you of your team within a few hours," Daalman told her. "You'll have a shuttle and probably ten Marines. Try to bring them all back intact, Lieutenant Commander."

"Of course, sir."

Roslyn was busy pulling together the information she had from the MISS agents to identify a starting point when the admittance buzzer for her office went off. She concealed the data with a wave of her hand, then studied the door in silence for a moment.

She hadn't heard anything from Captain Chiyembekezo Dickens—courtesy promoted to Major aboard a starship to avoid confusion with the ship's Captain. She wasn't entirely sure how the Marines would handle an assignment like this, though—she had limited experience with the Royal Martian Marine Corps.

"Enter," she ordered.

The door slid open to reveal what she realized she'd been expecting: A Marine Sergeant in shipboard blues. The woman snapped to perfect attention as the door opened, giving Roslyn the preemptive salute both her rank and her Medal of Valor required.

"Mage-Lieutenant Commander Chambers, sir?" she asked in greeting.

"Come in, Sergeant," Roslyn replied. "And you are?"

"Staff Sergeant Borislava Mooren," the dark-haired Slavic woman introduced herself. "I lead First Squad of First Platoon for Major Dickens, and my squad has been assigned to you for a special project."

"Come in, Sergeant," Roslyn ordered. "I'm assuming the Major didn't give you much to work from?"

"No, sir," Mooren confirmed. "We're assigned to your protection and discretion until ordered otherwise, with the understanding that everything you tell us and everything we do are completely classified."

"That's about all I've got, yeah," Roslyn said with a chuckle. "This is locked down at some of the highest levels of bullshit, Sergeant. I have no idea how dangerous it's going to get, but I can tell you that multiple very capable people are already dead.

"Once I brief you and your squad, you can never breathe a word of any of this unless I or the Prince-Regent authorizes it. Do you understand?"

Mooren managed to somehow get straighter as she stood in front of Roslyn's desk. She was at least five years older than Roslyn, the Lieutenant Commander judged, and she seemed somewhat taken aback by Roslyn's certainty.

"We are Marines, sir," Mooren told her. "We do the job. Sometimes, that means we never talk about the job again. Whatever you need, whatever we're ordered."

"All right. I don't want to have to repeat myself, so why don't you arrange for your squad to meet me in a secure conference room?" Roslyn suggested. "No one even aboard *Huntress* is to know about this."

"I will make it happen, sir," Mooren assured her. "No one will ever know we were gone."

CHAPTER 9

"SETTLE IT DOWN, Marines," Mooren barked as Roslyn stepped into the room.

The Mage managed not to visibly shake her head as she realized what Mooren had picked as a "secure conference room." She was almost certainly correct that the security around the Marines' ready room was as good as any secure conference room, but the age-old space of lockers and benches certainly didn't feel professional.

Still, the ten Marines in the room were on the benches and paying attention within seconds of the Sergeant's order, and Roslyn surveyed them calmly, hopefully concealing her own momentary discomfort.

At least half of the squad was older than she was, and all of them were hardened veterans of assault operations in the war against the Republic. She'd taken some time to review their records before this meeting, and she'd been impressed.

"All right, people," she said to them. "Major Dickens apparently assigned you to me because you're the best he has. Are you going to live up to that?"

"Oorah," ten voices echoed back at her, and she had to grin at their enthusiasm.

"Good. You're going to be living in my back pocket for the next few days at least as I investigate the situation on Sorprendidas," she told them. "Since we're going into an unknown threat environment, I want to make sure you know almost as much as I do about the situation. Hence, this."

She waved around.

"What's the threat, sir?" one of the older Marines asked. "We can prep for anything."

"Threat is unknown," Roslyn repeated. "But it will likely involve either or both of Mage war criminals and Republic covert-ops Augments."

The room suddenly silenced and she realized she had everyone's attention.

"Let's start at the beginning, shall we?" she asked. "For those of you who missed it, the inventor of the Prometheus Interface was a Mage named Dr. Samuel Finley. Prince-Regent Montgomery killed him—before he was Prince-Regent, obviously.

"But there were other Mages involved in the Prometheus Project. We've identified twenty-six and we've only brought eleven to justice," Roslyn told the Marines. "That's fifteen war criminals, Mages who voluntarily helped the Republic murder thousands of other Mages and extract their brains to fuel their warships."

Now the silence was *angry.*

"After the war, the Mountain sent out imagery of every one of those Mages we had to every asset we had in the former Republic," she continued. "The Red List, it's called. An MISS long-term plant here in Sorprendidas identified Finley as a recurring visitor and even flagged several businesses that he was involved in.

"Then that agent went silent. A second agent sent to follow up was killed in a car crash. Two more sent to follow up on *that* have also gone silent. Four MISS covert operatives—primarily spies but still expected to handle themselves—are missing. Presumed dead."

"And you think they found something?" another Marine asked.

"I'm not sure they did," Roslyn admitted. "I have all of their reports prior to them going dark, and there's no smoking gun in there. But I think they each got close enough that someone decided not to take the risk.

"That tells me there's something *active* here, not just a few businesses that took investment from the worst war criminal of the last few centuries," she told them. "The Prince-Regent thinks there's a secret laboratory somewhere on Sorprendidas—and if there's a rogue Prometheus lab, it likely has rogue Prometheus *Mages*.

"We want to find the Mages. Find the lab. Capture the Mages. Shut down the lab. And not die doing it."

The room was silent for longer than Roslyn expected.

"We're not really equipped for fighting Mages, sir," Mooren finally admitted. "Not without full exosuit combat armor, anyway."

"You have a blank check from Captain Daalman for any gear you need that *Song of the Huntress* carries," Roslyn replied. "We have a shuttle at our disposal until the mission is over. We load it with exosuits and everything else you can think of.

"I don't know what we're going to be facing, so I suggest we make certain we can take on *anything*." She spread her hands. "I can take on most Mages," she admitted.

Roslyn Chambers was a Mage by Blood, able to trace her bloodline to the survivors of Project Olympus, the victims of Mars's pre-Mage-King Eugenicist rulers. Even for a Mage by Blood, she was powerful.

There were few Mages she wouldn't be confident in her ability to handle. Assuming a fair playing field or one tilted in her favor, at least— she'd been tranquilized and captured by a Mage traitor once, after all.

"Can I make an argument for an assault shuttle?" Mooren suggested. "Can we trust local backup?"

"To a point," Roslyn said. "An assault shuttle is too much for theoretically friendly landings on a Protectorate world, Sergeant. And while I suspect our target has at least partially co-opted local authority, the government of Sorprendidas would probably be just as horrified to discover a secret Prometheus lab as we are."

She shook her head.

"We will cooperate with the local authorities, but we are the RMN and RMMC," she told them. "We have the authority and the orders to investigate and handle this situation. We will do so covertly and quietly while trying not to draw attention to ourselves...for as long as we can."

"And then we kick down doors in exosuits?" Mooren asked.

"Exactly."

"Where do we start?" the Marine NCO asked.

"The last agent I have a location on was staying in a rental apartment in Nueva Portugal," Roslyn said. "I need to access the records for the rental company, but at least theoretically, his lease isn't up yet.

"I plan to check that out first."

"Then what are we waiting for, sir?" Mooren asked. "Corporal Knight can breach any lock ever built." She gestured to a petite Black woman who was listening patiently and nodded firmly at the gesture.

"We're waiting for you to decide what you need on the shuttle, Sergeant," Roslyn replied with a chuckle. "I expect to be intermittently on the surface and back up on *Huntress*, but I suggest you load for bear...and for a long stay."

CHAPTER 10

"NUEVA PORTUGAL Spaceport Control, this is shuttle *Huntress-Charlie*. We are on the provided vector and slowing to land. Do we have a pad assignment?"

Roslyn listened to Lieutenant Alvina Herbert talking to the ground control while studying the city beneath them through the shuttle's cameras. Nueva Portugal had been well named in several ways. It was built on a peninsula that stuck out into Sorprendidas's warm oceans, with vast white beaches visible from the air.

A mountain range at the east end of the peninsula provided readily accessible raw resources, while the peninsula itself was covered in farms suggesting fertile soil—and the oceans were likely a rich source of aquaculture and fish.

All of that supported Sorprendidas's second-largest city, a metropolis of two million people. The peninsula supported almost five million total souls, making up the region of Nueva Portugal as opposed to the city itself.

The spaceport was on the western extreme of the peninsula, with clearly marked water docks for larger landing-capable ships. For shuttles like theirs, a hundred floating pads were hooked up to piers that stretched out into the water.

"Understood, landing pad forty-four," Herbert told the ground control. "Stay is currently indefinite; we're on Navy business."

The redheaded pilot paused.

"No, I'm not going to explain further," she said. "Navy business. If it becomes your business, we'll tell you."

"Be nice, Lieutenant," Roslyn murmured. "We're supposed to be making friends here, not enemies."

She wasn't going to allow Herbert to actually tell ground control what they were up to, but that didn't mean they had to be *rude* about it.

The pilot waved her off, continuing to listen to her headset.

"I understand, I understand," she assured ground control. "We've got our course set for forty-four. The shuttle will be secured against intrusion as our team goes into the city. Can we arrange vehicle rental?"

There was a pause.

"Really? Well, my boss will be sure to pass on her thanks. Nice working with you, NPSC."

With no visible change, Herbert turned to Roslyn and raised an eyebrow.

"There's apparently several vehicles already waiting for us, organized by the Nueva Portugal Guardia," the pilot told her. "Did we arrange that in advance?"

Roslyn sighed and shook her head.

"No, we didn't," she admitted. "Not unless Captain Daalman or Major Dickens didn't tell us something, which seems unlikely."

She turned to look into the back compartment.

"Mooren, I'm going to need backup when we touch down," she told the Sergeant. "Everybody else stay aboard until the Sergeant and I have talked to the locals."

Her day was messy enough. This was a complication she could have lived without.

There were *six* vehicles waiting on the floating dock next to their landing pad, Roslyn realized. Only two of them would be capable of hauling her entire team—and somehow, she didn't think showing up in an armored utility vehicle with bright gold and blue Guardia coloring was going to help her need to be subtle.

An officer in a similarly brightly colored uniform was standing in front of the collection of vehicles. He wasn't visibly armed, but he was tapping a hand impatiently on his hip—which probably also expressed the mood of the two more drably dressed tactical officers behind him with the stunguns.

"Officer, we didn't request an escort," Roslyn greeted the man as she and Mooren crossed the small-but-disconcerting gap between the floating launchpad and the long fixed dock. "May I ask what's going on?"

"I am Lieutenant Celio Oliveira," the young man greeted her. His tone was more servile than his body language suggested. "The Guardia wishes to provide any necessary support for the RMN's operations in our city...so that you can leave as quickly as possible.

"The presence of Martian military personnel is going to be an active irritant to several segments of our population and create potential difficulties for the Guardia," he concluded. "We wish only to help you complete your duties and return to your ship as efficiently as possible."

Roslyn eyed him for a few seconds, then sighed.

"I appreciate the effort, Lieutenant Oliveira," she told him. "But I can't make any promises as to how long my duties here on the surface are going to take. I *can* provide you with my contact information to make sure that we coordinate with the Guardia as necessary, but I'm tasked with matters of the Mountain's security, and I can't delay or abrogate that mission."

"I see," he said stiffly. "I hope that transportation will help?"

"It will, though I'll admit that marked vehicles will not," Roslyn told him. She studied the vehicles. There were only two unmarked vehicles, and they were standard electric sedans. They could *maybe* fit all twelve members of her team into the two cars, but it would be a squeeze.

"On the other hand, if the Guardia would like to assist, I could use access to your computer systems," she continued. "We can travel to a Guardia station with you, and you can arrange unmarked transport for twelve."

Unless they had some kind of low-profile unmarked armored personnel carrier, Roslyn didn't think that Lieutenant Oliveira could manage that.

"I should be able to arrange that, sir," he admitted. "Both access and vehicles, Mage-Lieutenant Commander..."

"Chambers," she told him, somewhat surprised by his managing to read her insignia. "If the Guardia can be quietly helpful, I suspect that will serve both of our purposes best. I would prefer to keep the operations of my team under wraps, but I understand the Guardia's legitimate concerns.

"As much as I can, I will accommodate them."

So long as the Guardia remained helpful, at least. She certainly wasn't planning on telling them *everything*—but she also suspected the Guardia could tell her whether Angus Killough's apartment had been rented to someone else.

"That is the most we can ask, I suppose," Oliveira admitted. "You have more people aboard the shuttle, then?"

"Two years ago, this world was actively at war with the Protectorate, Lieutenant," Roslyn said gently. "For the same reason you're worried about our activity in your city, my Captain insists that our officers travel with Marine escort.

"We will make use of whatever unmarked vehicles you can loan us," she continued. That would allow the Guardia to track their movements, so they'd *also* want to acquire other vehicles—but the appearance of cooperation was worth a lot.

"We only wish to serve," Oliveira told her.

"And *observe*," Roslyn said pointedly.

To her surprise, that got an honest chuckle from the young man. Maybe they could get some value out of the partnership after all.

CHAPTER 11

TWO HOURS LATER, Roslyn and her team were equipped with two large gray SUVs that hopefully wouldn't draw too much attention as they shuffled around the city—and the information that the lease signed by Andrew Jackson, Killough's alias, was still active.

"All right, take us past the address," Roslyn ordered. "Regular speed; let's look like we're going somewhere."

"Subtle peeping tom, right," Mooren replied. The Sergeant was driving the lead vehicle, with Herbert driving the following van.

"We don't know what happened to Mr. Killough," Roslyn pointed out. "It seems likely the apartment is watched."

"I was making commentary, not arguing," Mooren noted. A navigation system overlay appeared on the bottom half of the SUV's windshield as the Marine plugged in addresses. "There's a nice hotel in the suburbs of Nueva Portugal that we'd drive right past the apartment on the fastest route to," she noted.

"Sounds good," Roslyn said. "We'll probably need a home base for a bit."

She pulled up the holographic screen and keyboard on her wrist-comp and fired off a note to Abiodun back aboard *Huntress*. Booking hotel space for twelve definitely fell into the Logistics Department's responsibilities.

"What have we got on the apartment?" she asked. Corporal Knight was sitting directly behind her, and the electronic-warfare tech had been doing research for her in the public records.

"It's the third-floor unit in a five-floor complex inland from the main downtown core," Knight replied. "Villa-style complex, with two hundred units around a central courtyard. Reasonably midrange, mostly occupied by young professionals and new arrivals.

"Fourteen Guardia reports in the last year: minor domestics and a couple of break-ins. None were related to the unit we're looking at."

"Security?" Mooren asked.

"Artificial stupid silent alarm at the entrances," the Corporal replied. She paused. "That's an Artificial Sequential Intelligence," she clarified. "Pre-coded semi-learning algorithm, works through a logic chain to decide whether to call the Guardia.

"Nothing complicated or unusual," she concluded. "ASI alarm has never been triggered. This is quiet and boring, sir. Exactly where I'd rent an apartment if I was trying to stay under the radar."

"Wonderful," Roslyn murmured. "So, if we have to cause trouble, we're causing it for a bunch of the people we *don't* want to bother."

"They're all Protectorate citizens, aren't they?" Mooren asked, the Marine's voice calmly pointed.

"They are," Roslyn agreed. "We do everything we can to make sure we aren't *risking* anyone, but I prefer not to irritate the people who might have their local MP on speed dial."

Several of the Marines chuckled—but the Staff Sergeant cleared her throat.

"If you look out your left, we're coming up on the complex," she told them. "Time to peel our eyeballs, I think."

There was surprisingly little to see from the outside, Roslyn quickly realized. The complex was a square structure of white brick and red tile, with a gated accessway through to the inner courtyard with a stylish metal gate closing it off.

"Herbert, can you swing by the other side and see what the rest looks like?" Roslyn requested. There were balconies on the outside, but they had privacy screens to prevent exactly the kind of surveillance she was trying.

"On it," the pilot replied.

"Not much to see," Mooren agreed. "Can't slow down without drawing attention, either."

"Take us to that hotel," Roslyn ordered. "I'm going to see if I can get overhead from *Huntress*. Might not tell us much more, but everything we can get helps a little."

She was already considering her worst-case scenario: there wasn't going to be any way to tell if Killough was present from the outside. They were going to have to move in.

The suite Abiodun acquired for Roslyn at the hotel had clearly not been picked at random. It was excessively comfortable, in the Lieutenant Commander's opinion, but it had the virtue of having a seating area large enough for the Marines to all squeeze in.

Knight set up a few security devices to make sure they weren't being watched, and then Roslyn projected a hologram of the complex from her wrist-comp.

"This is what we've got," she told them. "It's not much. Right now, I know that Angus Killough rented a third-floor apartment in this building and the lease is still active. Someone is paying for it and the landlord doesn't think he's disappeared."

"Easy enough to pay in advance or set up recurring payments from an account with enough to cover it," Mooren pointed out. "And most landlords don't come around that often."

"Exactly," Roslyn agreed. "Last report I have from Killough is six weeks old. He believed our Prometheus lab was somewhere in Nueva Portugal, and was digging into some of the companies that the previous agents had IDed as working with Finley.

"It's *possible* he simply lost access to the drop box that got uploaded to the Link," she admitted. "But I haven't seen anything in the local data drops, either. So far as I can tell, he went dark six weeks ago."

"If his target moved against him, he may have just gone dark and not trusted his coms," Knight suggested. "But I'm not sure how to track him down if that's the case."

"I have emergency data drops that should have been secure in that case," Roslyn admitted. "They're empty. I have *nothing* suggesting that Killough is still alive except that the apartment is intact and untouched."

"Do we have the authority to just break in and kick his door down?" Mooren asked. "I mean, I'm up for doing it either way—though if he is alive, that will make for some interesting conversations."

Roslyn considered the parchment-wrapped datachip inside her overnight case. She probably didn't even need the Warrant for this, but...

"We have the authority," she said quietly. "But we don't want to draw attention to ourselves if we can avoid it. Covert, not exosuits."

"We left the exosuits on the shuttle, anyway," the Sergeant replied with a chuckle. "All we have with us is standard body armor."

"Which should more than suffice right now," Roslyn said. "I don't expect to run into Mages or Augments in Killough's apartment. I'm *hoping* for information."

Right now, all she could say with certainty was that all of the companies MISS had been investigating were either headquartered in Nueva Portugal or had major operations there. The city was a nexus of all of the potential players.

"There is one easy way to check it out," Knight suggested. "I've got a case of aerial drones locked in the SUV. They're pretty sneaky and they should be able to get us a peek into Killough's apartment without drawing too much attention."

"What else do we have in the van?" Roslyn asked. "That's a good idea, Corporal."

"Most of our gear is still on the shuttle, but we loaded everything we thought we would need quickly into the vans," Mooren told her. "We have armor, stunguns and carbines in the vans, plus some specialty gear like the drones."

Roslyn exhaled and nodded.

"I suggest we armor up and get those guns on hand before we send in the drones," she told them. "Just in case. I'm reasonably sure Killough is dead...but that means I also figure the people who killed him are watching his apartment."

CHAPTER 12

"WELL, ISN'T THAT a nice, quiet alley?" Mooren murmured to herself, pulling the van suddenly off to the side of the road.

Roslyn didn't say anything as the SUV came to a halt in said alleyway, out of view from anyone not directly in front of the exit.

"How close are we?" she asked.

"Forty meters from the back entrance," the Sergeant replied as the second SUV pulled in behind them. "A block of other apartments, but we can cross it in under a minute if we need to."

"We shouldn't," Roslyn said—but she accepted the black carapace chest-piece Corporal Knight absently handed her, leaning forward to pull it over her head. "But we'll prepare for everything, I guess."

"All right, everybody out," Mooren barked. "Knight needs space to work and we need to stretch our legs."

Roslyn waved the Marines out and slipped back to join Knight as the EW Marine opened up her case of toys.

The drones varied from a winged unit the size of a large bird to a sphere equipped with miniaturized vertical-takeoff-and-landing systems—and *hover* systems.

There were four of the VTOL spheres and Knight pulled them out. She set each one on a disk that appeared to link to her wrist-comp for diagnostics.

"Everything green, full fuel," she murmured. "These guys are quiet, Lieutenant Commander. Mix of ion engines and high-density air jets. They draw less attention than proper military drones, anyway."

"It's your specialty, not mine," Roslyn admitted. "Carry on, Corporal."

Knight nodded and started entering commands on her wrist-comp's holographic keyboard. The four drones lifted off, proving out their mistress's promises of their noise levels, and then flitted out the open side door of the SUV.

Roslyn could see the video feed from all four drones in the holographic display projected by the Marine's wrist-comp. They lifted up into the air, above the apartments, and swept toward their destination.

For a few seconds, the drones orbited the complex, allowing Knight to pinpoint their target.

"Fuel is limited," the Marine murmured. "Twenty minutes' endurance."

"All I need to know is if someone is in that apartment, Corporal," Roslyn said. "Then you can bring them home."

Nodding, Knight sent the four drones dropping slowly toward their destination. The unit had an interior balcony, opening out onto the well-kept gardens in the center of the apartment complex.

If the curtains had been open, they'd have had their answer almost instantly. As it was, the balcony doors were closed and the curtains were drawn behind them.

"That's a pain," Knight murmured. "But handleable."

Roslyn stayed silent as the Marine worked her technical magic. The four drones dropped onto the balcony, one of them moving up to the lock for the balcony door.

A new set of icons and commands popped up on the display for that drone as it extended a toolkit. Knight was focusing on that drone now, taking the little robot in closer as she prepared to pick a lock by remote.

Except the moment the toolkit touched the lock, all four screens died.

"What the hell?" Roslyn asked.

"Drone-killer pulse," Knight snapped. "Someone had a security system set up to stop us doing just that—and if the drone triggered that, it triggered an alarm."

The Marine shook her head.

"It shouldn't have," she admitted. "Not without my doing a lot more—not unless someone knew our gear *perfectly*."

"I *saw* that pulse," Mooren interrupted, sticking her head back in the SUV. "What happened?"

"Someone killed the drones with a focused EMP," Knight replied. "Are there still lights in the building? I half-expect—"

"Everything in the building is fine that Jacques can see," the Sergeant cut her off. "That's damn precise and damn specific." She turned her gaze on Roslyn. "Sir, they were waiting for Marine drones. We need to move *now*."

"Agreed," Roslyn decided instantly, jumping out of the SUV as she spoke. "Let's go."

The Marines took off at a steady sprint. Even in full body armor and carrying several weapons, they moved faster than Roslyn could have— but she had no illusions about that and instead stayed by the SUV, running a series of numbers through her wrist-comp.

Mooren stayed with her, presumably because she remembered they were *supposed* to be Roslyn's bodyguards, not her strike team.

"Coming, sir?" she finally asked as Roslyn finished her calculations.

"No," Roslyn replied sardonically. "I'm *leading*. Give me your hand."

The Sergeant looked at her in confusion.

"Give me your hand, Staff Sergeant, and remember that I am a Navy Mage."

Realization swept over Sergeant Mooren's face and she took Roslyn's hand. Power flashed over them as Roslyn *stepped* and they moved from the alleyway to the corridor outside unit 322 of the apartment complex.

"The door, please, Sergeant," Roslyn ordered as she took a deep breath to steady herself. Fifty-odd meters wasn't as draining as a full light-year— but on the other hand, she had the runic infrastructure of a starship's amplifier for *that* teleport. Any teleport was draining.

To her surprise, Mooren was only slightly off-balance. Most people who rode along on a personal teleport ended up vomiting. The Sergeant just took a moment to regather her senses before following Roslyn's order.

The presence of anti-intrusion measures was more than sufficient cause for Roslyn and her people to break into the apartment, and Sergeant Mooren was an apt student of the Royal Martian Marine Corps's method for forced entry.

An armored boot slammed into the door next to the lock. It was as much a test as anything else—a lot of doors would resist a regular human's muscles.

This one wasn't one of those, and the flimsy manufactured wood shattered under the Sergeant's boot, sending pieces flying into the room beyond as Mooren followed up with her entire torso.

Roslyn was right behind the Marine as the remains of the door crashed to the floor around the other woman. She had no time to take in the contents or state of the apartment as she realized there were *more* anti-intrusion measures.

She didn't know for certain what the black cylinder in the middle of the room was, but it looked like the kind of object that had THIS SIDE TOWARD ENEMY printed on it somewhere.

"Bomb!" Mooren shouted in agreement with Roslyn's assessment, charging forward to examine the black device.

Roslyn was right behind her, cursing herself for her failure to follow the risks all the way through.

"No time," she told the Sergeant, shoving Mooren aside to lay her hands on the device. That the bomb hadn't gone off already was probably due to the speed of the Marine's entrance, but Roslyn doubted they had any time at all.

Her magic flared to life again and pulsed through the runes in her hands. She *felt* the device heat as the explosion began—and then the bomb was gone.

The room was silent.

"Where did you send it?" Mooren asked quietly.

"Fifteen klicks straight up," Roslyn said. "I *really fucking hope* there was no one in that airspace."

CHAPTER 13

"SWEEP THE APARTMENT," Roslyn ordered the first Marines to join them. Coming down from the adrenaline high had occupied most of the minute it had taken the rest of the squad to reach them. The fire team certainly hadn't expected to find their two superiors waiting for them in the apartment and had entered with weapons drawn.

"Yes, sir," the Corporal replied immediately, gesturing for his Marines to check out individual rooms.

"I don't think we're going to find much, sir," Mooren admitted as she and Roslyn finally took the time to look around. "The EMP system will have self-destructed automatically—and so would anything linked to it."

The apartment was a solid midrange unit that would have looked perfectly normal on any planet Roslyn had ever visited. It was significantly nicer than the unit she'd lived in after leaving prison as a teenager, that was certain.

It was also a complete disaster. Someone had gone through everything. The tightly upholstered furniture had been sliced open with a blade. Every drawer in the kitchen had been emptied out on the floor. Anything in the main space that *could* be opened had been.

"Someone already went through here with a knife," Roslyn agreed. "But we'll see what we can find regardless."

She knelt down by where the bomb had been sitting and studied the impression in the carpet.

"The bomb was here for a while," she noted. "I guess that's positive."

"Positive?" Mooren asked.

"The bomb wasn't set for us, Sergeant," Roslyn said. "It was set for Killough and it was never detonated. That means he didn't come back here—and while that doesn't mean he's alive, it increases the odds of it."

Her wrist-comp started to buzz with incoming messages, and Roslyn grimaced.

"And now I need to explain why a bomb just went off above me," she noted. "What's your bet, Sergeant? Captain Daalman or the locals?"

"No bet, sir. It's the Captain."

Roslyn nodded silently and stepped away from the Marines as they continued to sweep the apartment.

"Lieutenant Commander, would you happen to know why a midsized explosive just detonated in the sky above Nueva Portugal?" Daalman asked calmly.

"Yes, sir," she said. "Because it was that or watch it blow up an apartment building, sir."

There was a long silence.

"That bomb was enough to level several city blocks," the Mage-Captain noted. "If you're in an apartment building, how many people just nearly died?"

Roslyn winced.

"Assuming half of the residents are away from home because it's only midafternoon, several hundred," she said levelly. "I was investigating a potential location for a contact, sir. And there were anti-intrusion measures."

"May I remind you, Lieutenant Commander, that the last thing we can afford is to cause trouble with the locals?" Daalman said. "Nearly killing several hundred people would count."

"I did not anticipate explosives, sir," Roslyn admitted. "I..." She breathed in sharply, glancing at the Marines and keeping her voice low enough that they couldn't hear her.

"I don't think I accurately assessed the risks," she confessed. "I didn't think a ground investigation would be dangerous in ways the Marines couldn't handle."

Of all people, Roslyn should have known better. She'd already been dragged into the wrong end of a Republic covert operation targeted at Crown Princess Mage-Admiral Jane Alexander, back when she'd been Alexander's Flag Lieutenant.

"How big of a disaster is this, Chambers?"

"It's under control. No one was hurt here and I *should* have got the bomb clear of anything in the air," Roslyn said in a small voice.

"Our scans say you're right. No one was injured, but that's a hell of a mess you're making, Chambers. I can't... I can't stand by while you risk civilians, Lieutenant Commander."

"I have no intention of risking further civilians, sir," Roslyn said stiffly. "I need to continue this investigation."

There was another long silence. Roslyn could use her Warrant to override the Captain if Daalman tried to shut her down, but that would ruin their working relationship.

"I trust you," Daalman said with a long sigh. "You have some contact with the locals now?"

"Yes, sir," Roslyn said, concealing her relief.

"Calm the waters," her Captain ordered. "Find out whatever you need to find out and then get back aboard *Huntress*. Please try not to find any more bombs?"

"I wasn't expecting to find this one, sir," Roslyn admitted. "If I find any more, well... Fifteen klicks up seems safe enough."

"I guess it does, doesn't it?" Daalman asked. "Be *careful*, Chambers."

"Yes, sir," she agreed quietly. The Captain cut the channel before she could say more, and she sighed as she saw that she now had a call from Lieutenant Oliveira.

"Mage-Lieutenant Commander," the Guardia officer greeted her politely. "May I inquire as to just what you are doing right now...and if it had anything to do with the explosion just reported above my city?"

"Classified, Lieutenant," Roslyn said as calmly as she could manage. "But I *can* tell you that if I hadn't been here, that explosion would have occurred rather closer to the ground."

Oliveira paused, seeming to chew on that.

"Then I guess I should thank you?" he asked. "May I ask that we avoid future explosions?"

"Believe me, Lieutenant, explosions are the second-last thing I want, behind major public attention," Roslyn told him, managing *not* to grit her teeth. "It will hopefully not repeat."

"I'm sure. Please keep me informed of what you can, Lieutenant Commander," Oliveira said plaintively. "Explosions do draw attention, after all."

This time, Roslyn cut the channel, feeling a little bad for the Guardia officer.

"What do we have?" she asked the Marines as they reconvened.

"Nothing," Mooren said grimly. "Place was occupied by one heavyset male of relatively decent taste. From the state of the food in the fridge, no one has been here in about five weeks. The search was professional and complete, if extremely destructive. Electronics on the EMP setup self-destructed when the device triggered. Neither the main bomb nor anything else were linked to the sensors, though."

The apartment was now stripped twice over.

"I'll let Oliveira know to come check it out once we're clear," Roslyn told the Sergeant. "Anything of use? At all?"

"One of the bedrooms had been turned into an office; looked like it had a computer console set up," Mooren said. "It's gone. Someone even cut a few test gouges in the table to make sure it wasn't hiding data.

"The people searching this place were *very* thorough."

"Fuck," Roslyn swore. "All right. Let's get out of here and head back to the hotel. Next step is going to involve a lot of financial records, so I hope *someone* has brushed up on auditing recently."

Mooren coughed.

"We're Marines, sir," she said delicately. "Only thing I audit is weapons inventory."

"Then you're the best I've got," Roslyn replied. "Get ready for paperwork, Sergeant. Tracing the ownership structures of the companies MISS flagged and seeing what they own in Nueva Portugal might be all we have left."

"I don't suppose giving up is an option?" the Sergeant asked, but there was no heat in her tone. She was looking around the wrecked apartment—and focusing on the impression in the carpet that had held a bomb capable of leveling the entire building full of innocents.

"We're looking for the people behind Project Prometheus, Sergeant," Roslyn replied. "What do you think?"

"I think we want to hang them high in the main square," the Sergeant admitted. "Alongside the son of a bitch who planted that bomb."

CHAPTER 14

THE NEWS REPORTS playing quietly in the background as Roslyn set to work in the hotel room were depressing. No one had been injured, but the lack of information about the explosion was leading to all kinds of ugly speculation.

She'd heard the news anchors blame everyone from *Song of the Huntress*'s crew to rogue Republic remnants to Mage-funded terrorists. The Republic-remnants theory was probably the closest, but the reporters weren't going to find evidence of anyone.

"I suppose if there were a smoking gun in these ownership docs, MISS would have found it ages ago," Knight opined drily. The Marine Corporal was suffering from the benefits of her skillset: while Roslyn could do the necessary analysis, she couldn't hack databases.

Knight *could*, though her cyberwarfare skills were usually more tactical.

"Well, I've pulled one thing out of it that MISS either didn't notice or didn't make it into the reports," Roslyn replied. "Take a look."

She expanded her holographic display and gestured Mooren and Knight over to her. "A few of the investments MISS managed to ID as belonging to Finley were run through numbered companies with this woman as a partner."

Roslyn highlighted the name: Roxana Lafrenz.

"MISS flagged Lafrenz as a potential interest, but they either didn't run the name against the list of known Prometheus Mages or my copy of the Red List is more complete than the one they sent to their field agents," she noted. The latter was entirely possible.

She was learning that the Red List was more segmented than the Protectorate liked to pretend. Any name on the Red List was dead-or-alive, no escapes permitted.

"Sir?" Mooren questioned, looking at the name.

The Navy Mage brought up a profile next to the list of ownership documents. A rotating holographic headshot of a blonde woman attached to a career record.

"Mage Ulla Roxana Lafrenz," Roslyn identified the headshot. "Mars-born Mage by Blood. Graduated from Curiosity City University's thaumaturgy program with a focus on biomagic. Proceeded to acquire a medical doctorate and become a Mage-Surgeon."

She grimaced as the two Marines reached the *next* part of Lafrenz's bio.

"At the age of thirty-two, she was identified as a member of the White Star Mage supremacy organization," Roslyn continued. "Accused of no less than six murders, she fled Mars less than six hours ahead of a warrant for her arrest and disappeared.

"Later intelligence showed that she appeared in the Republic as a protégée of Samuel Finley eight years ago," she concluded. "On the other hand, she vanished again from even most *Republic* records four years ago—around when her name started showing up in the local corporate ownership documents."

"We might just have our lab head?" Mooren asked.

"We might. At the very least, we have a senior Prometheus Mage, a Mage-Surgeon heavily involved in the development of the original brain-extraction technology, who appears to be on this planet," Roslyn told her subordinate. "If *all* we do here, Sergeant, is find Lafrenz, we will have made our efforts more than worth it."

She gestured at the pages of ownership listings they were looking at. Corporate ownership was a matter of public record in most human space, if not necessarily easy to access—or useful, unless you knew *exactly* what you were looking for.

"It also gives us a second name to look for in this damn haystack," she told the other two. Most of the Marines were just holding up walls at this point, but Knight and Mooren were helping.

Herbert *had* helped, but the pilot was now back at the shuttle making sure their gear was still where it was supposed to be.

"Somewhere in all of this is a pattern that explains *why* the man behind Project Prometheus bought up *half a billion* Republic pounds reliant worth of stock on the most isolated planet in the Republic of Faith and Reason."

Roslyn shook her head

"I'm not seeing it yet," she admitted. "But it *has* to be here."

Whatever pattern was hidden in the data didn't reveal itself after a single day of three analysts poring through it. Roslyn was able to pull out several more names of people who were involved in large percentages of the businesses and even numbered companies, but none of those appeared to lead anywhere.

She had three names of people who were definitely not in the Sorprendidas System—in one case because he'd been publicly tried and shot on Chrysanthemum during the slow dissolution of the Republic's government.

Two more names—a pair of sisters, she guessed—didn't seem to exist. At all.

One was a construction magnate with her fingers in practically every pie in Nueva Portugal. The woman wasn't necessarily untouchable— Roslyn had a Warrant of the Mage-Queen's Voice, after all—but she wasn't going to be the first place the Mage-Lieutenant Commander started hunting.

People who owned provincial governors were generally difficult to interrogate.

As night fell over Nueva Portugal, Roslyn was starting to think that Ms. London O'Berne was their best option. If nothing else, if O'Berne was innocent, she could provide them with a *lot* of internal documents from the companies in question. Documents that might just give them answers MISS hadn't been able to access.

"I do wish we had the work the MISS agents did," Mooren said grimly. "This is enough outside my area that I'm worried about missing things, but even if we're doing it *right*, we're duplicating work they already did."

"I know," Roslyn agreed. "But we have to do it anyway. None of the reports I had gave us a smoking gun and Killough's apartment was a public and wasteful bust."

The Marine grunted.

"So, what do we do?"

"We take a break," Roslyn decided. "Take Knight and half the team and go find a meal somewhere. I'll keep the other half here for security until you get back, then do the same."

She shook her head.

"There's no point in burning ourselves dry. We've been on-planet for a day."

"And we already blew up a bomb in the sky above the city," Mooren replied. "Aren't we making an impression."

With the Marines providing security or gone, Roslyn was alone in the hotel room. She was still staring at the data, trying to see if she could divine *which* of the several hundred construction projects Finley's people had been involved in had concealed a secret lab.

Nothing in the data was leaping out and providing exact information, and she sighed, pouring herself a glass of water as she looked at a holographic map of the city. If she had a *battalion* of Marines, she could send them off to inspect every site. With a squad, that wasn't happening.

There was everything from parks to office towers to entire residential suburbs on the list. Finley and Lafrenz had run everything through numbered companies, but the MISS agents had cracked open the ownership on those.

Without that starting point, Roslyn figured she'd have been *completely* lost, public corporate documents be damned. With it, she was merely convinced she was looking at a massive amount of data that *had* to have an answer buried in it somewhere.

Enough of an answer, at least, to have justified killing four Martian agents.

She sipped her water and was considering calling the hotel desk to have something stronger sent up when her wrist-comp buzzed.

The icon was from *Huntress*'s general communications department, which seemed...odd.

"Mage-Lieutenant Commander Chambers," she answered it crisply, allowing the device to scan her face for a holographic video call. An image of Lieutenant Commander Frost appeared in front of her, the blond officer looking amused.

"Commander," he greeted her with a lazy attempt at the salute her Medal of Valor demanded. "How's the surface?"

"Warm and cozy," Roslyn replied carefully. She couldn't speak about her mission or her frustrations. "What's going on, Frost?"

"I have a message that came in without any headers or directional information," Frost told her, his tone slightly more serious and surprisingly soft. "I managed to keep it under wraps on our end, as I suspect it's related to your mission—and all I know about your mission is 'it's classified.'"

He echoed Mage-Captain Daalman's tones perfectly.

"The message's header was simply: *to the idiot that nearly blew up Nueva Portugal.*"

Roslyn winced.

"While I hesitate to remotely support their description of today's events," Frost continued primly, "you are the only RMN officer in Nueva Portugal and, well, a bomb was teleported into the air."

"Your point, Commander Frost?" Roslyn asked.

"I'm presuming the message is for you," he told her. "Like I said, I kept it under wraps. Only myself and one of my Chiefs know about it, though I'll have to brief the Captain."

He grinned.

"Coms officers are used to seeing mail we're not supposed to read, Chambers," he said. "I haven't decrypted the message, but I have identified the cipher. It's an MISS code, our systems say, for covert operations.

"I'll send the decryption protocol along with the message." He shrugged. "If it *isn't* for you, let me know and I'll pass it on to the Captain. Seems the best compromise, yes?"

"It does," Roslyn agreed, shaking her head at the man's amusedly sardonic—but competent and sensible—approach to the odd message. "Thank you, Frost. I appreciate the care you're taking."

"You're welcome, Chambers. Forwarding now. Good luck."

The channel cut out, and her wrist-comp confirmed it had received an additional data transfer.

Opening the message and running it through the decryption that Frost had sent was the work of moments. The pure text message that followed was straightforward enough.

Please stop flailing around in the dark. Meet me.

That was followed by an address—a coffee shop twelve blocks from the apartment they'd visited—and a time. Eight AM local time the next day.

Roslyn shook her head. There was nothing to go on to make this sound legit or not—except that the code the message had been sent in was exactly what Ignác Frost had labeled it: an MISS deep-cover operative's encryption.

The encryption was both the only proof that the message was from an ally—and all the proof Roslyn Chambers needed.

Plus, well, even if it *was* a trap, that was still a lead.

CHAPTER 15

"WE HAVE EYES on the café," Mooren's voice said in Roslyn's earpiece. "Two hundred, three hundred and five hundred meters.

"Backup team is just around the corner with Corporal Knight. Exoteam is in the shuttle with Lieutenant Herbert. Current response time estimate is eleven minutes."

The Sergeant sounded disapproving to Roslyn.

"It takes five to warm the engines, Sergeant," Roslyn reminded her. "And if we do *that*, we attract more attention from the locals than we want."

She was walking down the street toward the café on her own. She was hardly defenseless, of course, and she knew that all three of Mooren's surveillance/sniper teams had her in sight as well.

"Any sign of our contact?" she murmured, speaking almost subvocally to make sure none of the other people on the busy sidewalk heard her.

"The café is pretty busy," the Marine told her. "I don't see anyone who sticks out as a spy, though that's what I'd expect. Any idea how you're going to flag them?"

"None at all," Roslyn admitted. "But they threw the invite my way, so I'm expecting them to have a plan."

She and Mooren were both feeling the limitations of their manpower. The three sniper teams took up half of the Marines available to them—including the Staff Sergeant herself. Knight's backup team was a single three-Marine fire team, including the Corporal. The team of Marines in exosuit combat armor aboard the shuttle was the last fire team they had.

Roslyn had seriously considered calling for more Marines, but that also felt like it would be overkill. Twelve Marines should be able to handle anything the secret lab's protectors could throw at her—especially if Herbert dropped an exosuited fire team in.

"It'll be fine, Sergeant," she subvocalized, smiling at the young woman standing at the hostess's lectern.

"Hi," she greeted the youth. "I'm looking to meet someone here? Eight AM reservation."

"Of course, ma'am," the hostess said, taking a quick look back through her patrons. "Table six, I think—that gentleman?"

Roslyn didn't recognize the slim dark-haired man in the blue suit, but she didn't have much else to go on.

"I believe so. Thank you."

She nodded to the hostess and headed into the open-air patio. The blue-suited man looked up at her approach and smiled. He looked gaunt compared to the imagery she had of him, as if he hadn't eaten properly in weeks, but he was definitely the man she was looking for.

"I wondered," he admitted. "Mage-Commander Chambers, I believe?"

"Mage-Lieutenant Commander," she corrected. "And you are?"

"Michael Hammond," he told her. "Or, to certain people not on Sorprendidas, Angus Killough."

"Ah," Roslyn breathed as she took her seat. She looked around. "This is rather...open for serious discussion, isn't it?"

"It is, I suppose," Killough agreed. "But I figured you'd want to have snipers on those rooftops in case I wasn't what you hoped." He waved airily at the buildings down the street—the buildings, Roslyn knew, where Mooren *had* placed snipers.

"And are you what I hoped?" Roslyn murmured.

"Well, you were in my apartment yesterday, looking for something," he told her. "I haven't been back there in a bit, as you clearly saw. Things got...hot. Communication channels were compromised."

She raised an eyebrow at that, and he shrugged.

"A bit too public for details," he conceded, "but there were some back doors we missed. Once I have *secure* coms, we'll need to address that."

"I'll admit, I didn't expect to meet you," Roslyn murmured. "Your message was promising, but...we had every reason to believe you'd joined your predecessors."

She wasn't even sure what the best way to talk around the situation was—but she *was* sure that the people at the table next to them could overhear them without difficulty.

Roslyn also hadn't ordered anything, so she was surprised when a robot trundled up with two sets of coffee and waffles.

"I took the liberty of ordering for us both," Killough told her. "Feel free to decline, Commander, but I have no more control of this restaurant than you do."

"Less, I think," Roslyn murmured. "Snipers."

"Do *not* eat that," Mooren's voice snapped in her ear. "We did not have a chance to sweep the kitchens."

Roslyn chuckled and leaned back.

"I am being advised not to touch the food," she said. "So. What do you want, Mr. Killough?"

"I suppose asking just *what* you were thinking yesterday would be rude," he said drily. "I can put together the logic chain, I suppose, but it very nearly got messy."

"I'll admit that I didn't expect to find a bomb in the apartment of a man we thought was dead," Roslyn said. "I think we handled it relatively well after that."

"Fair," he conceded. "It could have been much worse. I had a security setup in the hallway that they missed, so I knew they'd stripped and rigged the apartment. Safest thing to do was leave it the hell alone.

"I figured they'd eventually either remove it themselves or send in an anonymous tip," he told her. "*My* plan was to send an anonymous tip before the landlord tried to take possession."

"Could have been messy," Roslyn agreed.

"Thankfully, I had a backup plan and options," Killough told her. "They just didn't extend to retaining most of my damn tools. Hence reaching out once I realized you were poking at the same problem."

"Lafrenz," she noted.

"Among others, yes," he agreed. "I see you have access to our reports and some data."

She glanced around at the other patrons. They weren't paying attention, but this conversation could still be dangerous for them to overhear.

"I think we need to move this somewhere quieter," she told him. "Just realize our observers are coming with me."

"Of course," he allowed. "May I bring *my* coffee at least?"

"Sure," she said.

"All right," Mooren said in her ear, the Sergeant's voice resigned. "We also have visibility on the park one block south of your location. Backup team can move with you covertly and I'll only need to relocate one sniper team."

"Walk with me, Mr. Killough?" Roslyn said, eyeing the sidewalk Mooren was suggesting. It would work.

By the time they reached the park, Knight and the other two plainclothes Marines had fallen in around them. The five of them entered the green space and found a modicum of privacy there.

"Talk, Mr. Killough," Roslyn ordered. "You're alive where three other people are dead, but you went dark six weeks ago and everyone thought *you* were dead."

"It turns out that the Link is still compromised," he reiterated. "I don't know how, I don't know where, I don't even know how they picked our reports out of the traffic running through the civilian net to the Core.

"But they IDed us based on our reports and moved to neutralize us as quickly as they could." He shook his head. "I don't know how many Marines you brought, Commander Chambers, but I guarantee you that you have underestimated the threat level.

"My analysis suggests we're looking at at least three Mages and somewhere in the region of twenty covert-operation Augments," Killough laid out swiftly. "At least one Mage appears to be primarily security while the others engage in their research."

"That's a larger security force than I expected, yes," Roslyn conceded. "How big *is* this lab?"

"Big," he said bluntly. "I *believe* we are looking at one central location with maybe a dozen satellite facilities for...processing. The satellite facilities are irrelevant. Only the central facility will have access to their data, and it's where the Mages are hiding."

"How big?" she repeated.

He shrugged.

"Around sixty active people, including security and researchers," he told her. "It was designed for five times that, so the facility itself has to be significant. I *think* I know which sector of the city it's buried underneath, but I haven't had the eyes and the analysis tech to find it."

"That large a facility should be detectable from orbit," Roslyn countered. "That seems...unlikely."

"This might have been a rogue op under Finley himself, but he was drawing on Directorate resources throughout," Killough reminded her. The Republic Intelligence Directorate had proven themselves again and again to be one of the best covert-ops organizations in human history.

"They know how to hide their shit."

"So, what do you know that *isn't* in the reports I have?" Roslyn asked.

Killough sighed, glancing around to be sure the Marines had bought them enough privacy for this conversation.

"I don't think the missing-persons analysis made it into anyone's reports," he said grimly. "That was why they rushed the job on Yuan. They'd been talking to the Guardia and recognized the pattern—so the lab's security rushed the op and Yuan was publicly killed instead of disappeared.

"Whoever is in charge of security here is fond of making people disappear," the MISS agent concluded. "It's a Mage, but that's all I know. I'm not even sure where they *found* Mages for this shit."

"Finley had a lot of things to teach," Roslyn guessed. "Some people were willing to do anything, I think, to learn from him."

"Yeah." Killough was silent for a few seconds, then sighed. "Here, that *anything* is running somewhere around six hundred people."

It took Roslyn a moment to put together the pieces of what he'd said.

"Wait, you're saying they've killed six hundred people?" she demanded.

"Excess-missing-persons analysis," he told her. "Compared to the prior decade and similar cities elsewhere on Sorprendidas and in the Protectorate, the last two years have seen at *least* six hundred extra people go missing...and never be found."

"My god," Roslyn murmured. "But...why?"

"I don't know," he admitted. "Experimentation is my guess, but I haven't seen any excessive jump in morgue counts. It's like they completely disappeared. Not even their bodies found."

"So, they're either still alive or the researcher moved the bodies elsewhere and disposed of them to keep them *disappeared*," Roslyn concluded. "But what are they even doing that would require hundreds of human subjects—and *killing* them?"

"It's something to do with the Prometheus Interface," Killough told her, shaking his head. "I don't know what, but Lafrenz was one of the critical people building the neural-interface component of the system. Without her, Finley would never have managed to get the captive brains talking to computers or vice versa."

Roslyn swallowed a moment of nausea. The realities of the Republic's Prometheus Interface jump system were still sickening to her.

"Building a better drive? Or some kind of...reverse interface?"

"I don't know," Killough admitted. "But I *do* know that Ulla Lafrenz is directly responsible for thousands of deaths and *needs* to be brought to justice."

"I can't argue with that," Roslyn agreed. "I want to see your data, Killough."

He tapped his wrist-comp.

"It's all in here. I've had nothing else to work with for weeks. Staying in hotels and suchlike, under false IDs." He shivered. "Even for me, it's been a rough month."

"Sounds it," she said gently. That explained the weight loss from the file imagery all right. "We need to work together."

"Agreed. You're assigned to the new destroyer in orbit, right?" he asked. "I need access to her sensors. I'd *love* access to her computers to crunch some of the analysis I've been poking at, too, but I *need* her sensors."

"That's not entirely my place to give," Roslyn warned.

"Without it, this could take weeks," Killough said. "I can theoretically bring you up to speed and have you do the work, but that will take time. And from what I've seen, every day we waste is killing people."

She exhaled and nodded.

"I have to talk to my Captain," she told him. "I can probably get you aboard ship and access, but it's not entirely my call," she repeated.

"Fair." He tapped a command on his wrist-comp, and her own device chirped receipt. "That's everything I've got so far, just in case something happens to me. I *think* I've managed to avoid notice from the lab's protectors, but meeting with you has made us both vulnerable."

Roslyn nodded, considering the situation.

"Sir, I hate to interrupt, but you need to listen in on the Guardia channels," Mooren suddenly told her. "I don't know how much attention you and your friend have drawn, but there's a *riot* headed this way that did not exist twenty minutes ago!"

CHAPTER 16

ROSLYN'S TEAM didn't have official access to the Guardia network, but she was somehow unsurprised when Mooren uploaded her a full link to the local police service's operations map.

She projected it into the air between her and Killough, with Knight and the other two Marines closing in to see what was going on. It took her a moment to sort out the iconography—she'd been trained on standard Protectorate police symbology at one point, but she'd never *used* it before—but even the obvious factors were bad.

The entire region around them was lit up with calls for violence, break-ins and vandalism. The icons were shaded by severity, and even as Roslyn watched, more icons flashed to red—and new icons were appearing.

They were clustered in several locations, one of which was now covered by a rough circle in the map with a new code attached to it: the one Mooren had flagged.

Riot in Progress.

"What the *hell* is going on?" she whispered.

"I don't know, but look at the geography, Chambers," Killough told her. "Where did that bomb go off?"

"Directly above the apartment building," Roslyn said. It couldn't be... but a chill horror was spreading through her soul as she followed the MISS agent's logic.

"Wind patterns would have spread it to the east," Killough continued implacably, drawing a pattern in the hologram with his hand...a pattern that nearly overlapped with the chaos suddenly overwhelming several square kilometers.

"Some kind of...rage toxin?" Knight asked. "Included in the bomb's casing, to spread it as far as it could go?"

"It can't be related," Roslyn said weakly. The logic was too neat. It explained too much.

"Occam's razor, Chambers," Killough said grimly. "The simplest solution is often the correct one. If there *had* been some kind of toxin in the bomb, we'd be seeing a pattern like this. Depending on the weight of the molecules, it could have taken until this morning to take effect."

"Or most people were breathing it in while they were asleep and we're only seeing a critical mass of people affected now," Roslyn pointed out.

"Mooren, get your people down from the rooftops. Fall back on my position. Avoid attention if you can."

"Understood," the Sergeant replied. "We're coming in."

Roslyn looked at the map again and shivered as the cluster of red icons marking the riot continued to move in her direction. There were four clusters in the affected region, each seeming to gather new people as they moved.

"I need to talk to the Guardia," she decided. "Watch our backs."

Knight and Killough nodded simultaneously, exchanging a grim chuckle as they realized what they'd done.

"The Marines are in charge, Killough," Roslyn told him. "This situation is...weird."

She stepped away from her companions and switched her wrist-comp to pure communications and tried to raise Lieutenant Oliveira.

It took over a minute for the young Guardia officer to respond to her call—a minute in which she started to be able to *hear* the shouting. It... wasn't a coherent noise. If there were words there, she couldn't make them out at this range.

"Commander, I'm afraid I'm rather busy. How can I help you?" Oliveira asked, doing an admirable job of trying to conceal his stress. He wasn't managing it, but he was *trying*.

"I was hoping I might be able to help you if we trade information, Lieutenant," Roslyn replied. "I'm at the Tres Plantas Parque and everything around me appears to be going crazy. What's going on, Lieutenant...and can the RMN help?"

There was a pause.

"We're facing a series of riots for unknown reason," the young officer told her. "I don't know if you can help, but *we're* barely sure of what's going on."

"Have you connected with *Huntress* yet?" Roslyn asked. "If nothing else, my people should be able to provide you with better overhead. Captain Daalman also has Marines and access to Nix supplies."

Nix solutions were the Protectorate's tailored knockout gasses. Self-neutralizing above certain concentrations, they were *almost* perfectly safe. Of course, knocking large groups of people unconscious was dangerous regardless of how safe the drug used was, but it removed one potential problem.

"We have some stocks of Nix of our own, but we're hoping not to get to that point," Oliveira told her. He hesitated, then continued grimly. "There's a Guardia precinct station two blocks to the west of you, Commander Chambers. We've lost contact, but there's too much going on for my superiors to spare a ground unit to check it out.

"If you and your Marine escort could investigate, we would be... grateful."

"We can do that," Roslyn said, glancing over to confirm that Mooren had joined them. "Does the precinct station have a shuttle landing site? Several of my people are still at the dock along with our heavier gear."

"It does," Oliveira replied. "Commander...while I understand that I have no ability to give you orders, *please* do not use lethal weaponry. The situation is still under control."

"I wasn't planning on it, Lieutenant," Roslyn said. "But...Oliveira, we have reason to believe the riots may be linked to the explosion last night. You may be looking at some kind of chemical or even biological weapon.

"Your priority has to be containment."

He was silent for several seconds.

"That isn't my call, but I'll pass the suggestion up the chain," he told her. "And the recommendation to call your Captain. We'll see."

The channel closed and Roslyn shook her head as she rejoined her people.

"Guardia realizes something odd is going on," she told them. "We've been asked to investigate a precinct station that's out of coms. I don't like the sound of that...but they don't have the time to check it out.

"Please tell me we have stunguns," she asked Mooren.

The Marine Sergeant grimaced.

"Knight's team has full-size weapons, but the rest of us just have SmartDart sidearms," she admitted. "We were expecting to be countering an ambush by Republic covert ops, not...whatever the hell we're doing."

Roslyn had the same weapon, an oversized pistol that fired the intelligent taser darts. The problem was that it took two SmartDarts to reliably disable an adult human—and the pistol only held eight.

"We've got what we've got," she told the Marines and Killough. "Let's go find out what happened to the local cops."

CHAPTER 17

THEIR FIRST SIGN that something was even more wrong than they'd anticipated arrived just after they left the park, in the form of a girl of *maybe* seventeen, who charged out of the bushes with an incomprehensible scream.

She was on one of the Marines before Roslyn and the others could even react, clawing and screaming in rage as her hands scrabbled on cloth-covered body armor. The Marine tried to pull her off of him and she went for his eyes.

The sharp *crack* of a stungun carbine echoed through the park as Knight opened fire. Three SmartDarts appeared on the teenager, their calibrated electric shocks flinging her away from the Marine and onto the ground.

SmartDarts were locally networked, identifying how many of them were in the target and synchronizing their shocks for the size and weight of the victim. Like most nonlethal weapons available to the Protectorate, they were nearly perfectly safe and nearly perfectly effective, expected to disable a target for a minimum of five minutes.

Everyone in Roslyn's team was moving on when the girl got right back up and charged at Knight. Clawed fingers tore across the Marine Corporal's neck, and Roslyn saw blood as Knight went down.

Roslyn flung out a hand and threw power across the edge of the park, picking up the teenage girl and suspending her in the air. The child hung there, still trying desperately to claw at the nearest Marine with madness in her eyes.

"Move," Roslyn ordered the Marines, maneuvering the girl out of the way. "Someone check Knight's injuries."

"I'm just scratched up; she didn't have long-enough nails to do more," the Corporal told her.

"Check them anyway," Roslyn snapped. "We don't know if the toxin can be transferred."

The girl's eyes met Roslyn's and she shivered. There was *nothing* there. No personality. No sense. Just mad rage.

"Cuff the girl," she ordered. "We'll bring her with us. I can't..."

"We can't leave a kid tied up in a park when we have no idea what's going on," Mooren agreed, already producing a set of collapsible manacles from inside her fatigues. She approached their prisoner carefully, watching for the spasms as the girl *still* tried to lash out at whoever was near her.

Once the cuffs were on the child's wrists and ankles, Roslyn released her from the magic.

"I'll carry her," Killough offered. "I'm not armed."

The agent scooped the girl up into a fireman's carry with ease, despite her attempts to squirm around and bite him.

"This is nuts," the Marine who'd been jumped muttered. "She's *way* too strong."

"Not as strong as tempered steel," Mooren replied. "Come on, people. I don't know if there are answers at the Commander's precinct station... but I do know that Lieutenant Herbert is bringing our *armor* there."

They managed to make it to the Guardia station without any more surprises—mostly by actively avoiding people. There was no way to be sure if anyone they ran into was going to react like their prisoner, and they couldn't handle large numbers of prisoners.

The station itself was deathly still...the appropriate term, Roslyn realized, when she saw the doors had been torn from their hinges. It took a moment to recognize the *chunks* scattered amidst the debris of the front entrance as having once been a Guardia officer.

"I'm going to be sick," Knight said, her voice surprisingly level.

"No time for that," Mooren snapped. "Team, forward. Stunguns out." She took a breath. "Shoot anything that moves. We can apologize later if we tase a Guardia officer."

The reception area past the wrecked doors was worse. Several physically dismantled bodies were scattered across the benches, and there was blood everywhere.

"What the hell happened here?" Roslyn demanded. "I thought things only started going crazy a few minutes ago."

"Like you said, people inhaled whatever it was when they were asleep," Killough noted. "But where would you have a lot of awake people?"

"A precinct station," Mooren said grimly. "Shuttle pad is on the roof. Do we split up?"

"Hell, no," Roslyn replied. "Move as a group, sweep up. Look for more data."

The door to the first stairwell they found had been wedged shut from the other side.

"Leave it," Roslyn ordered. "There's got to be another set of stairs, and I don't want to risk surprises."

By then, Knight had a map of the building loaded into her helmet and pointed wordlessly.

"This is a fucking nightmare," Mooren murmured. "I *think* I'm at nine dead, but I can't be certain. Plus, I'd say only half were in Guardia uniform."

Roslyn nodded grimly as she followed Knight.

"Probably Guardia, prisoners and people being processed were all hit," she said. "There might still be people in the cells, but everyone who was mobile...was affected."

"Whatever that entails," Killough said grimly. "Did they all end up like her?" He gestured at the teenager he carried, who was *still* occasionally trying to bite him.

"We'll find out," Roslyn said, then held up a hand as Knight stopped at a door.

The Corporal paused next to the door, listening for a moment before she pushed it open. Nothing happened immediately, so Knight stepped through.

"Stairs are clear," she reported. "I think I'm good all the way up."

"Let's move as a group," Roslyn repeated. "Fire team Delta, then Killough with the prisoner, then everyone else."

She hadn't even introduced the MISS agent. Everything had gone chaotic so quickly, she was hoping her people were keeping up.

The other two Marines of Knight's fire team joined her, heading up the stairs, and then Roslyn and the others followed. The station was still and quiet as they moved.

"Sir, this is Herbert, we are inbound on the precinct station," the pilot reported. "I'm linked in with the Guardia, and they are establishing a perimeter around the affected region. No one is quite sure of the limits, but they're blocking roads and moving in riot trucks."

"Good," Roslyn replied. "There should be a pad on the roof. We're going to need to improvise a cell. We've got one prisoner who I want delivered to *Huntress* for medical examination under full quarantine protocols."

There was a pause.

"Sir, if we're engaging quarantine protocols..."

"Then everyone in the ground is already locked down, I know," Roslyn confirmed. "We'll need full medical work-ups on everyone on my team before we go aboard ship. You are to act as if we are infectious until then; understand, Lieutenant Herbert?"

"Yes, sir," the pilot agreed. "This is terrifying from above, sir. It's like half the people in the region just went mad."

"We know," Roslyn said quietly. "Leave it to the Guardia perimeter for now..." She sighed. "Can you link me to whoever is in charge? I need to update them on their precinct station."

No one was going to enjoy that conversation.

"What do you mean, *dead?*" the officer on the other end of the channel demanded. He paused, swallowing hard. "Apologies, Commander, but that seems..."

"I haven't pulled the station's security feeds," Roslyn told him. She hadn't got a name yet for the man in charge of the Nueva Portugal Guardia effort to contain the disaster she'd unintentionally caused. "But we haven't seen anyone alive in here. It appears that everyone in the station was...affected by whatever is causing this and they turned on each other in extreme violence."

She heard the swallow.

"I see, Commander Chambers." He paused. "I am Captain Victoriano Bolivar. I normally head up our tactical response team, but this is...beyond anything we're prepared for. I'm pulling officers in from their days off to run barricades, and basically leaving the rest of the city to fend for itself."

"Are you in contact with my commanding officer?" Roslyn asked. "*Huntress* has many tools that should be able to assist."

"We're getting a sensor feed, but the regional Governor has forbidden us to call on further resources than that," Bolivar admitted bluntly. "You're on the ground, Commander Chambers. What are you seeing?"

"So far, a horror show," she told him. "I've got a teenage girl in manacles who attacked two of my Marines with her teeth. She's still *trying* to bite anyone who gets near her. Your precinct station has multiple people physically torn to pieces, and I haven't dared send anyone down to check on the cells.

"My shuttle is landing now and, thankfully, has exosuit armor aboard for all of my Marines," she said. "*I'm* going to have to settle for combat armor and a biohazard seal. I think you have to assume whatever is in play is infectious, Captain, until you have data showing otherwise."

"No one is leaving the perimeter until we've tested them to see if we can find anything," Bolivar agreed. "This is madness, Commander. What was *in* that explosion?"

"I don't know, Captain," Roslyn said. "A nightmare. My intent is to secure the precinct station once my Marines have full armor and heavy stunguns. Otherwise, I am standing by for orders from Captain Daalman."

"Understood," Bolivar told her. "You are authorized to secure the station, but asking you to do more would violate my Governor's orders. What I could use is blood samples from your prisoner."

"We're going to be sending her into orbit under full quarantine protocols," Roslyn told him. "That means a vacuum-barriered pod on the flight deck, not even sharing air with the rest of the ship.

"I'll request that Captain Daalman forward you all of our results as soon as we have them, but I don't think we can risk dropping off actual samples." She paused, swallowing hard herself. "We need to assume that anything that has entered the zone is potentially contaminated. Do you have biohazard gear, Captain?"

"Not in the numbers I need for this," Bolivar said grimly. "The regional Governor is holding off on requesting help from the Cardinal-Governor in the hopes we can contain this."

"You have more data than I do, Captain. How bad is it?" she asked.

"Best guess is that eighty percent of the population has locked themselves in their homes and is hiding from this disaster," the Guardia officer told her. "The *other* twenty percent are in the streets, attacking people and wrecking buildings, and I don't know why.

"Even in the relatively limited area we're looking at, that's ten thousand people, give or take," he concluded. "We'll be moving in to try and secure the area and take prisoners shortly."

"If you don't have biohazard gear, that could be dangerous," Roslyn warned.

"I know," Bolivar said calmly. "But if I have ten thousand raging mad-men in the streets, that means I have forty thousand terrified civilians hiding in their homes, Commander. I have to rescue them—even if that means Nix-gassing a mob of thousands."

"If it's what we think it is, Captain, even the mob are innocent," she said quietly.

"I know," he repeated. "And the best thing I can do for *them* is to stop them hurting themselves."

Roslyn had just closed the channel and was turning to look up at the shuttle flying toward them when she heard the crashing sound of a door being flung open.

She turned toward the noise and realized it wasn't the stairwell they'd come up that was open. It was the other stairwell, the one that had been wedged shut...at the bottom. It had been battered open by two men in Guardia uniform, falling sideways with the lock clearly broken as the Guardia rushed out.

Roslyn's greeting died unspoken on her lips as she registered the complete *nothing* in their eyes—and the multiple bullet wounds the lead man was ignoring.

"Hostiles!" she snapped, summoning a barrier of solidified air to contain the two attackers. They moved so quickly, she missed one. The second Guardia man was pinned inside her barrier, clawing uselessly at an invisible shield, but the first was *on* Roslyn before she could recover.

He leapt on her, the weight of his body driving Roslyn to the ground as the breath was crushed from her lungs. A stungun cracked and her attacker spasmed, but he was still on top of her, clawing at her uniform and trying to bite at her face.

Her own hands were up, Roslyn's basic martial arts training suffi-cient to keep his teeth away from her skin. She couldn't focus on her magic with someone pinning her to the ground, and the mild aura effect of the SmartDarts left *her* twitching against the shock.

"Watch the other!" she heard Killough shout—and then a familiar sound she'd hoped *not* to hear echoed across the rooftop as at least two of the Marines opened fire with battle rifles.

Her own attacker was flung aside by the high-velocity rounds that punched through his flesh. Injured, probably dying, he still managed to snarl and lunge back at Roslyn.

She couldn't disagree with the Marines' decision to go to lethal force—and followed suit. Her hands flashed out, channeling power as she summoned lightning and force in a hammerblow that could take out a tank.

Her target went flying over the side of the roof and vanished, not even screaming as her power incinerated his flesh.

Magic still flared around Roslyn as she turned to the remaining Guardia man. He had been flung backward by multiple gunshots but was getting up again—at the edge of the roof.

Mooren was there before Roslyn could act. The Sergeant was unarmored, having stripped to her skivvies to enter her exosuit, but she held a fully automatic combat shotgun in her hands as she stepped between the madman and her Marines.

The gun *cracked* three times in as many seconds, slamming heavy lead pellets into the rising Guardia officer and hurling him off the roof to join the first man.

The rooftop was suddenly very still and very silent.

"I didn't authorize lethal force," Roslyn said quietly. "But...well done, Marines."

"Fuck this," Mooren said harshly. "Exosuits up; cover the accesses with heavy guns. Everybody *else*, get in a fucking suit of armor."

"No exosuits for myself or Killough," the Mage pointed out.

"We have body armor and hazmat helmets," Mooren countered. "We have one sized for you, and I think Killough can fit in my armor."

The MISS agent gave the tall Marine a frank but nonsexual glance up and down and then nodded.

"Probably," he agreed. "Might have to adjust here and there, but I'll take it over these poor bastards trying to eat my eyes."

"Hurry," Roslyn ordered. "That kid we have in cuffs aboard the shuttle is the best chance we have of working out what the hell is going on. Mooren—pick a fire team to send up with her and Herbert.

"They stay aboard the shuttle until Medical has cleared them. Full quarantine," she repeated for the tenth or eleventh time.

"Sardonis, go," Mooren ordered instantly. "We'll armor up and sweep the building.

"What are the locals doing, sir?"

"Securing the perimeter of the neighborhood and arguing with politicians," Roslyn replied. "But they're about to start moving in with riot vehicles and nonlethals."

She shook her head, looking at the smears of blood where her Marines had shot two functionally rabid Guardia officers.

"Good luck to them," she murmured. "We provide what support we can. I'm going to talk to Daalman...because Major Dickens needs to be ready to start dropping Marines for civil support. This is about to get very, *very* messy."

She hated herself for it, but she was grimly certain that whatever plan the Guardia had wasn't going to cut it. Whatever the *hell* was going on, she doubted water cannon, sonic dispersers and SmartDarts were going to bring calm.

CHAPTER 18

"WE'VE ACTIVATED the security shutters on the exterior accesses," Mooren reported once they'd completed their sweep of the precinct station. "No one is getting in. We can still get out, though our control is pretty manual. Someone needs to be inside to open and close the shutters."

"Better than nothing," Roslyn said. The hazmat helmet felt claustrophobic, limiting her visibility and head motion in every direction. She'd *never* worn full body armor outside of training exercises. All her hand-to-hand combat had been...insufficiently planned to call for that.

"Agreed." Mooren loomed in the exosuit combat armor, looking out over the neighborhood from the station roof. "We checked the cells, too. Everyone is still contained."

There was an edge to her tone that Roslyn didn't like.

"But?" she asked.

"We'll have to recommend that the Guardia recheck the filtration systems on their air handlers," the Marine said quietly. "The ones that are still alive are definitely affected and have tried to physically bash their way through the bars. None of them are in good shape...and those are the ones that were in solitary."

"And the others?"

"The drunk tank is a slaughterhouse," Mooren said, her voice forced level. "I eyeball that there were fifteen prisoners, at least, in the cells. Maybe five are alive and they've all hurt themselves. Badly."

"And we've still got most of the population hiding in their apartments and the locals have contact with the other precinct station," Roslyn observed. "This must have been one of the epicenters."

"Most of the chaos seems to be concentrating on the park where we started," the Marine replied, pointing down the street. "The affected don't seem to be attacking each other anymore, either. The...wreckage here says they did at the beginning."

Roslyn nodded quietly, glancing down at her wrist as her comp buzzed. It was Bolivar, and she tapped a command to link in the Guardia officer, sending audio only from her end.

His video feed was more compressed than it had been, a narrow square around his head. Behind him she could clearly see some kind of vehicle.

"I figured you'd want to be in the loop, Commander," Bolivar told her. "We're flagging a concentration of the...affected near your location, and we're moving a secondary perimeter in on the south side."

He shook his head.

"Primary perimeter will now act as a quarantine zone. No one leaves the zone without full medical work-up, blood, bioscans, the works. We need to know what we're looking at and that it won't spread."

"I agree," Roslyn told him. "My Captain is standing by to provide any medical or other assistance you need."

"I know," Bolivar confirmed. "Right now, however, my Governor is refusing to even call in planetary resources, let alone Protectorate resources. 'If we can secure the crisis alone, we have no need to call on others.'"

The last sentence was a clear echo, but Bolivar managed to say it with a mostly straight face.

"*Officially*, I cannot provide a full update to Captain Daalman," he continued. "However, you're in the area and I see a full need for both of us to be sure you're informed.

"How many Marines do you have, Commander?"

"Nine, all in exosuits with both nonlethal and antipersonnel ordnance," Roslyn replied. "I didn't think we needed to bring real heavy weapons, so they stayed on the shuttle."

"I'm not going to ask *why* you have heavy ordnance on your shuttle, Commander," Bolivar said drily. "I'm forwarding you an access program for a full tactical link. You should be able to see us move in and interface with our sensors and video feeds.

"I am trusting you not to forward that data to Captain Daalman; do you understand me, Commander Chambers?" the Guardia officer told her.

"I understand completely, Captain Bolivar," Roslyn agreed. She understood that he *wanted* her to relay everything to Daalman, just in case things went very, very wrong.

"For now, I want you and your Marines to remain in position and provide a backup surveillance from inside the zone," he continued. "Hopefully, we will meet in person very shortly, Lieutenant Commander."

"Good luck, Captain Bolivar."

The live channel closed, and Roslyn looked over at Mooren.

"We're getting a tactical feed from the Guardia," she told the Marine NCO. "Can you or Knight set up a relay to get it to *Huntress*?"

"Of course." Mooren paused. "They're moving in, then?"

"They are. Bolivar says we should see them shortly," Roslyn said. "Bullshit."

"That's what he's afraid of, yes."

By the time the Guardia vehicles rolled in, Knight had interlaced the data from the locals with the overhead from *Song of the Huntress* and provided them with a stunningly detailed view of Nueva Portugal's attempt to restore order.

Whatever the situation might be, the Guardia had a standard set of protocols for escalation of force. Massive loudspeakers ordered the crowds to disperse—but only seemed to draw the attention of the small crowds of victims still scattered through the southern half of the neighborhood.

Dozens, then hundreds, of bodies gathered toward the sound of sirens and loudspeakers. There was a standoff as the lead vehicles, armored riot vehicles that could pass for light tanks, came to a halt ten meters from the crowd, continuing to bellow orders to disperse.

Instead of dispersing, the crowd on Knight's holographic projection surged toward the vehicles. New icons flashed up on the hologram as the lead pair of vehicles activated their sonic dispersers, noisemakers that were supposed to act on subconscious instincts to send humans running.

The crowd kept charging. Roslyn grimaced as she watched the civilians storm onto the riot vehicles, clawing mindlessly at the armored panels and trying to break into the pseudo-tanks.

The officers behind the riot vehicles opened fire with stunguns, but Roslyn already knew what was going to happen there.

"We told them," Knight said grimly. "What the hell are they going to do?"

"That," Mooren said grimly, pointing as the video feed showed gas vents opening on the exterior of the riot vehicles. "Nix solution. It's a last-ditch defensive measure for exactly this situation."

Except it wasn't working. The hologram was interpolating imagery from multiple sources and gave Roslyn and her people a clear image as one of the people swarming the lead riot vehicle tore the access hatch open. Half a dozen people fell into the opening within seconds—and the Nix solution came with them.

"My god," Roslyn whispered. "What... What do we *do*?"

More SmartDarts cascaded over the crowd as the Guardia officers opened fire with everything they had. The SmartDarts' shock settings were still managing to bring people to the ground, temporarily disabling them...but Nueva Portugal had been an UnArcana World. The local police didn't have Mages to pin people down as Roslyn had incapacitated their one prisoner.

The second wave of vehicles and officers began to pull back. It wasn't a planned thing. It was a wavering step backward. Then another. Then three.

Then people were running—and like predators sensing weakness, the crowd came after them.

Seventy-plus officers abandoned their vehicles and fell back toward the outer perimeter. At least three hundred theoretical civilians came after them. Even from several kilometers away, Roslyn *heard* the incoherent keening scream as the affected victims charged the Guardia.

She knew what had to happen next and forced herself to keep watching. Everyone who was going to have to live through this was innocent, attackers and Guardia alike. They deserved her witness.

The vehicles of the barricade were pulled aside to let the fleeing officers through. There were still maybe forty Guardia on the perimeter, and Roslyn could feel their hesitation. More loudspeakers were blazing. Sonic dispersers were active.

The icons of Nix grenades scattered across the charging crowd as several automatic grenade launchers opened up, but the supposedly perfect knockout gas did nothing. Flash-bang icons, their overwhelming sound audible even from Roslyn's perch, seemed to slow the charge...but only for a moment.

The gunfire was inevitable, and it broke her heart anyway. The Guardia didn't even *have* a lot of lethal weaponry—very few Protectorate police forces carried lethal weapons by default—but they'd issued automatic rifles to the outer perimeter.

It took a moment for Roslyn to realize they'd opened fire too late. Even automatic weapons couldn't slow a charge by ten times as many attackers as defenders when they only opened fire at twenty meters. The mob were *among* the Guardia far too quickly.

"Incoming," Mooren suddenly snapped. "Heads *down.*"

Roslyn obeyed instinctively—only looking up to see two of *Song of the Huntress*'s assault shuttles come screaming in a moment later. Their engines flared white-hot as they slammed into a jet-fueled hover above the chaos.

Twenty-millimeter ground-support cannon opened up moments later, the two assault shuttles strafing the streets as exosuited Marines leapt out, plunging to the ground like angry meteors as they charged to the Guardia's rescue.

"Chambers, you there?" Daalman's voice asked, clearly having overridden her way into Roslyn's coms.

"I'm here," Roslyn said in a shaky voice.

"This is a nightmare," the Mage-Captain said in a disturbingly calm voice. "You're on the ground; I'm linking you to Dickens's command and control.

"We had two shuttles up just in case, but I wasn't going to defy the regional Governor until things *really* went to shit. We've got the feed you forwarded us, but Dickens is going to need eyes on the ground."

There was a long pause.

"I am assuming the situation is sufficiently diffuse that *Huntress's* weapons will only make things worse, correct?"

"Yes, sir," Roslyn confirmed. "I think the locals are going to be willing to accept your help now, sir."

"I don't care if the locals are *willing* anymore," Daalman said grimly. "I don't actually have to listen to them. It's just *rude* to drop Marines without permission."

CHAPTER 19

MORE SHUTTLES delivered the rest of *Song of the Huntress*'s Marines over the next half-hour, doubling up the perimeter and making sure nothing left the quarantine zone.

Roslyn and her people remained on the rooftop, watching the tactical displays.

"I wish we could be more help," Mooren muttered. "There's still a lot of unaffected people in the area, and I don't know how safe they are. Without something to lash out at, that mob is going to either start breaking into buildings or breaking out of the perimeter."

"I know," Roslyn said. "Keep your eyes peeled for movement toward the apartment buildings. We're going to have to do *something* if the civilians are in danger."

Something was probably going to be air strikes from the assault shuttles. That was the last thing Roslyn wanted to enable or order, but what could they do?

"All of the Marines are down," Mage-Captain Daalman informed her. "I don't suppose you have any clever ideas, Lieutenant Commander?"

"Nothing that leaps to mind, sir, except seeing what the medical report says on the prisoner we sent up," Roslyn replied.

"I just got that," Daalman admitted. "The blood sample is normal. Bioscans are normal. Girl is now in a coma, and Dr. Breda thinks we might lose her."

"How is she *normal?*" Roslyn demanded. "She got back up after being SmartDarted, sir. There is *something* going on."

"I agree. But our medical systems can't detect whatever it is. That's a problem, Commander, as we try to establish who we can let out of quarantine."

"Yes, sir," Roslyn agreed. "Sir...I think this may be related to my investigation. Specifically, to the bomb."

She was responsible for this. The Guardia and Marines had already killed dozens of people. Dozens more had killed *each other*. All of this was because Roslyn had rushed into Killough's apartment and found a trap.

Daalman sighed.

"I suspect the same," she admitted. "But *this*, Lieutenant Commander, was not something you could have anticipated. You reacted to the clear and present danger in an entirely appropriate manner.

"This? This you can't hold yourself responsible for. This is down to the bastards who placed the bomb. Please tell me you can find them."

"I don't know yet, sir," Roslyn said. "I have a lead, a contact, but I need access to *Huntress*'s sensors and computers...and you can't risk bringing us aboard."

"So far, quarantine protocols on your shuttle suggest that there is no active infection risk," Daalman told her. "The medical work-up on our prisoner is perfectly clean, after all."

"Can you have Dr. Breda send that to me?" Roslyn asked. "We might find something she missed... I have an idea of what the people here were working on that I can't share."

"I'd argue that the doctor needs to know, Commander Chambers," Daalman told her.

"That depends on if I find anything to suggest a connection," Roslyn said. Given the orders she had from the Prince-Regent, she was going to err on the side of caution for a bit longer.

"Fine. We need to start planning to extract you, regardless," the Mage-Captain said. "Lieutenant Herbert is still in isolation, so sending her back down should be fine."

"I feel like I should be here until the end, sir."

"Permission denied," Daalman said bluntly. "I'm leaving the ugly choice of whether to risk the unaffected civilians by waiting a day to see if the effect fades or going in now to the planetary Cardinal-Governor.

"I expect him to make that call in the next ten minutes. You, Lieutenant Commander Chambers, are *not* going to be in there overnight or while the Planetary Army storms the quarantine zone.

"This is not a discretionary order."

"They almost seem to be drawn to each other, like there's a marshaling order in their heads telling them to attack the perimeter en masse."

Knight's voice sounded more sick than analytical as she watched the display with Roslyn. The deaths of dozens of the affected as they'd rushed one section of the perimeter appeared to have rippled through the remaining people in the quarantine zone.

Now the park to the north of them had been filled with a cluster of at least five thousand people, all making an awful keening noise that tore at Roslyn's ears and sanity alike.

"Clear the landing pad," Herbert told them over the radio channel. "I am coming in."

"Pad is clear," Mooren replied, letting Roslyn continue to look at the holographic display and wallow in her guilt.

The sound of the shuttle descending finally cut off the horrific keening of the victims of her mistake.

"There it is," Knight suddenly said.

"There what is?" Roslyn asked.

"The Cardinal-Governor's orders. He's going on air in ten minutes, but the first wave of orders just went out: the entire peninsula is being quarantined until further notice. Units of the Sorprendidas Planetary Army are moving in by helicopter to secure the roads and ports."

"Makes sense," Roslyn said grimly. She looked over at Killough. "Any clear sign in those medical reports?"

"No," the MISS agent replied. "I'd say whatever it *was* dissolved underneath medical examination. So, standard bioscans should be a treatment, but...getting people into them would be almost impossible."

"That's disturbing," she said. She stepped away from the hologram as the shuttle touched down behind them, looking up the road to the park she knew was full of rabid innocents.

"If we could disable them somehow, it would be an option," she said. "But...SmartDarts only knock them down. Nix gasses do nothing. It might fade in a day or two, but...there's enough innocents in the quarantine zone that I doubt the Governor is going to risk it."

"The only thing I'm seeing out of the ordinary is silver carbonate," Killough told her. "The quantity is...nothing, but it shouldn't be there at all."

Roslyn blinked.

"That's what we make runes out of, isn't it?" she asked.

"Not quite," Killough said. "It's a decay product when the polymer breaks down. *You* would have silver carbonate in your bloodstream at a slightly higher level than this, but you have Jump Mage runes that your body is trying to metabolize.

"This girl has no runes, and silver carbonate isn't something that most people encounter."

"It's something for the quarantine line to look for, at least," Roslyn told him. "Let's keep it in mind. For now." She gestured to the shuttle.

"It's time for us to go."

CHAPTER 20

THE NEW DESTROYERS had enough space that Mage-Captain Daalman had been able to set aside a section next to the shuttle bay to act as a temporary quarantine zone. Medtechs in full-body hazmat suits guided Roslyn and her team into the designated rooms.

"How long?" she asked Dr. Breda, once she'd managed to identify the squat woman amidst the support staff.

"Well, the good news is that it doesn't seem to be contagious," Breda told her. "Certainly, there's nothing coming through the class five biosuits.

"It also looks like about an eight-to-twelve-hour onset, so you're probably already fine," the doctor continued. "We're going to keep you quarantined for twenty-four hours just in case."

"What's the Cardinal-Governor ordering?" Roslyn asked.

"No one is leaving New Portugal for two weeks," the Navy doctor replied. "I believe we're providing sensor support as well as medical aid as needed."

"I see the planetary Governor likes us better than the regional one did."

"Not really," a new voice interrupted. Roslyn looked around to see Mage-Captain Daalman, identifiable by her height even in a class five biosuit. "Cardinal-Governor Fulvio Guerra is just more desperate than his local subordinate.

"He *did*, after all, just have to order the death or internment of thousands of his citizens to save *tens* of thousands," Daalman said grimly. "Our Marines are going in. It's...ugly."

"I thought I saved them by teleporting the bomb," Roslyn said quietly.

"If you hadn't done what you did, several thousand people would have died in that moment," her superior pointed out. "And *then* we would still have had to deal with this.

"I've had our systems people set up full access to our databases and scanners from the quarantine section, linked to your authority," Daalman continued. "You and your...contact should be able to do whatever you need to do.

"Thank you, sir," Roslyn replied. "I'm...surprised you still trust me."

"You misjudged and charged in, but you also handled the result in the best way possible," Daalman pointed out. The older woman shook her head. "I would have preferred you to put in the work to *know* there was a bomb, but I won't pretend I see a better way to handle what you found.

"The blame sits on the murderous assholes who designed and deployed this goddamn modified rabies virus or...*whatever* it is," she said. "Find them, Lieutenant Commander Chambers.

"We don't execute people for much, but I'm going to *enjoy* watching these assholes swing. Find them for me," she repeated.

"Yes, sir."

Every piece of analysis they'd done on the surface was in Roslyn's wrist-comp, easily fed into *Song of the Huntress*'s computers as Killough downloaded information from his own machine.

The Marines, finally stripped out of their bulky armor, left the tactical officer and the MISS agent alone with the computers. They seemed to focus on the *showers* that had thankfully been included in the quarantine quarters.

Roslyn, on the other hand, had panicked at the sight of the showers until she'd confirmed the water was being contained and not fed back into the ship's main supply.

"The key that I found, shortly before everything went to hell for me, was that Lafrenz and Finley and their partners owned enough of one of the local construction companies to make Lafrenz CEO at one point," Killough told her. "They had enough ownership of other companies to bury the supplies needed to build a facility, but they needed machinery and people.

"They found them in Triple Q Commercial Construction. They bought three-quarters of the company through assorted fronts, turfed the entire senior executive staff and put Lafrenz and what I assume were carefully selected allies in their place."

Data on Triple Q was running across the screens as Killough spoke. Most of it was very high-level, the general information submitted to stock exchanges and suchlike around the company's projects.

"So, if Triple Q built it, we need to find out which project they buried it in?" Roslyn asked.

"Exactly. Which is a problem, because Triple Q no longer exists," Killough told her. "The files and paperwork that would give us those answers are locked behind a court filing in a secure judicial server.

"They appear to have overstretched themselves and failed to deliver a third of their projects on time or on budget. Penalty clauses wiped them out a year ago, tying up thirty-two construction projects in Nueva Portugal alone in debts and lawsuits."

Roslyn winced.

"Lafrenz did that intentionally, I'm guessing?" she asked.

"Probably. At this point, the work crews have scattered to every other construction company on the planet, one by one. Any listing of staff below the executive level is in those confidential files the court won't release."

"What about the executive level?" Roslyn said. "They can't all have been Lafrenz's patsies."

"Fifteen names listed in the last annual report," Killough said after a moment. Those names floated in the air between them. "Obviously, we have failed to track 'Roxana Lafrenz.' I should have data on some of the others."

"I'll see what's in the public files," Roslyn told him. "Let's see what we pull together."

The answer was a litany of blatant lies, unexpected deaths and people who'd never existed at all. Five of the names joined "Roxana Lafrenz" as being aliases. Six of them had *existed* but had already been off-planet when they'd been listed as part of the final executive staff of Triple Q Construction.

The remaining six were dead. Two heart attacks, one cancer, three car accidents.

"Normally, I'd trust natural causes," Roslyn said as she and Killough went through the results together. "Except that Lafrenz is a Mage-Surgeon and I have to wonder if she could give someone cancer."

"Fucked if I know," Killough admitted. "Though that is a terrifying thought."

He shook his head.

"If the people aren't the answer, the projects have to be," he told her. "What I didn't manage to pull together was a list of projects they completed. That's what I wanted *Huntress*'s computers for.

"If we can search the public construction records and flag everything Triple Q was involved in over the last five years, that gives us a starting point," he continued. "We can then try an analysis to see what was big enough for them to have hidden a lab of the scale we're talking about.

"I'm *assuming* it's underground, but to be honest, that's just an assumption."

"If they set it up right, they could just as easily hide it in an office or even a residential tower," Roslyn agreed. "Or just in the basement of a tower."

"Or bury it when they're laying the pipes, power and pavement of a residential suburb," Killough said. "There's a lot of places and ways they could have hid this project, Commander. But I think *Huntress* has the computers and access to find all of their projects in a way that a rented console in a library can't.

"The bastards swapped my analysis setup for a bomb, after all."

"I'll start the searches," Roslyn told him. "You..." She sighed. "Can you take a look at what happened in the quarantine zone? We know that's related, so I want to see what comes out of it.

"I'm just not sure I can bring myself to look."

The construction permits and licensing of a midsized city were a massive amount of information that were rarely properly organized, scanned or stored. All of it was at least digitized, but the search Roslyn had set for *Huntress*'s computers was far from as straightforward as it should have been.

And that was *before* the fact that even a legitimate construction company would often bury their involvement behind numbered companies or subordinate contractors to keep competitors in the dark about what was going on.

Roslyn's involvement as the computers crunched was wading through court files and legal filings to identify the other companies Triple Q might use to hide their involvement and adding those to the search.

It kept her mind engaged and away from the horror show they'd seen on the surface—at least until Killough stepped back into the room with her and sat down heavily.

She looked up at the newly tight lines on his face and swallowed.

"That bad?" she asked.

"Yeah," he told her. "The quarantine zone is secure, though the locals still aren't letting anyone out. One hundred and twenty-two Guardia officers are dead. About that again wounded."

The Nueva Portugal Guardia had responsibility for five million souls. If they had the usual ratios of Protectorate police departments, two hundred and fifty casualties were over a tenth of the entire Guardia.

"And the victims?" she asked quietly.

"Current estimates are over four thousand dead," he said flatly. "Current reports are that they managed to disable and contain about eighteen hundred, but processing them is being a nightmare.

"Most of the ones they've managed to get into bioscanners have... Well." Killough shook his head. "Like the one you sent aboard *Huntress*, they're in comas with mixed prognoses. Like her, though, they seem clean *after* the bioscan."

"So, whatever we're looking at is actively killed and dispersed by the radiation used in a bioscanner," she said. "How did something *that* fragile survive an explosion?"

"Different stages in the life cycle?" the MISS agent guessed. "I'm not a bioscience guy. I'm a *spy*, Commander. The locals are starting mass autopsies on the Cardinal-Governor's orders...and then the bodies will be burned."

Roslyn grimaced. Despite Daalman's assurances, she couldn't shake the feeling this was her fault.

"Let's hope the autopsies show something we can use to protect people," she told him. "*Anything*. This is a nightmare."

"I wish it was a nightmare," Killough said. "I'm a lucid dreamer, Commander. I can *fight* my fucking nightmares. I can't fight this, and I won't wake up from this."

The room was silent, and Roslyn glanced back at her data search.

"It's going to be an hour or so before we even have our first-wave search results," she told Killough. "I suggest you try that sleep business. See if you *do* wake up."

He snorted.

"Fair. What about you, Lieutenant Commander?"

"I need to keep going," she told him. "My nightmares are bad enough most days. I'm not looking forward to these additions."

"A word of advice?" Killough offered. "Go rest yourself. Taking a few more hours to look at the data isn't going to change anything, and even nightmare-ridden sleep is better than working yourself to death.

"And once you've done that, talk to the damn ship's doctor. I'm assuming she knows how to handle trauma."

Roslyn already had regular sessions with Dr. Breda. The RMN was *very* specific in their doctors' training.

"She does." Roslyn sighed. "You're probably right. I just want my damn answers."

"Even this data search just kicks off a wave of analysis which just tells us where to point *Huntress*'s sensors," Killough pointed out reasonably. "None of this is going to be fast, Chambers.

"We'll be better at the analysis if we're both fresh. Go rest."

CHAPTER 21

ROSLYN'S SLEEP was as bad as she'd feared, but she *did* sleep. New night-mares of Guardia officers full of bullet holes trying to tear her apart joined her old nightmares of cells aboard Republic warships and space stations.

When she woke from a dream where a bullet-filled Guardia offi-cer tried to sexually assault her *in* one of her old cells, she decided enough was enough. She'd never actually been sexually assaulted while a Republic prisoner—it was a low bar to clear but one the Republic co-vert-ops team that had captured her had managed.

Checking her wrist-comp, she saw that she had managed to sleep for five hours. Her data search had finished three and a half hours earlier—and she had a video message waiting for her from Dr. Breda.

She hit Play on the message as she donned a fresh uniform. She'd presumably be back in her own quarters that night, which would help with some of the stress level.

"Lieutenant Commander Chambers, I figured you'd want to see the summaries of the autopsies the locals have been carrying out," Dr. Breda told her. "As I'm recording this, they've completed just over two hundred and seventy individual autopsies of affected individuals, and there are def-initely some visible signs of what happened.

"The reports they sent up are attached, but I wanted to give you my own take on it all as well," she concluded. "The major thing to realize is that we are looking at something with a clear and significant effect on the brain stem and nervous system.

"As with the bioscans, there is limited sign of any *cause* of the damage by the time of the autopsy," Breda warned. "But the dead don't heal. We can see patterns of damage and...integration, for lack of a better term.

"Whatever affected these people was directly linking into their nervous system in a way that's rarely seen with viruses or bacteria. That kind of intrusion is more usually linked to a larger-scale parasite—but it *has* been incorporated in artificial viruses."

Breda's face was perfectly professional, but something in her voice and eyes told Roslyn she was worried by what she was seeing.

"We are continuing to see the presence of silver carbonate as you flagged in the bloodwork of our own patient," she told Roslyn. "Both in the dead and the living prisoners.

"Most disturbing of all, though, is that several autopsies show clear signs of postmortem damage," Breda said quietly. "I do not believe that either the locals or our Marines were intentionally shooting corpses, which means in some cases it at least *appeared* that an affected individual was still threatening the containment teams while already dead.

"Given the pattern I'm seeing, it is possible that the nervous-system integration allowed an affected individual's body to continue moving *after* blood flow and brain function had ceased," she concluded. "I do not believe, given the degree to which even blood samples are clear of the infection, that situation would last very *long*...but it is a possibility in the short term.

"That could be why Nix and SmartDarts have no effect," Breda concluded. "Potentially, the brain *is* being disabled...and the virus is puppeting the victim."

The doctor paused.

"Unfortunately, our own prisoner will not be able to answer questions," she said quietly. "Despite our best efforts, her body is shutting down. We are doing everything we can, but keeping her unconscious and in a state of partial hibernation is the only thing buying her time.

"If she can be saved, Commander, we *will* save her. But this kind of coma is hard to predict or counteract. If I had an intact sample of the damn virus, I would be able to identify just what it did to her body and be certain I could save her—and, in saving her, save the hundreds the locals have in the same state.

"As it is..." Breda shook her head. "I know you're doing *something* classified that I suspect is related to this mess. I hope it's finding the bastards who did it. If there's anything I can do to help, let me know.

"There's a comatose sixteen-year-old girl dying in quarantine in my medbay, and she's just one example of this mess. Someone has to pay."

Roslyn grimaced as the recording stopped. There wasn't much she could say to that—and she agreed *completely* with the doctor's sentiment.

CHAPTER 22

ULLA LAFRENZ'S FINGERS had woven through every corner of Nueva Portugal.

The data analysis that Roslyn had left running gave her the answers she needed, but she wasn't sure how helpful they were. Triple Q had become one of the largest single builders in Nueva Portugal over thirty years—right up until the moment they hit penalty clauses on seventeen contracts within six months and collapsed.

Roslyn had the authority, one way or another, to access the company files locked behind the seal of the courts. Not many people *would* have that authority, though, which made the bankruptcy and ensuing lawsuits an effective screen against acquiring data on Lafrenz's activities.

The problem was that she didn't know *when* the lab had been constructed. Triple Q had collapsed about six months after the war ended—they had been far from the only major corporation in the former Republic worlds to come apart despite the Protectorate's best efforts to arrange a smooth transition.

On the other side, Finley and Lafrenz had taken control of the company shortly before the actual Secession. That left a period over four years long in which they'd controlled a major construction company and been able to do whatever they wanted.

"I wish I knew when they finished the Prometheus research," she said aloud. If the lab on Sorprendidas had been intended to carry out research expanding on the brain-interface work Project Prometheus had done, then logically, they wouldn't have built the lab before that was done.

But...they wouldn't have moved into Nueva Portugal with enough money and influence to secure control of Triple Q until they'd been planning on building the lab, so she could assume that the lab would have been built as quickly as possible after they took control.

She had no idea at what point Lafrenz would have decided to cover her tracks by destroying the company, but it would make sense that they'd have started building within, say, six months of her taking control of the company as CEO.

Roslyn ran that into her data as a filter. That brought her down to a *mere* twenty-eight construction projects across the city. Three neighborhoods, seven apartment complexes, four parks, two hotels, a casino, and eleven office towers.

She pulled up a holographic map of the city and marked those twenty-eight locations in red. Between the parks and the neighborhoods, there were several large swathes of Nueva Portugal lit up in red—plus the casino complex, in one of the exurb communities several dozen kilometers outside the city itself.

None were in the quarantine zone. *That* area had more to do with where Angus Killough had set up his base than with anything the secret lab was doing.

At least with only twenty-eight targets, they could actually start pointing *Huntress*'s sensors at the locations and see what they could pick up. The rogue Republic lab would be well concealed, but there were *limits*.

"I see you couldn't sleep very well," Killough observed from the door.

She looked up at him and snorted.

"I had nightmares *before* this," she said. "If anyone ever told you naval service was a joyride, well, they lied."

"I know a few people who would have figured being the Crown Princess's protégée would be," Killough said. "Though, as I understand it, you were captured with her."

Roslyn shivered.

"Yes," she confirmed shortly. "And that's as much as I really want to talk about that."

Being imprisoned and stripped of her magic for weeks had been one of the more unpleasant aspects of her life—and she'd spent two years in the care of Tau Ceti's "Juvenile Rehabilitation Program."

To give them credit, the JRP had tried to live up to the R part of their name, but she'd still lived in a detention center for those two years. It wasn't something she talked to most people about, and it ranked *well* above being a prisoner of war in terms of experiences.

"Fair," Killough conceded, stepping around to study the map of Nueva Portugal. "What are we looking at here, Lieutenant Commander?"

"Everything Triple Q started construction on in the six months after Lafrenz took control of the company," Roslyn told him. "It gives us a first cut at potential locations, but doing detailed scans of each of the sites could take days."

She shrugged.

"I'm prepared to spend those days," she admitted. "But if you've thoughts on narrowing it down, I'm listening."

The MISS agent stood across the hologram from her, studying the image of the city in silence.

"Power and victims," he finally said. "We know there's been people going missing. We can't necessarily map the *excess* over what we should be seeing, but we can map roughly where missing people disappeared from.

"Give me a few minutes."

"And power?" Roslyn asked.

"Even if they have their own power-generation facilities, they're better off with access to the grid to help bury their emissions if nothing else," Killough said. "If you want to map up the power grid, I'll map up the missing people. Let's see if that narrows it down any, shall we?"

"I've had enough experience with drugs and gamblers in my life that my *first* urge is to mistrust a casino," Roslyn admitted fifteen minutes later as their three-layer map took shape.

"It's not a perfect match," Killough said. "I don't see a perfect match on here, but I agree it looks...fishy. Right on the main transmission line from the fusion plant at Nuevo Habanero and definitely the highest density of missing people outside the city."

"That could just be regular organized crime," she pointed out. "Not to lean on stereotypes or anything, but casinos aren't always the cleanest of organizations in any sense."

"Agreed," he said. "They're also just off the main transport routes off the peninsula: highway and monorail alike."

The monorail stop was probably part of why the casino was situated where it was. It was only walking distance from the casino if you were determined, but a few seconds' search told her there was a free automated shuttle running a ten-minute loop between the station and the casino.

"Enough traffic and power flow that no one is going to question anything in terms of supply trucks or movement," Roslyn concluded. "If they're even a little careful, they could conceal a truck dock somewhere underground and have everything they need."

"Guns, guards, supplies and power," Killough agreed. "Enough to start with, yes?"

"Enough to run deep scans of the area, at least," Roslyn said. "We're not landing Marines until we know more."

The MISS agent snorted.

"May I suggest that there can be at least *one* step between those two?" he asked delicately. "You and I, for example, can be *much* less attention-drawing than a platoon of armored boots."

"Assuming the place is even open right now," she pointed out. "Let's get the sensor data first, and then start planning next steps. There might be nothing there."

Daalman had set her up with access to the ship's sensors from the same office. It took Roslyn a minute or so to bring up the tactical operating system—and longer than she'd like to find the sensor controls in the new software.

Having Killough watching over her shoulder made her self-conscious of the way the new system slowed her down.

"Let's start with the basics," she said aloud. "Overhead."

The hologram of Nueva Portugal vanished, replaced with a new image of the casino. Vehicles and people were moving around the structure of the complex as the destroyer's optical sensors trained on it.

Huntress's computers were already going through the data for anomalies as Roslyn looked at the image herself. It took a moment for the sensors and computers to catch up and build a three-dimensional model of everything they could see, but then they had a nearly perfect visual of the casino at that moment.

"Matches up well to the plans, so far as I see," Killough noted. "That's suspicious on its own, to me. *Nothing* matches the plans."

Roslyn chuckled as the analysis sweep completed.

"Oddities there and there," she pointed, highlighting two sections. "Nothing clear that we can resolve without putting drones or boots on the ground, but there's *something* off on the north side of the surface parking lot and the north side of the building."

Killough moved to examine that chunk of the hologram more closely, zooming in with a gesture.

"Looks like a concealed entrance of some kind on the parking lot," he noted. "Underground access for trucks. Not supposed to be there, though." He looked at the section of park in question and shook his head.

"I don't know what the computer is seeing there," he told Roslyn. "Could just be landscaping. Or a security bunker. Can't be sure."

"Bringing up everything else we've got for passives," Roslyn replied. "Thermals and spectrography should give us a bit more."

The complete *lack* of anything on thermal at the two points that had looked odd to the computers was probably a sign on its own. They looked perfectly normal in infrared.

The spectrographic analysis, though...

"Yup, definitely a concealed parking entrance," Killough noted. "They've got a good seal on the door, but every time they open it, they mix up the material composition of the dirt around it."

"And the other anomaly?" she asked.

"Nothing," he admitted. "Might *be* nothing. Somehow, though, I think it's the edge of an underground structure."

"Well, I guess the question is how good you think their scanners are," Roslyn told him. "I can do a radar pulse and get a pretty decent map of the underground, but they're going to *know* we did it if they have any kind of anti-radiation system."

"They can't stop you doing it, but they can know you did it," he agreed. "And we need to know. Damn."

"You're the spy," she said. "I'm inclined to scan them and let them panic, but it's not subtle."

"Um." Killough looked at the hologram again. "It's not like we can go poke at holes in the ground without drawing attention, I suppose," he admitted. "And yet I still feel like a subtle ground mission might be the better idea."

"Angus...there's a comatose sixteen-year-old girl dying in our med-bay," Roslyn told him quietly. "Hundreds in the same state on the surface. If we can find out what these people did, we might be able to save their victims."

The office was silent as Killough studied the hologram.

"Are we still quarantined?" he asked. "If we find something, who do we send in?"

"Good question," Roslyn admitted. "I'll talk to Dr. Breda, but my inclination would be that you and I go in first, with Mooren's squad as backup aboard the shuttle. No need to break up a team that worked, after all."

CHAPTER 23

IN THE END, Roslyn and her team were back aboard the shuttle when the radar pulse was activated.

"Drones are in position, sir," Mage-Lieutenant Jordan told her. "We've got them at each cardinal point, ready to double-check the return from the radar ping. If there's anything in the site, we'll pick it up."

"Thank you, Lieutenant," Roslyn replied. "Herbert, what's our drop time?"

The pilot chuckled.

"We're pretending we're en route to the NP spaceport," she replied. "We'll detour from that as soon as we have an update. Depending on where we are on the path, anything from three minutes to thirty seconds.

"I don't think anyone is going to know we're coming."

"That's the hope," Roslyn said. "This isn't going to be subtle."

She and Killough were back in light body armor and hazmat helmets. The Marines were in full exosuits, carrying ugly-looking shotguns with under-barrel stunguns.

The *plan* was to take their targets alive, but they weren't going in without real weapons and armor this time.

"You're coming up on your closest approach, sir," Jordan said. "We are pulsing the site...now."

The lightspeed delay *shouldn't* have registered to human senses, but the fractions of a second before the data processed seemed to take forever.

"Confirm we have a concealed underground complex," Jordan reported. "Downloading maps to your computers and flagging entry points. One is through the casino, linking in to the underground structure we IDed from above. Another is from the parking lot, large enough for vehicles and even small shuttles.

"At least four more personnel-sized entrances are scattered around the complex. Looks like four or five levels, mostly buried under the casino basement. Probably just dug deeper than anyone announced."

"Understood," Roslyn said grimly. "Herbert: hit the parking lot."

"Inbound," the pilot replied. "Shall I knock on the door, sir?"

The odds that this was their target were high...but it wasn't a *guarantee*. Opening the trip with armor-piercing missiles could cause all kinds of trouble.

On the other hand, the Nueva Portugal Guardia had over a thousand people who were going to die if Roslyn didn't find answers very, *very* quickly.

"Knock away, Lieutenant," Roslyn ordered. "Make a road."

She brought up a feed from the shuttle's lead cameras running on her helmet heads-up display. The HUD had the outline of the underground complex highlighted on it—and the armored and concealed door blinked in red as Herbert dropped the shuttle's targeting system on it.

"This is *Huntress* shuttle seven," the Lieutenant announced on the Navy tactical channel. "Rifle One. I repeat, Rifle One."

A single air-to-ground missile blazed away from the shuttle, accelerating at speeds no spacecraft carrying a human could match, and slammed into the highlighted door at several times the speed of sound.

Armored or not, the missile warhead *shredded* the access point. It had been designed to rise out of the ground and uncover a ramp down into the underground complex—and now only the ramp remained, covered in debris as Herbert brought the shuttle down *into* the hole she'd just created.

"We're down," she reported. "Access is clear. Good luck, Marines."

There was no way Roslyn was going to lead the charge out of the shuttle. Even if she'd been so foolish as to try, the Marines wouldn't *let* her.

But she was still the Mage in the team, and that meant she was in the middle, following two three-Marine fire teams out into the now-uncovered tunnel. Powerful shoulder-mounted lights from the exosuits lit up the cavern, showing a ramp descending into the ground toward the casino.

"Negative contacts, negative contacts," Knight reported crisply on the tac channel. "Moving forward."

"Don't go too far," Roslyn admonished. "You may want to protect me, Corporal, but I can protect *you* as well."

"Never stray too far from the Mage, right," the Marine replied with a chuckle. "Sending drones ahead; scanning for life signs."

The drones that Knight threw into the air were bigger than the ones they'd investigated Killough's apartment with, pigeon-sized robots with enough wingspan to keep airborne without rotors or jets.

"Move up, move up," Mooren ordered. "Stick with the Commander but keep moving. Something is down here, and if it's our target, we're expecting Augments and we're expecting them *fast*."

The Marines moved. Roslyn moved with them, keeping a mental eye on Killough as the spy brought up the rear. Like her, he was only armed with a standard stungun. Unlike her, he wasn't a Mage capable of handling almost any threat unarmed.

"Drones have contacts," Knight snapped. "Multiple drones down, but we have contacts moving up the tunnel. They're bringing vehicles with them as cover—what scans I have suggest the vehicles are armed."

"Hold position," Roslyn ordered. "Covering."

Her hands flared out in front of her, palms forward, as she wove power through the air ahead of the Marine squad. Air concentrated and stopped moving, forming a solid barrier that could resist incoming fire.

She managed it just in time, as three ordinary-looking vans appeared out of the darkness at speed. The drivers knew what they were doing, twisting the vehicles in a synchronized maneuver that blocked the entire

tunnel—and allowed the van's side panels to swing open, revealing tri-
pod-mounted penetrator rifles.

The high-powered weapons fired discarding-sabot tungsten penetrators, designed to go through the heavy armor Roslyn's Marines were wearing. Trapped in the tunnel without cover, the three automatic weapons
could have easily mowed down Mooren's entire squad in seconds.

Instead, the tungsten darts hit Roslyn's magical barrier and stopped
dead. Dozens of rounds hung in the air for a few moments before they
clattered to the ground, but the heavy rifles kept firing until their magazines ran dry.

"Nix!" Mooren barked, the Marine Sergeant lifting the automatic
grenade launcher she'd kept for herself.

"Clear," Roslyn replied, measuring her timing carefully. She wasn't
as good at this part as a proper Marine Combat Mage would be, but she
knew the theory.

The launcher made a sharp triple cough, firing a burst of gas grenades down the tunnel, and Roslyn opened a hole in her barrier for the
weapons to pass. A second triple cough followed, Mooren sending that
burst over the vehicles into the approaching hostiles behind them.

The gun teams in the vans hadn't been expecting the gas. A follow-up
round of penetrators started—and then trailed off as the neutralization
solution took effect and the defenders fell unconscious.

"Move up," Mooren barked. "Hostiles are unarmored; stunguns *first*."

Roslyn was tempted to argue—the penetrator rifles could have easily
wiped out the entire squad in seconds, and the defenders were *not* playing nice. It was the Marine's call, though. Roslyn wasn't going to micromanage her escort.

The vans were modified civilian vehicles and were easily moved aside
by the powered muscles of the exosuits. With the pathway cleared, it became obvious that Mooren's Nix grenades had been the right call.

"Andrews, hold your team with K and secure the prisoners," Mooren
ordered.

Corporal Natal Andrews led the fire team at the lead with Killough,
who apparently was being referred to by initial to pretend some level of

discretion. They gestured for their Marines to fall in around them and began shuffling through the storage compartments on their armor for cuffs.

"Everybody's down," the Sergeant continued after a moment. "Watch for a second wave; teams one, two, three, keep moving with me and the Commander."

Nine Marines moved forward with Roslyn as they carefully stepped around the unconscious defenders.

"No Augments," Mooren murmured on a private channel to Roslyn. "Regular mooks, mixed weaponry, no body armor, no gas masks. They had the vans with the rifles, but I wonder if those were meant for Marines or the Guardia's armored cars."

"What are you thinking, Sergeant?" Roslyn asked, glancing over at the unconscious bodies. The woman closest to her was wearing standard worker coveralls without markings.

"I don't think this is our target, sir," the Marine admitted. "On the other hand, they shot at Marines without saying anything, so I figure we're in *a* right place."

"Let's see what we find," Roslyn replied. "Keep pushing forward."

The lights were now picking up a set of heavy security doors. Clearly designed for standard transport trucks, they were easily large enough for all three vans to have come through at once.

They were also now closed and sealed. Roslyn considered the doors for a moment, then turned to Mooren.

"Standard civilian security. Do you have this?"

"Of course," Mooren replied. "Fast or clean, sir?"

"Fast," Roslyn said immediately.

Exosuits completely encased their wearers from head to toe. They were *very* bad at transmitting body language, but Roslyn somehow picked up the Marine's amused glee at that order.

"Fall back; sticky grenades," Mooren barked. She lifted the grenade launcher and aimed carefully. Eight single shots followed, the grenades sticking to the door as their name implied.

The Staff Sergeant glanced around, checking her people's distance.

"Fire in the hole!" she announced—and all eight grenades detonated simultaneously in the white-hot flash of thermite explosives.

Most of the door fell backward, away from the Marines. The exosuited troopers were already moving when the metal crashed to the concrete floor, leading the way into the main target of the complex.

As soon as Roslyn stepped over the wreckage of the door, she knew that Mooren was right. They were *definitely* in the wrong place. The facility was definitely illegal—concealed, defended with restricted weapons, etc., etc.—but it was a shipping-and-storage facility.

Not a laboratory.

"Well, that's been an annoying waste," Roslyn muttered. "I guess we finish the job, since we're here."

"Spread out," Mooren ordered. "Sweep for security and anyone in charge. Herbert, are you airborne?"

"I am," the pilot replied. "Watching the exits. No one has made a run for it yet, but... What's the call?"

"Commander?" the Sergeant asked.

"Call in the Guardia, Lieutenant," Roslyn ordered with a sigh. "Track anyone who emerges, and pass the chase off to the locals. We appear to have broken a smuggling ring...not a secret ex-Republic lab."

"Damn. I suppose that's still a win?" the Lieutenant asked.

Roslyn looked around the massive, automated racks containing hundreds of containers of likely illegal guns and drugs.

"I suppose," she conceded. "But it's not helping our victims."

CHAPTER 24

"SIR, I THINK WE HAVE someone who wants to talk to you," Knight's voice said drily over the tac channel. "We've found the offices. They're mostly empty, but one gentleman was sitting waiting for us."

Roslyn hadn't been expecting that.

"Sergeant?" she asked Mooren.

"We're secure if you want to go chat with the locals," the Marine replied.

Herbert hadn't spotted anyone leaving, but the facility was almost entirely empty. The defenders who'd ended up gassed had likely been planning to provide cover for an evacuation rather than to truly hold off Marines for an extended period.

"Most people left through the casino and we have no ability to separate them from the crowd," Roslyn noted. "Why would someone *stay*?"

"Either they figured we were going to ID and catch them anyway, or they think they're invincible," the Marine told her. "Or both."

Roslyn snorted.

"Well, I guess I'll find out," she told the Marine. "Knight, flip me a waypoint? This place is big and confusing."

"There you go," Knight replied. "Do we have any good news, sir?"

"There's no *people* in those containers," Roslyn said grimly. "That was my first concern."

Despite everything the Protectorate—and the Republic, during its existence—could do, sex-slave trafficking was a continuing problem. Most of the victims were teenagers from worlds across human space, convinced they were signing up for a better life somewhere else.

Some went to the Core, some to the Mid and some to the Fringe. The point wasn't so much supply and demand, as Roslyn understood it, as to separate the victims from any potential support structure they knew of.

The Protectorate would *deal* with the organized criminals running guns and drugs, or evading taxes and tariffs, but they reserved their harshest punishments and most dramatic efforts for the human traffickers.

That thought carried Roslyn across the underground warehouse to the office, where Knight's fire team gestured her to an office they'd barred shut. Knight herself was standing guard over the door, though the wires from her armor to one of the warehouse consoles suggested she was multitasking.

"What have we got, Corporal?" Roslyn asked.

"John Doe, wanted to speak to our commanding officer," the Marine replied. "He was calmly sitting in the office when we arrived and hasn't moved. He's acting like he's in control of the situation, which strikes me as particularly nervy."

"Indeed," Roslyn murmured. "Well, let's go see what he has to say. Back me up, Corporal? You're a far more visible threat than I am."

"Can do."

The two women entered the office in step. Knight remained by the door, turning her blank faceplate to focus on the prisoner in a clear glare.

The office was much nicer than Roslyn had expected. Unlike the concrete floor of the rest of the warehouse, it had been carpeted in a thick, soft material she didn't recognize. The walls were decorated with what Roslyn suspected were original art pieces by Sorprendidan artists, and a pair of cat statues sculpted from a glittering local black stone stood on either end of the desk.

The man behind the desk stretched languidly, like one of the cats the statues depicted, as Roslyn approached. He was a dark-haired and stunningly pale-skinned man dressed in an all-black suit and wearing silver rings on all of his fingers.

"At last, some decency and etiquette," he observed. "You invade my place of business, abuse my people, damage my facility and you don't even have the grace to greet me in a timely fashion."

He shook his head.

"The galaxy has gone so downhill. Now tell me, whoever you are, how exactly are you planning on justifying this blatantly illegal invasion of private property?"

"It isn't private property if it doesn't exist," Roslyn replied with a chuckle. "This entire facility is missing from all official records. That's questionable enough, Mister..."

He glared at her in silence.

"And that *questionable* suffices for probable cause, given the use of a bioweapon in Nueva Portugal," Roslyn told him. "The Royal Martian Marine Corps is operating on the authority of the Protectorate to investigate the use of a weapon of mass destruction.

"You will find, I'm afraid, that under the authority we are granted in that circumstance, our actions are entirely within our remit."

Some of the glare faded, but the man did a good job of concealing his surprise.

"You have no grounds to decide that this *warehouse* is a source for bioweapons," he argued.

"That's a discussion for the courts," Roslyn noted. "But believe me, we have more than sufficient grounds to investigate *any* unregistered covert facility in Nueva Portugal with whatever level of force is necessary."

She gestured around.

"Even the most basic scans of the contents of this warehouse suggest a long list of felonies we can level against everyone involved," she told him. "I don't know what game you think you're playing, but I do believe you lose."

The pale man chuckled and spread his hands.

"I own this casino, officer," he admitted. "I have no desire to flee Sorprendidas as a penniless vagabond, so I must defend my property one way or another.

"I see that our final battle shall be in the courts, but I think you still overstate your position. This illegal incursion could easily render all of your evidence against me invalid."

"You're stretching," Roslyn warned. "And it won't save you. If you have nothing of value to offer, I suggest you begin planning your discussion with your lawyer."

"Wait." He held up a hand as she turned to leave. "While I am a...casino owner, let us say, I am also a citizen of Nueva Portugal and Sorprendidas. I was once a citizen of the Republic and am now, as I understand, once again a citizen of the Protectorate."

"Your point?" she asked. That was as close as he was going to get to saying he was neck-deep in organized crime.

"I voted for reintegration, officer," he told her. "I believe in a unified humanity and that I have civic responsibilities. I will assure you, with absolute certainty, that no bioweapon of *any* kind has ever been transported through this facility.

"I have no idea what kind of weapon was used in my city, but I have no desire to see the people I rely on as customers injured in this way. If there is a way I can be of assistance, before you throw away the key, I would be delighted to help."

Roslyn glared at the mob boss. He wouldn't be able to see her glare through the hazmat helmet, but she suspected he got the idea.

"*Someone* used Republic resources to build a secret laboratory in this city roughly around the time of the Secession," she told him. "They've been kidnapping human test subjects from Nueva Portugal—and probably the rest of the planet. Any ideas, Mr. 'Casino Owner'?"

He looked at her in silence, his hand still languidly raised as he considered.

"I assume you have access to the Guardia prison population?" he asked slowly. "There is a woman—I will neither grace her with the title of *lady* nor say I ever worked with her—who is serving a prison term for trafficking.

"While I cannot be certain of anything, it is *possible* that the organization she was working with cut her off and provided evidence to the Guardia of her activities because she was causing trouble close to home," the man said. "It is *possible* that she was engaging in more aggressive personnel acquisition than that organization would tolerate, and it is *possible* that she wasn't kicking enough cash upstairs to justify her actions."

"Possible, huh?" Roslyn said grimly. She'd hand the recording over to the Guardia. The lack of trafficking victims *currently* in the warehouse didn't mean that no one had been trafficked by the man she was facing.

"Her name is Josephine Jackson," the mob boss told her with a flick of his hand. "You may make of the possibilities what you wish, officer. I will say nothing further until I have seen my lawyer."

"Given everything the Guardia is dealing with, that may take a while," Roslyn warned. "I hope you like cells."

CHAPTER 25

CAPTAIN VICTORIANO Bolivar was not quite what Roslyn had expected from his voice. He was surprisingly young, *maybe* thirty, and wore a perfectly tailored uniform that showed off the results of a lifetime of working out. Dark-skinned, dark-eyed and dark-haired, Bolivar was eye-catching even *without* the muscles and the gorgeous black uniform.

Roslyn had more important things to be doing when they met at the Guardia headquarters than eat the eye candy, but she still had to appreciate the man's effort.

"Lieutenant Commander Chambers," he greeted her in the plainly decorated lobby of the building, bowing over her hand as they shook. "I appreciate your efforts in the quarantine zone and the assistance of your Captain Daalman.

"It's been a hellish few days."

"I didn't expect any of this when we arrived for a glorified show-the-flag tour," Roslyn admitted. She gestured to her companions. "This is my escort, Marine Staff Sergeant Borislava Mooren, and my aide, Ensign Rodrigo Borst."

"Borst" was actually Killough, but the MISS agent had insisted on pretending to be a junior Navy officer. His uniform had been quickly fabricated to fit him, and he'd fiddled around with some kind of disguise kit to give his cheeks a youthful chubbiness and smooth complexion that left *Roslyn* thinking he was maybe twenty.

"Sergeant, Ensign." Bolivar nodded to both of them. "This way, please, all of you."

Roslyn fell into step beside the attractive Guardia officer.

"The Planetary Army has set up a full blockade around the Nueva Portugal region," Bolivar told them. "We have had additional incidents over the last twenty-four hours, but those have thankfully been isolated.

"Our analysts think we're still seeing concentrations of the toxin from the explosion drifting around the city and occasionally reaching critical mass." He shook his head. "That results in an individual or several becoming incoherent and violent. The pattern is consistent with the quarantine zone problem though, gracias a Dios, much more contained."

"Do you have any more data on what we're looking at?" Roslyn asked.

"I was hoping you did, Commander," he said. "I'm uncertain why you asked to see Ms. Jackson. She is not exactly a...pleasant person."

"We found evidence in that damn underground warehouse that potentially links her to the source of the toxin," Roslyn told him. "I can't tell you much more than that, I'm afraid. We're operating within some strict classification instructions from Mars still."

"You'll forgive me if I find that almost as terrifying as the zombie plague," Bolivar said quietly, using a word that Roslyn hadn't let her brain use yet.

"The people are victims—and still alive. I'm not sure *zombie* is the right word," Roslyn pointed out.

"Look up the origin of the term," he suggested. "For now..." He sighed. "We've brought Ms. Jackson here for interrogation. We will want to record the interview."

"Denied," Roslyn said quietly. "My conversation with Ms. Jackson will be recorded, but I will not be certain if I can *release* those recordings to the Guardia until afterward.

"You have my word, Captain Bolivar, that anything of relevance to the Guardia will be provided to you," she told him. "But there are reasons for the secrecy. You will have to trust me."

She could argue need to know for the local police, except...the existence of a secret, Mage-run Republic lab was a political firestorm waiting to happen. Project Prometheus itself had come close to triggering atrocities on the part of the RMN, held back only by professionalism and Damien Montgomery.

From the flip side, Sorprendidas had been an UnArcana World and was still unreconciled to those rules being stripped away. While so far, everyone was assuming a technological source for the toxin, that was hardly guaranteed.

A lot of high-end Protectorate biotech work involved magic, after all. The presence of a fully qualified Mage-Surgeon like Ulla Lafrenz suggested all kinds of unpleasant possibilities to Roslyn. While it would still take a solid understanding of DNA and RNA to build an artificial virus with magic, that virus could be made to do things with magic that would be impossible with regular genecoding.

Roslyn could *not* tell the locals what she was looking for. The risk of chaos was too great, even if she trusted Bolivar.

So, she needed Bolivar to trust *her*.

Fortunately...so far, so good.

Even clad in a prisoner's shapeless jumpsuit—a sight that brought back memories for Roslyn, few of them pleasant—Josephine Jackson was stunningly attractive. The jumpsuit did little to disguise the woman's generous curves, drawing side glances from the male half of her prison-guard escort.

"Leave us," Roslyn instructed the guards. "Only my team will be in the room. Disable all recorders."

"Sir?" the security officer looked at Bolivar.

The Guardia Captain looked unhappy as he turned his gaze on Roslyn. He still sighed and nodded.

"This is the Protectorate's interview, not ours," he conceded. "Good luck, Mage-Commander."

Roslyn concealed a mental snort at the promotion. The "Lieutenant" part of her rank was often dropped as a courtesy, but that usually came with dropping the *Mage* part. Bolivar was trying to intimidate Jackson.

As the last of the Guardia trooped out, leaving Roslyn and her escort alone with the prisoner, Roslyn figured Bolivar's efforts hadn't achieved much.

"Double-check the recorders are off," she instructed Killough. "And check her bindings," she told Mooren. "Let's not have any surprises."

The prisoner eyed them with curiosity as they worked. She was cuffed to the chair and her hands were cuffed together, though that gave her enough slack to run a hand over her short-cropped hair.

"They can't even let me grow out my hair," she complained. "I don't suppose you can do anything about that, *Mage-Commander?*"

"Probably not," Roslyn said genially. "If they're shaving your head, you were doing something unwise with it. I kept my own hair in your place."

That got her *looks* from both Mooren and Killough, but she figured the extra bit of connection couldn't hurt.

"A Mage-Commander who's been in jail? Mierda," Jackson replied.

"Juvie. Long string of trouble as a kid," Roslyn told her. "Not, you know, human trafficking. They let me out. I'm not sure they're planning on letting you out."

The woman rolled her eyes.

"Thirty-six years," she told them. "Twenty until the first parole hearing, so I have *limited* interest in playing nice for at least another decade. Not sure what the point of all this is."

"The point of all this is that I believe you were supplying human test subjects to a secret lab working on Project Prometheus," Roslyn said flatly. "Which would be enough, Ms. Jackson, to get you a second trial...for *war crimes.*"

The prisoner lost some of her composure, staring directly at Roslyn.

"Mierda," she repeated. "I did not... They were not... *FUCK.*"

The curse word echoed off the interrogation chamber walls until it faded to silence.

"Well, Ms. Jackson?" Roslyn asked. "You seem to know what I'm talking about, though it also seems like somewhat of a surprise."

Jackson raised a hand.

"You want to know what I know," she said. "I don't *have* to tell you shit. You know what omertà is."

"I know it doesn't apply to third parties like this," Roslyn pointed out. "Even the first Mafia helped fight the Nazis."

The room was silent for several seconds.

"I want immunity for anything we talk about and ten years off my sentence," Jackson said flatly. "Or I don't say a fucking word."

Roslyn hadn't even sat down yet, and she smiled mirthlessly.

"I don't think you have anything worth that," she noted. "Shame to have wasted both of our time."

She turned back to the door.

"Look," Jackson said behind her. "You do not do what I did by asking questions or being squeamish. I've been *convicted* for enough that I won't pretend otherwise. While I didn't think about it then, I can guess which of my clients is most likely to be your problem.

"I can tell you names, rendezvous points, bank accounts. Stuff I *won't* break for anything else," she told Roslyn. "If they're what you say they are, omertà doesn't apply. If they *aren't* and I betray them, I'm a dead woman.

"Either way, I'm still in jail for longer than you've been *alive*, kid."

Roslyn grimaced. Clearing that off her face and fixing her eyes and lips in a neutral expression, she turned back to Jackson.

"I can guarantee immunity for anything we discuss," she conceded. She didn't necessarily *want* to—the woman across the table had kidnapped dozens of people and fed them into a bioweapon lab for human testing, after all—but she'd trade that for *finding* the damn lab.

"I have no control over your existing sentence from the Sorprendidan authorities," she told Jackson. "The Royal Navy doesn't have that authority."

Roslyn could manage it with the Warrant she carried, but if she could get through this mess without using that, she would.

"*If* your evidence is useful, I will ask that the locals reconsider the time before parole hearings, if nothing else, and consider your cooperation," Roslyn promised. "I cannot do more."

The interrogation room was silent for a good minute, then Jackson bowed her head.

"Fine," she conceded. "Sit down, 'Mage-Commander.' And start whatever recordings you need. I'll tell you as much as I can."

Roslyn took the seat. Just sharing a room with Jackson made her feel dirty. She was going to need to shower after all of this.

"We're already recording," she told Jackson. "Tell us everything."

The human trafficker nodded, inhaling as she marshaled her thoughts.

"The most likely person for what you're looking for is a contact who went in our files as Six-Eight-Three-One," Jackson noted. "I met her twice, both times she introduced herself simply as R. Tall woman, blonde. Mixed ethnicity, skin tone much like yours."

"Mars-born," Roslyn concluded. That fit the profile for Ulla Roxana Lafrenz, at least.

"She was paying well below market rate for cargo," the trafficker continued, her tone brushing calmly over what *cargo* meant in this case. "But she didn't care about condition, and having a local purchaser buying in bulk was handy initially.

"It got harder as she wanted larger numbers and a greater variety. Normally, we focus on quality cargo—young and attractive. She wanted samples of every age and health we could find."

Jackson shrugged.

"Turns out that a lot of middle-aged sick people will jump at chances for jobs and new starts even more readily than kids will."

It took every scrap of self-control Roslyn had not to pin the other woman to the wall with magic—or her fists. The callous disregard for the lives Jackson had ruined—dozens, even hundreds of people sold into slavery or delivered to Lafrenz's experiment—beggared belief.

"How many."

The two words Roslyn ground out didn't sound like a question to her, but Jackson got the point.

"Hard to say; I wasn't involved at that level of—"

"*How many*," Roslyn growled.

"Several hundred. No more than five."

"Dear god," the Mage-Commander whispered, staring at the utter monster sitting calmly across from her. "You kidnapped *five hundred* people for them without asking what they wanted them for?"

"Over three years," Jackson countered. "It wasn't like R walked up to me and asked for a statistically viable random population of five hundred cargo in the first meeting! She was our largest on-planet client, but..."

The trafficker cut herself off before admitting that "R" hadn't even been the majority of her business, but Roslyn picked it up. Against even a small planetary population, several hundred missing people a year was nothing, but the scale of the woman's operation was horrifying.

"You said you could give me names, account numbers, locations," Roslyn said flatly. "Start."

"I don't know R's name," Jackson conceded. "But I did learn the names of several of the subordinates I dealt with. There were four regular contacts, named Iole Man, Kane Unkle, Miluse Shriver and Iracema Jain. Not all of those might be real names, but they should give you a starting point from records, yes?"

"Keep talking," Roslyn said shortly. The more the woman said of value, the more she was going to be able to justify this to herself at night.

"They picked up a new boss shortly before I got arrested, just after the war ended," Jackson continued. "I met him once, damn pretty man but no soul in his eyes."

That was rich, coming from Jackson.

"I wasn't *supposed* to know his name—he was introduced to me as 'C,' but we overheard a few phone calls and got the pieces. They called him Connor ad Aaron."

Even with Roslyn already exercising ironclad self-control not to violently injure the woman in front of her, that made her jump. She'd hoped Connor ad Aaron was dead. He'd been somewhere in the fortifications at Hyacinth when Mage-Admiral Jane Alexander had destroyed them, after all.

The rogue Mage had been a member of the Republic Intelligence Directorate and the mastermind behind kidnapping Alexander—and Roslyn.

"Names don't help much," Roslyn pointed out after a moment. "Anyone can say their name is anything. Locations. Details. If you don't know where the damn lab is, Ms. Jackson, I'm not sure we've done much other than make me ill."

The criminal chuckled.

"Such a squeamish stomach for a naval officer," she replied. "Are you bothered by little old me?"

"I am bothered, Ms. Jackson, by the effort it requires not to kill you where you sit," Roslyn said calmly. "I have faced battlefleets unarmed and Republic combat cyborgs in my underwear. Please stop wasting my time."

The interrogation room chilled again as Roslyn held the other woman's eyes until Jackson finally looked away. Roslyn wasn't sure the criminal knew how deathly serious she was being, but her point appeared to be made.

"There were supposed to be individual new drop-offs each time," Jackson said quietly. "After the first eighteen months, they stopped being quite so careful, though. There were six repeated locations. They didn't always use those six, but they kept showing up, so I think they had to be convenient to the lab."

"Ensign, get us a map," Roslyn told Killough. A moment later, a holographic map of Nueva Portugal appeared between the two women. "Show me, Ms. Jackson. We'll take the account numbers afterward—those might come in handy as well—but I need those locations."

CHAPTER 26

"DID SHE HELP?" Bolivar asked as Roslyn and her escorts left the interrogation.

"She tried, at least," Roslyn conceded. "And I managed not to throw her into a wall, which I consider a small personal triumph." She sighed. "I promised I'd tell you she was cooperative and helpful and that should be considered in future assessments of her sentence."

"I'll pass it along," he agreed. "Will we need her again or should I have her sent back to her cell?"

"We're done with her," Roslyn said after a moment's thought. Either the locations and account numbers would help, or they wouldn't. There was no way that they were getting anything else useful from Jackson— the presence of ad Aaron confirmed they were looking for the right people.

"You look like you've seen a ghost, Mage-Commander," Bolivar noted. "Is there...anything we should be looking at?"

"Yeah." She gestured to Killough. "Ensign, give Captain Bolivar the account numbers that Ms. Jackson provided us. The Guardia is going to be better able to trace the money than we are—and following the transactions might help them roll up more of her former organization, as well."

Killough quickly loaded a datachip and passed it over to Bolivar.

"What happens now, Commander?" Bolivar asked.

"I take the data Ms. Jackson provided and compare it against every-thing we've already pulled together on these people," Roslyn told him.

"Then, if we're only moderately lucky, I go kick down another set of secret doors that *actually* has a bioweapon lab behind them."

Bolivar grimaced.

"The last set of doors is giving me a headache," he admitted. "The lawyers aren't going to *succeed* in arguing against probable cause on your part, but they're already set up to try and have filed an injunction to have the prisoners released on the grounds of violation of their habeas corpus rights."

"No offense, Captain, but the local mob isn't my problem," Roslyn said. "By no means do I *mind* that we accidentally ripped apart a major smuggling operation with links to human trafficking, but my focus is on the source of this damn weapon."

"I hear you," he conceded. "I *will* need statements from you and your Marines on the warehouse eventually, though."

"I'll have Captain Daalman forward appropriately redacted versions of our reports," she said. "I'm afraid I can't offer better right now. That said, I don't expect *Huntress* to leave Sorprendidas soon unless something goes very wrong.

"We'll be available when you actually end up in court...assuming my main mission is resolved."

"Aren't you supposed to be *Song of the Huntress*'s tactical officer?" Bolivar asked.

"Any officer of Her Majesty's Navy must be prepared to handle ancillary duties as required," Roslyn replied virtuously. "I cannot really say more than that."

"Fair." He sighed. "My superiors have asked me to pass on the request to tell us *before* you launch an aerial assault in the city next time." He chuckled. "I recognize the value of surprise and the complexity of the situation, but it *does* help us provide backup if needed."

"Captain Bolivar, if I find the people I'm after, calling the Guardia in for backup is only going to result in more dead Guardia," Roslyn said quietly. "The only people I'm going after these bastards with are Marines.

"I may not have found my enemy yet, Captain, but I know who they are, and I will *not* underestimate them."

Connor ad Aaron was a name to conjure with in her head, after all. The man had successfully hacked *every* record needed to infiltrate his team of Augments as Mage-Admiral Alexander's security detail from the *Protectorate Royal Guard*. He'd kidnapped Jane Alexander and Roslyn Chambers from the middle of a Protectorate battle fleet, leaving everyone believing them dead.

Part of her was grimly certain that if he'd remained responsible for their security at Styx, the Republic's continuity-of-government station in Chrysanthemum, she never would have escaped.

Instead, it seemed, he'd ended up here. Roslyn wasn't sure what to do about that...but she *was* sure she couldn't underestimate him again.

Back in the shuttle, Roslyn leaned against her chair and took a moment to close her eyes and attempt to decompress. Instead, a slew of memories of meeting with the big Mage who'd held her captive for weeks of transit flickered across her mind, and she exhaled a long sigh.

"I'm guessing ad Aaron is a name that means something to someone," Killough said in the silence.

"Run Jackson's locations against the map from Triple Q," Roslyn ordered, ignoring the question. "Mooren, is the squad ready?"

"Give us five to lock into exosuits, and we're ready to drop and rock at your order, Commander," the Marine replied. "Do we have a target?"

"It'll take us more than five minutes to answer *that* question," Roslyn replied. "I need to record a message back to *Huntress* to send on the Link. Ad Aaron was presumed dead in the destruction of Styx Station."

"RID?" Killough asked quietly.

"Yeah. He was the son of an ass who kidnapped Mage-Admiral Alexander," Roslyn said. "And me. I remember him and none of it's pleasant."

That wasn't *entirely* true, but the fact that she'd crushed on the attractive Royal Guardsman Mage before finding out what he really was contributed to the sense of betrayal. And now, he'd been involved in this kind of monstrosity?

"If people have been going into that facility, they have to have been coming out, right?" she continued, her eyes still closed as she struggled with her memories and her traumas. "Mooren, did we see an increase in...I don't know, John Doe bodies?"

"I'm not as good at this as you are, but I'll take a look," the Marine replied. "Looping Knight in."

"I ran the analysis already," Killough admitted. "Plus...well, Jackson's numbers still don't cover the full excess-missing-persons number, even if all of her kidnapping was here in Nueva Portugal."

"Which it wouldn't be," Roslyn sighed. "How many people are we looking at here, Killough?"

The shuttle headrest made for a solid physical focus as she tried very hard to keep her mind on the moment and the task in front of them, but past and present horrors were rushing together far too quickly.

"Over the last four years, at least a thousand from Nueva Portugal alone," he told her. "And no, there's no statistically significant increase in John and Jane Doe bodies. Those people have just completely fucking disappeared.

"Unless the lab is bigger than I think it is, they're not *alive* in there, either."

Roslyn nodded, focusing on the spike of sheer anger that gave her.

"So, these fucking murderous *monsters* have killed a thousand people in their goddamn lab," she whispered. "And then went on to kill thousands more with that bomb in your apartment. I don't... I can't... *Why?*"

"Because they're convinced that they are better," Killough said, his voice very quiet. "Because they're convinced non-Mages don't matter—that even other Mages sometimes don't matter. Because the science and the possibilities are so incredible to them that the consequences and the prices of their actions don't register.

"It's not even the Republic," he noted. "The Republic you could respect; they had an ideal...They lied and manipulated, but at least they stood for *something*. Finley didn't. Finley was in it all for his own power."

"Thankfully, someone put a bullet in *him*," Mooren replied. "But these feel like the same mold. What do we do?"

"We find them," Roslyn said firmly, finally opening her eyes and studying the holographic map that Killough was creating. "We find them, and we capture them—and then we give them scrupulously fair trials and then we shoot them.

"Because we are *better* than them and we will do it *right*," she told the Marine and the spy. "But before that, before anything, we need to find the fuckers. So, tell me, Agent Killough, what does the map look like now?"

It didn't look like an answer; that was certain.

The six red splotches of Jackson's rendezvous locations formed a lopsided circle some fifteen kilometers across. Inside that circle were at least four of Triple Q's projects, including half a neighborhood—elementary school included—a large park and two apartment complexes.

It didn't include any office towers, but there were two just outside it.

"Well, that cuts our targets pretty significantly," Killough noted. "Four projects, assuming we're only looking at the ones that would be convenient to all six locations..."

"Or Lafrenz and ad Aaron could be intentionally creating a pattern to fool the mob," Roslyn pointed out. "From what our contact said, the mob was already getting twitchy about Jackson's methods. Our targets might have realized that and set up a false trail."

"Agreed," the spy said. "But we don't have anything else to go on. We'll need to start working through Triple Q's construction projects eventually, and this gives us a place to start."

"We have the same problem with ground-penetrating radar as before," Roslyn said. "Plus, if we fire it across the entire zone, people are going to notice. It won't cause a *lot* of trouble, but enough burnt-out microwaves and cheap electronics, and people might notice a pattern."

"The alternative is we see what overhead we can get from *Huntress* and look for oddities," Mooren suggested. "That's what you did at the casino, and it helped confirm there was something there, right?"

Roslyn nodded slowly.

"Overflight by the shuttle is going to draw just as much attention as the radar," she admitted. "More, probably. But *Huntress* can get into position and give us an orbital view. It's a starting point."

"And what happens if there's nothing visible from above?" Killough asked. "There's a school right there. We can't exactly go in shooting the same way."

"If we're *certain*, we can bring in the Guardia to evac the school as we move in," Roslyn replied. "But if we're quiet, no one on the surface ever needs to know anything."

She studied the holographic map again and sighed.

"Herbert," she called the pilot. "Can you get us down in that park without drawing *too* much attention?"

"There's a Guardia precinct on the south edge, opposite the school," the pilot reported after a moment. "If we ask nicely, do you think they'll let us borrow their shuttle pad?"

"I think so," Roslyn agreed. "All right, people. Let's move."

Maybe a rooftop view would bring answers the orbital view didn't.

CHAPTER 27

NOTHING. There was *nothing* on the orbital overhead that stuck out as unusual. It was a suburban park, three kilometers square of mostly untouched wilderness surrounded by stormwater ponds.

To the east, toward the main continent, there was a suburb that Triple Q had built. To the west were a slew of apartment complexes, including two built by their target.

North was a low-sprawling commercial district of shops and some small apartments and office towers. The far northern side was marked by a pair of Triple Q-constructed office towers.

The south was a light industrial district, with the Guardia station they'd landed the shuttle on.

Nothing about the region screamed "secret evil lab" to Roslyn, but based off what Jackson had told them, more than two hundred people had vanished in handovers around the area—and it was one of their three highest-density areas of Triple Q construction.

"Triple Q built the suburb here," Knight told them, the cyber-Marine having joined the analysis now. "They also built these apartment complexes directly across the park, and about forty percent of the storm drain system for *everything* around here. All funneling to these drainage ponds to help sustain the natural wetland."

"And the park?" Roslyn asked quietly.

"Triple Q put in the paved pathways and the two security-and-maintenance stations," Killough said. The agent stroked his stubble thoughtfully and then tapped a structure well away from everything else.

"Water processing plant," he noted. "They use the stormwater ponds as a counter-flood reservoir as well, but the water goes back into the city system eventually and has to be treated.

"It's not on our Triple Q list but let me take a look."

A minute ticked by. Then another. Roslyn was pulling up data on the stormwater drainage system around the park and then stopped.

"Oh, fuck me," she murmured. "Or is it supposed to be *Eureka?*"

"Commander?"

In response to Knight's query, Roslyn threw the drainage map onto the hologram. All six of their rendezvous locations for the human traffickers' contacts with the lab were within a block or two of a maintenance access to the drainage tunnels.

"How big are those sewers?" Mooren asked.

"They're storm drains, not sewers," Knight replied. "This is almost a monsoon-esque area, isn't it? They have a rainy season... Figure the storm drains are big enough for a truck?"

"Easily," Killough said grimly. "What *isn't* visible from the air and wasn't on our list because Triple Q didn't build it was the reservoir."

"The reservoir?" Roslyn asked.

The MISS spy tapped a command and added a new orange oval shape under the park.

"Surface stormwater ponds are handy, but as Knight pointed out, this is a monsoon area," he told them. "Rainy-season storms have rainfall measured in centimeters. Despite everything we do, water that washes down our streets isn't safe to go into the ocean without treatment, and they can only treat it so fast.

"So, there are reservoirs positioned throughout the city. The newest of them is here, under the surface-water ponds. Designed to hold approximately twenty-five *cubic kilometers* of water, the excavation was done with off-angle drilling to keep the surface park untouched."

"How easy would it be to fudge the numbers on how much fill you removed?" Roslyn asked quietly.

"Easy," Killough replied. "*Especially* if you're funneling the fill over to other major construction projects and not reporting it as disposed. Triple Q didn't just help them hide materials incoming; it also helped them hide the fill coming *out* from the project.

"The company that did the work isn't on our list," he continued. "But they *subcontracted* it...and the company they subcontracted to was privately owned and appears to have only existed to do this one project.

"We don't know who owned it. We don't know where the equipment came from or where the equipment went, but they were drilling in the right place at the right time *and* installing a massive underground concrete structure."

"And with access to that and Triple Q's materials orders, they could have built a second structure alongside or under it," Roslyn concluded. "I think you found them, Killough."

"Your catch on the drainage network says they have at least *some* access from there, but that wouldn't be reliable," the agent said. "They couldn't be sure it wouldn't flood."

He sighed.

"It gives them a lot of ways out. Too many for us to cut off."

"But not too many for *Song of the Huntress* to watch from orbit," Roslyn told him. "That means we can't call in more Marines. If the shuttles and the rest of the Marines are needed for containment, it's just us going in."

She shook her head, looking at the orange highlights of the underground drainage system hiding their enemies.

"I'll talk to Daalman and Dickens. We'll make it work, try and pull out another squad, but we'll have to do," she said grimly. "Any idea where the best entrance to bring in exosuits is?"

"Here," Killough replied, tapping the water treatment plant that had sent them all in the new direction. "It's a secured, automated facility. A lot of material goes in, but there's only *people* there when trucks go in and for weekly inspections.

"If they have control of the security, they can run any number of people in and out. The main access is concealed in the park, so no one will really question the numbers."

Roslyn sighed.

"That's right next to the damn school, Killough," she said. "We're going to have kids drawing exosuits for weeks—and that's assuming everything goes smoothly.

"We can go in at night," Mooren suggested.

"It's noon, Sergeant," Roslyn replied. "Every hour risks the lives of hundreds of people waiting for some kind of answer to the toxin these people built.

"No. I'll make the call upstairs, and then you see if you can borrow something from the Guardia that will let us get to the door unnoticed. There is no time.

"We go in *now.*"

The shuttle barely had the space for Roslyn to find a private corner to establish a link with *Huntress*. A proper assault shuttle would have, but this was a light transport with token armament. Assault shuttles were designed to carry entire platoons of Marines, after all, not a single squad.

"Daalman," the Mage-Captain responded when she finally connected with her superior. "What is going *on*, Chambers? That last stunt turned out to everyone's benefit, but you're starting to look a tad rogue here."

"Sir, we are facing a serious threat," Roslyn said quietly. "I believe that the toxin used to send several thousand of Nueva Portugal's citizens into madness originates from the same location I was looking for under my orders from the Mountain."

"I'd guessed," Daalman told her. "Commander, we are well past the level where I am comfortable with one of my officers operating independently and under secret orders. I trust you and I have faith in the Mage-Queen, but this is too much."

Roslyn paused for a moment, considering how to approach this. She had Daalman's support so far, but she believed the Captain—and she *needed* Daalman's full support going forward.

"Then you need to know," she concluded quietly. "We're pursuing a secret laboratory set up by rogue Mages from the Republic's Project Prometheus. I now suspect they were working on alternative uses of the basic brain-interface technology used in the Promethean Interfaces.

"At the very least, we are looking at a high-level Mage-Surgeon and one of the RID's handful of Mage operatives," Roslyn continued. "We both know I'm operating under orders from the Mountain, sir. Neutralizing this lab and taking the Mages into custody is absolutely necessary—and doing so without it becoming public knowledge is critical to maintaining the fragile peace we have with the former Republic worlds.

"If it comes out that rogue Mages murdered thousands of people on a former Republic world, it's not going to matter that those Mages worked for the Republic," she said quietly. "It should...but it won't."

The channel was quiet.

"Well, I should know by now that you don't pull punches," Daalman finally said. "You're talking multiple names from the Red List *and* an active Prometheus lab?"

"Yes, sir," Roslyn confirmed. "We believe we have located the lab, but we have confirmed they have a *lot* of ways out."

"You have a plan," Daalman said flatly. It wasn't a question.

"Yes, sir," she said. "I'm taking my team in through what we believe is the main entrance. I'm forwarding you a map of the drainage tunnels they have previously used for entering and exiting the facility. The network is large enough to handle transport vehicles.

"I need *Huntress*'s Marines to move against anyone who exits from that network as we move in. I don't think we can afford the time or the risk to bring in the Guardia or the local Army."

"No. This has to be Martian," Daalman agreed. "You're talking about kicking in the front door with twelve Marines and one Mage, Chambers. Surely—"

"We're looking at over a hundred potential exits, sir," Roslyn interrupted. "I need Major Dickens's Marines to make sure no one escapes. I trust Sergeant Mooren and her people to back me while we punch through whatever they have.

"They can't have an army down there. They couldn't have hidden that from the locals—and all of this was as hidden from the Republic as it was from us."

Daalman sighed.

"All right," she agreed. "But I'm moving Navy Mages in with the Marines, and you *will* call for backup if you need it, Commander. I've got your back, to the end of the line.

"Let's not fuck this up."

"I'm not planning on it, sir. I will keep you in the loop as much as I can."

"You'd better. At the end of the day, if this goes wrong, the court-martial will string me up right next to you," Daalman told her.

Roslyn chuckled bitterly. They both knew the truth: if this went wrong, Roslyn would be *long* dead before any court-martial took place.

CHAPTER 28

"WE DON'T HAVE much that fits exosuits," the young Guardia Lieutenant said nervously, watching as twelve Marines, each augmented to a full two meters in height by the battle armor, crossed his precinct's front yard.

"Do you have *enough?*" Roslyn asked gently. She couldn't be much older than the Guardia officer, but experience mattered as much as years sometimes—and there was a vast gulf between her experience of war and conflict and the local cop who'd never left his world.

"We can fit four in the back of one of our SUVs, but the suits won't fit in the front to drive," the youth told her. "You'd need three SUVs and three drivers..."

"Well, we've got two drivers," Killough replied, stepping up beside Roslyn. Like her, he was dressed in the same lighter combat gear they'd worn before. There just hadn't been *time* to fit anyone in exosuit armor, let alone train them.

Roslyn had left the Academy with a field promotion long before she'd been supposed to receive exosuit training, and the armor training given to a Navy officer was perfunctory at best, regardless. The MISS spy had *no* training.

Light armor and hazmat add-ons, it was.

The hazmat helmets Killough was carrying drew the Guardia officer's gaze, and he swallowed as Roslyn took hers from the spy.

"I'll ask for volunteers to drive the third vehicle," he offered. "I don't know if we have the proper hazmat—"

"That won't be necessary, Lieutenant," a rich baritone said from behind them. "I brought my own gear, and I'll drive the Lieutenant Commander's people."

Roslyn turned to find Captain Bolivar having just emerged from a Guardia car at the edge of the precinct yard. She caught herself smiling brightly at the man, his presence a breath of hope in a difficult situation.

"You didn't brief us that you were pulling off another stunt, Commander," Bolivar continued as the Lieutenant skittered half-consciously away. "Can we help, beyond providing cars?"

"*Huntress*'s people are standing by to capture anyone who runs, Captain," she told him. "If we're in the right place, your people aren't ready for this fight."

"There's only three things in the universe I won't back my tac-teams against," Bolivar said drily. "There were four, but you guys dissolved the Space Assault Regiments."

"Mages, Augments and Marines in exosuits?" Roslyn asked.

"You didn't even need two guesses," Bolivar agreed. "And from that..."

"Your people aren't ready for this fight," she repeated. "I can't say more."

The Guardia officer whistled softly.

"Read and understood, Mage-Commander," he told her. "I'm just the driver, then, but I think Sorprendidas has the right to have *somebody* in this operation, don't you?"

"It's not the worst plan," Roslyn agreed. "You get the back car."

"The most protected one, huh?" the Guardia Captain noted. "Who's driving the one in front?"

"Who do you think?" she asked.

The drive from the precinct station to the water treatment facility was probably the safest part of the trip. Roslyn had no intention of taking their borrowed vehicles—two of which were marked Guardia trucks—into the drainage tunnels. They were unlikely to be attacked on their way *to* the lab.

Which was good, as overhead and commentary hadn't quite given Roslyn the true scale of the school they were driving past. It was the crowning jewel of the suburb Triple Q had built there, a solidly built complex that had to be home to at least two thousand kids.

"I do *not* like how close that school is to this," she murmured on a private channel to Killough and Mooren. "We need to keep that in mind. If things go sideways, we need to pull any action away from the school."

"I wanted to wait until nightfall," the Marine reminded her. "But you were right. A lot of people could die if we wait."

"Or Lafrenz could escape," Killough added, the spy's voice grim. "If she gets away, all of this might end up being for nothing."

"Let's try to keep the fighting underground," Roslyn told them. "Swift and surgical. This ends today."

The water treatment plant's security gates happily gave way to their vehicles' Guardia codes, the automatic systems pulling the entrance open to allow the three vehicles entrance into a parking lot concealed amidst a carefully manicured collection of trees.

The plant itself was a low-slung bunker only visible as a structure—as opposed to a hill slowly growing new trees—from this angle. Roslyn pulled her vehicle into the empty lot and turned it off.

The other two vehicles slid to a halt around her and she drew a deep breath.

"Sensor check?" she ordered.

"Nothing pinging so far," Mooren replied. "There's nothing in the parking lot, but the building itself is solid enough to defeat our mobile passives."

"Is that normal?" Roslyn asked. "Because that doesn't sound normal to me."

"Most water treatment plants are built with twenty-centimeter concrete shells so they can do things like plant trees on top," the Marine replied. "But most *don't* have a lead lining, and I'd say this place does."

"Right," Roslyn said drily. "I think this is the place." She switched to the squad channel. "Lock and load, everyone. Remember: we want prisoners, but we are expecting serious resistance.

"This is effectively a Republic Intelligence Directorate facility. Whatever the RID would have packed in, we can expect the rogue Prometheus Mages to have packed in—*and* we know there are at least two Mages in here.

"We have backup if things go sideways, but I *don't* expect to face resistance in enough force to hold off a full squad of Marines," she told them. "They hid this place from the Republic, from the Sorprendidas government, from us. They couldn't risk an army, and it isn't big enough for one.

"They almost certainly know we're coming, but they have no idea what they're dealing with," Roslyn said. "Let's remind them why *everyone* fears the Royal Martian Marines!"

"Oorah!"

CHAPTER 29

"I'VE GOT THE DOORS," Bolivar promised as Roslyn reached the entrance to the treatment plant. "I'm sure you've got six ways in, but I'd rather we minimize the property damage."

She chuckled and waved him forward. The Guardia officer wore very similar hazmat and light armor to her and Killough. Like them, he was dwarfed by the Marines in their exosuits, but all of them were equally anonymous now.

With properly fitted armor, even Roslyn's chest was flattened into androgyny. Modern armor handled that surprisingly comfortably, while rendering the team utterly uniform except for height.

The doors opened within seconds as Bolivar tapped a command sequence into the door, then stood back and gestured the Martian personnel forward. He was clearly *not* so foolish as to go first when there were people with exosuit armor around.

"Clear," Corporal Andrews announced as their team swept the first area. "Treatment plant itself seems quiet, but there's enough machinery to muck with the motion and heat sensors."

"Keep the mark one eyeball peeled, then," Mooren ordered. "Marines, move up! Rest of you...follow on."

Roslyn chuckled at the *rest of you* designation—though she didn't exactly follow the instruction, either. She was in the middle of the pack, with half a dozen of the Marines ahead of her and six behind. Power flickered around her hands, invisible even to her, ready to shield the entire squad *when*—not if—their enemy made a move.

The water treatment plant was an entity of open pools and massive pipes, with machinery humming efficiently and ignoring the mere humans who wandered through its depths. From the statistics she'd seen, it could handle over a trillion liters a day. At that rate, it would *still* take three weeks to empty the massive reservoir installed under the park—and Nueva Portugal had *four* similar facilities.

And the new one had been installed out of clear need. The rainy season on this section of Sorprendidas brought enough water that each district of the city had its own drainage system leading to a reservoir-and-treatment facility like this.

Roslyn was glad she wasn't visiting the city *in* that rainy season, even if it would have made this job a lot easier if the drainage tunnels were full of water. Right now, the machinery around her was running at less than five percent of capacity, almost quiescent against the thunder that the plant must be filled with during the rainy season.

"Anyone seeing anything other than tanks, pools and piping?" she asked. "All of our estimates and guesses say they have to have an access in here."

"Nothing at this level," Mooren admitted. "Knight, get some drones up. I'm guessing we need to go down."

"Two more levels under us," Roslyn told the Marine. Tactical drones launched from several of the Marines' suits, the pigeon-sized winged robots flickering out across the facility. "And not a soul. I understand the logic, but damn, is it creepy."

"A team of thirty does a full inspection on one of these plants every day," Bolivar said quietly. "Five days a week and they take weekends off. This one was inspected yesterday, and the report was clean. Nothing out of the ordinary."

"Yeah. There's nothing here that wasn't built when the plant was," Roslyn agreed. "And somewhere, I'm guessing on the very bottom level, is a door that's either hidden from the inspection team or the team just takes for granted now."

"We'll find out," Mooren replied. "Marines! Map says the stairs are in the middle. Do *not* split up."

It seemed Roslyn wasn't the only one feeling twitchy.

The waste treatment plant had large freight elevators to handle replacement parts, but it was clear that the main method of reaching the two lower floors was the stairs Mooren had sent everyone to. Wide enough for six exosuited Marines to walk down abreast, the shallow steps spiraled down a large opening descending twenty meters into the earth.

"Skip the middle level," Roslyn ordered. "Scan for threats with the drones, but I'm betting our access is on the bottom."

No one verbally acknowledged her, but four of Knight's drones flashed away as they passed the first sub-level, and the Marines kept tramping downward. Each ten-meter-high level was a duplicate of the one above, with a few large cylindrical tanks descending the full height of the treatment plant.

The bottom of the plant was the same smoothed industrial concrete as the two floors above it. Nothing about the facility yet indicated that it was a cover for a secret bioweapon lab—but that, Roslyn supposed, was the point.

Secret labs shouldn't *look* like secret labs.

"Stick to a group, move north, circle counterclockwise toward the reservoir," Mooren ordered. "Knight, keep the drones sweeping for anything we might miss. I would rather *not* get ambushed in this mess."

"I don't know; there's lots of cover in here," Killough said drily. "Speaking as one of the people in the *light* armor, cover sounds better than wide open corridors."

"Yes, but think of the property damage," the Marine replied. "We'll take it out of your paycheck."

"I think I might still be legally dead," the spy said. "They'll have to fix that before they can dock my pay!"

Roslyn smiled to herself as she moved with the Marines. At least everyone was in good spirits, even with the vaguely depressing silence of the mechanical plant. This floor was almost entirely shut down at this time of year, it seemed.

She had an overlay of the map they'd put together of what they thought was under the park on her HUD, and slowed to a halt after they'd circled around a quarter of the bunker.

"Stop," she ordered. "The reservoir is directly west of us. Most likely the lab is on either the north or south side of the reservoir, dug out in the same project and built at the same time. So, we are now into the area where I expect to see the access point."

She gestured to the south, where several massive pipes emerged from the exterior bunker wall.

"That's the reservoir link," she reminded them. "We *know* they're using the drainage tunnels to the reservoir itself as passageways, so we've got to be close."

"Knight, those drones can rig up a short-range penetrating-radar pulse, right?" Mooren asked. "Sequence them into the wall. I'm *betting* some of this wall moves aside with the right commands, but we don't have the network codes."

"Setting them up," the Corporal replied. "This will take a minute. Do we want to sweep the rest of the west wall while I work?"

"Don't split up," Roslyn and Mooren said simultaneously.

Several of the Marines very clearly swallowed chuckles in response to that.

"Form up around Knight," Mooren ordered. "Keep your eyes peeled and watch for incoming hostiles. We don't know what kind of defenses or security are in place, but there is *no way* they don't know we're in the treatment plant."

The drones converged on them once again. Each of them flew forward and attached itself to the wall as Roslyn watched. Within a few moments, they'd formed a wave pattern on the wall, and Knight made a small gesture with her armored hand.

Roslyn didn't feel or see anything, but new data immediately appeared on her HUD as the maps updated with the radar data. Knight had calibrated the pulses carefully, and only about ten meters behind the wall was illuminated—and that was enough.

"All right. Everyone stand back," Roslyn ordered as she studied the location of the passageway. "Like you said, there's almost certainly some kind of code or command we can give, but we don't have time for that."

The Marines got out of her way in a flash. Every one of them had seen a Combat Mage make a door before, and they were *not* going to be in the way. It took Bolivar a few seconds longer to realize what was going on, but ten seconds after her HUD updated, Roslyn had a clear line of sight to the wall concealing the door.

Explosives would be equally brute-force as Roslyn's plan, but they would take longer. Time was everything and Roslyn was worried. They *needed* the data on the damn toxin to save the affected people who were still alive.

She didn't know how much time those people had left—but she did know that none of them deserved what the Prometheus Mages had done to them. She let that anger flow through her, pushing her power as she flung her magic against the concrete barrier in front of her.

Concrete could never stand against a trained Mage. The wall was dust in moments, revealing a heavy steel vault door concealed behind it.

The door didn't last much longer as Roslyn stepped forward with blades of force answering her will. Steel parted like paper against an edge forged of pure force, and the heavy vault door fell backward into the tunnel.

She exhaled a long breath and nodded to herself, holding a shield across the entrance as the Marines moved up.

"No lights," Mooren murmured. "Probably killed them when they realized we were coming. Go thermal, people. They're *definitely* waiting for us."

CHAPTER 30

ROSLYN WAITED for the Marines to lead the way again, falling once more into the middle of the column. The dark tunnel was foreboding, even with the thermal vision and infrared lights lighting it up ahead of them.

It descended at a shallow angle toward the reservoir. Initially, one side of it was clearly the outside of the big pipes moving water up to the treatment plant. The infrared flashlights only gave them fifty meters or so of visibility as they headed deeper, and a deep chill settled into Roslyn's spine.

"Think it's *supposed* to be this creepy?" she murmured.

"Nah, but it's a nice side effect from their point of view," Killough said. "Keeps us on edge."

"We've got a break in the tunnel ahead," Knight reported. "It curves right, and the descent gets steeper. Watch your step. This tunnel definitely wasn't meant for vehicles."

"Move up to the turn and hold position," Mooren ordered. "Keep together."

That kept getting reiterated, but Roslyn understood. They had too small of a force to risk getting separated when they knew almost nothing about the layout of the complex they'd entered.

The turn was enough to detach the tunnel from the pipes as Knight had said. The path curved away from the reservoir systems and headed deeper into the ground.

"I think you might be wrong on the vehicles," Roslyn noted, flashing her infrared lamp over the roof. "There's a power line up there for lights and a tram of some kind. Permanent installation to make the transit up and down easier.

"Probably means this trip is longer than we thought."

"We thought it was a half a damn kilometer," Mooren pointed out. "That's quite the walk, boss."

"Wait," Knight snapped. "Drones have picked up motion headed our way...and I'm guessing it's the Commander's tram."

"Against the wall; stand by weapons," the Marine Sergeant snapped. Her people leapt to obey, with the non-Marines only a few seconds behind.

There was no visible trail on the concrete floor to show where the tram usually ran, but with the attack team pressed to the walls, they were *probably* safe.

Roslyn swallowed hard. She had a carbine slung across her back, but she had no intention of *using* the weapon. Power ran through her limbs as she summoned her magic. Whatever happened next was going to be... interesting.

The tram came hurtling up the slope with its lights disabled, only barely visible in the infrared lights as the SUV-sized vehicle whirred up to them on electric motors—only to violently careen over onto its side half a dozen meters ahead of them.

It wasn't quite large enough to fill the tunnel from side to side, but it *was* large enough that the nearest fire team was in active danger.

Except they were in exosuits. Corporal Andrews bodily stepped into the oncoming vehicle, leaning their shoulder into the vehicle and smashing it to a halt with a resounding crash.

Two figures leapt from the vehicle as it ground to a halt, moving with blurring speed as they swung penetrator rifles toward Andrews. Unfortunately for them, there was a *reason* the Corporal had stepped forward alone, and their fire team opened up on the attackers.

Augments weren't faster than bullets. Tungsten penetrator rounds hammered into the roof, but none struck the Corporal before their attackers were down.

"Danger close," Andrews reported sharply. "Explosives in the tram!"

The Marines recoiled as one, and Roslyn threw up a defensive barrier between them and the vehicle—barely in time. Multiple explosives had apparently been linked to the Augment's life signs and detonated simultaneously, spraying intentional fragments and tram debris alike toward Roslyn's attack team.

None of the deadly spray made it through the shield of solidified air and pure force Roslyn put in its path, the antipersonnel mines failing in their lethal purpose as she protected her people.

But there was a *second* purpose to the explosions, and that was made clear moments later as gunfire hammered into the barrier. Two Augments had ridden the tram forward to try and take Roslyn's team by surprise.

The rest had dismounted farther back and brought portable cover with them. Distinctive *snap-hiss-crack* sounds marked the deployment of foxhole grenades, laying out chest-high barriers of bulletproof foam as the lab's defenders moved up in full force.

Her people had the same grenades—but they also had Roslyn Chambers.

"Grenades," Mooren snapped. "Hold on the Mage's order—Commander?"

"Launch," Roslyn agreed, opening a gap at the top of her barrier as the Marines hurled their weapons forward. The grenades weren't the armor-piercing weapons they might use against exosuits—but those weapons required greater accuracy than this mess was going to allow anyway.

Their own waves of deadly shrapnel scythed down the corridor, buying time for Roslyn's Marines to move up and take what cover they could against the wreckage of the tram. Several more foxhole grenades went off amidst the debris, turning the vehicle's hulk into useful cover even for the exosuits.

"Locking in targets," Knight reported. "I make it fourteen. All appear to be Augments, carrying penetrator rifles with medium body armor."

There were very few unaugmented humans who could carry the big automatic penetrator rifles with their discarding-sabot rounds. Roslyn had encountered the stripped-down version used by the Protectorate Secret Service, but those guns cost more than the exosuits they were supposed to take down.

The Republic had gone for Augment cyborg soldiers instead, with upgraded bones and muscles that could carry and fire the heavy weapons. Now over a dozen of those super-soldiers were dug in ahead of Roslyn's people.

"Your call, Sergeant," Roslyn murmured. "I can hold the shield for a while yet."

She'd pay for it later, but Roslyn was a naturally powerful Mage, of some of the strongest bloodlines out of Project Olympus. A hail of tungsten darts wasn't going to cause her problems.

"We can't shoot back through the field, and grenades didn't do shit," Mooren replied. "Marines, on my mark. Commander, drop the shield on...*mark.*"

They couldn't have done it more smoothly if they'd practiced a thousand times. The Marines probably *had* practiced the drill, but with Marine Combat Mages.

She dropped the defensive barrier at Mooren's command, and the Marines opened fire in the same instant. Killough and Bolivar joined the fire a moment later with their own lighter weapons.

Half of the Marines carried the same heavy penetrator rifles as their opponents. The high-speed tungsten darts from those went right through the foam of the foxhole grenades, sending Augment soldiers sprawling backward.

Two more had grenade launchers, dropping a mix of armor-piercing and shrapnel grenades behind the defenders' cover. The last four Marines had big auto-shotguns designed for specialty munitions. They were firing heavy shot, each "pellet" the size of a smaller shotgun's slug and punching through armored soldiers like they were made of paper.

The exchange of fire lasted a few seconds after Roslyn dropped the barrier, then everything fell silent.

"Move up," Mooren barked. "Secure prisoners and watch for a second wave. That's only *half* an Augment Corps platoon!"

Unspoken was the warning that the *other* sixteen cyborgs were almost certainly somewhere in the base. They'd met the first line of defense and overcome it without losses...but that didn't mean they were done yet.

Far from it.

CHAPTER 31

THEIR TRIP DOWN the rest of the tunnel was uninterrupted until the very end. That was when Knight's drones, scouting ahead of them, ran into the same kind of targeted anti-drone pulse screen as had been set up in Killough's apartment.

"Drones are fried," the Corporal reported. "I have a second set, but they're going to run into the same thing. Visual I got says they weren't playing games at this end of the passageway."

The tunnel had taken them six hundred meters to the west and almost two hundred meters down. They were now on the north side of the reservoir and almost halfway down its mind-boggling depth.

There was a reason the lab had been built with a tram, though Roslyn was still wondering where the power for all of this came from. She supposed they could be hijacking the treatment plant's power lines—or just running a fusion plant using the water from the reservoir, for that matter.

Sorprendidas had a lower-than-normal ratio of heavy water, but enough was running through the drainage and reservoir for the lab to pull oxygen and deuterium from the system easily enough.

And even a small fusion reactor would power what she saw in Knight's half-second-long video clip.

"Active sensors here, here and here," Mooren told everyone, flagging them in the image they'd quickly thrown together. "These four units up here are combat lasers. The Republic's personal laser weaponry was always better than ours, so those can almost certainly punch through your suits.

"And if *those* didn't scare us enough, *this* pair down here are eight-barrel twenty-millimeter gatling railguns," the Sergeant continued, marking two more objects on the screen. "At that size, it doesn't *matter* if they're firing penetrators or not. A hit will turn you to jelly *inside* your armor.

"All automated, but it's not like we brought an EMP bomb with us."

Roslyn snorted. That was a terrible idea on multiple levels.

"We could call in a bunker-buster strike from *Huntress*," Knight suggested. "That would end this whole situation real quick."

"And potentially spread their toxin across half a continent, even if we ignore the fact that we're right next to a park, a suburb, several apartment complexes, a school..." Roslyn didn't finish the list. She didn't need to.

"I know, I know," the Corporal conceded. "What do we do about the door? Mage-shield close enough for AP grenades?"

"Doable," Roslyn confirmed. "Sergeant? This is your area of expertise, not mine."

The guns were around another turn in the passage, denying anyone approaching the ability to engage at long range. They'd turn the corner and find themselves within fifty meters of the weapons platforms. The corner itself would give some cover but not enough.

"Mage-shield is an option," Mooren agreed. "But we know there's Mages in there, sir. How are you doing?"

Roslyn mentally poked at her internal "gas tank."

"If I have to face another Mage, I'd really rather not push things more than I have to," she admitted. "I can handle it, no problem, but if we have another option..."

Mooren grinned.

"That's what I figured. And as for this, well, there's a reason they sent Augments out to stop us before we got to it. The Republic knows *damn* well that Marines can handle this, clever as the setup is."

The answer, obvious even to Roslyn in hindsight, was grenades. Lots and lots of armor-piercing grenades, combined with the exosuit-clad

Marines' ability to target through the optics of the weapon without exposing themselves to fire.

They suffered accuracy-wise, but by the time the two Marines with grenade launchers had walked several magazines of armor-piercing grenades across the heavily fortified door, there wasn't much left.

"Grenadiers, fall back," Mooren ordered, stepping back and lowering her own weapon. "Penetrator rifles up; target anything still moving."

Six Marines moved forward. Roslyn followed them, but only enough to stand next to the Marine Sergeant, thoroughly aware that Mooren would stop her from doing anything stupid.

"Seems straightforward enough," she murmured as the heavy rifles spoke in the corridor, ripping apart the single still-operating turret with their high-velocity tungsten darts.

"Straightforward, yes," the Marine agreed. "But we are now out of armor-piercing grenades, so if we run into any defenders with exosuits, it'll be down to the penetrator rifles to handle them."

"That's what they're *for*, isn't it?" Roslyn asked.

"Yup. But I'm always more comfortable with a backup option," Mooren told her. "And since *I'm* one of my grenadiers, I'm always aware of the grenade magazine levels."

"Fair," Roslyn allowed. "We clear?" The firing had stopped.

"Hold on."

The Marine NCO stepped forward to check on her people. After a few seconds, she waved the rest of the squad forward.

"One wrecked door, Lieutenant Commander," she reported. "Now we see what the hell they decided to hide down here."

The door itself had seemed impressive enough, but it had failed in the face of Marines with sufficient aggression. Roslyn crossed the last few meters of corridor gingerly, with exosuited guardians all around her, but it was clear that the automated defenders hadn't even fired a shot.

As Mooren had said, the lab's defenders had sent Augments out to fight them in the corridor because they'd been all too aware of the vulnerabilities of the fortifications against Marines. The Marines weren't the Protectorate's best—that title was reserved for the handful of elite forces that guarded the Mage-Queen and supported her Hands—but they were *damn* good.

"Open sesame," Mooren said drily as she stepped through the wreckage her grenades had made. "Knight, get new drones up. I'm pretty sure we blew the crap out of the anti-drone systems, and despite the pretty foyer we just made a mess of, I don't see a map anywhere."

Mooren's description of the space they were entering was surprisingly accurate—both in the "pretty foyer" and the "mess" aspects. There was a tram dock—empty for obvious reasons—to Roslyn's left, but the right side of the room could have been the entrance for any large corporate office, with a reception desk and a set of comfortable-looking chairs.

Those chairs had been ripped to shreds by shrapnel from the door's destruction, and the reception desk wasn't in much better shape. Roslyn doubted anyone had ever shown up at this entrance to the lab with anything so mundane as an *appointment*, but they'd been set up for it.

"I don't see a receptionist, so I think we're going to have to find our own way around," Roslyn agreed. "Knight, are there any intact data ports there?"

The cyberwarfare Marine and her drones were already most of the way to the desk when Roslyn asked. Exosuit gauntlets tore through the remnants of the desk, and Knight snorted on the squad channel.

"Data connections are trashed," she replied. "And it doesn't look like anyone has even sat in this chair in six months. Whole place was probably just decorative."

"Decorative or not, where are the rest of the Augments?" Bolivar asked. "The Augment Corps works in platoons of thirty-two, as you guys said. This place is...weird."

"This place is a covert bioweapon lab, Captain," Roslyn told him with a sigh. There was only so much she could hide from the Guardia officer now. "And everything you're seeing down here is classified. Your Guardia report is going to be very, *very* short."

Bolivar chuckled.

"I'd guessed," he said. "Both parts, unfortunately. Three entrances deeper into the lab. Where do we go?"

"In the absence of a map, left-hand rule," Mooren replied. "Do we want to make sure nobody gets out, sir?"

"Even foxhole grenades can be cut through without leaving guards, and we're not splitting the team," Roslyn said. "Leave exit security to Major Dickens."

She paused.

"Speaking of, hold up here one moment. I'm going to check in."

A few commands on her wrist-comp later, she stared at a red alert on her HUD and swallowed a curse.

NO CONNECTION.

"We're blocked," she told the others. "Not sure if it's jamming or just the construction. Our enemy probably has boosters and a com network linked to an off-site relay."

That kind of thing was *her* job, not the Marines.

"We'd need special equipment to transmit out, and we didn't get that dropped," she said aloud. "Should have anticipated it when we realized the treatment plant was shielded."

Of course, it had already been too late at that point. The only option they had was to finish the job.

"We can't risk anyone running, so load up, people," Roslyn said grimly. "Left-hand rule it is, Sergeant Mooren. Let's move."

CHAPTER 32

THE LEFT-HAND OPTION led them into a collection of board-rooms and offices, all empty. They were well set up with tables, desks, chairs...all of it covered in a faint coating of dust.

"Has anyone been in this area *ever*?" Killough asked.

"The corridor has been used," Knight told him. "But these offices and boardrooms..."

A drone zipped through an ajar door into one of the boardrooms, then settled down on top of the long black table.

"Electronics aren't even hooked up to a network," the cyberwarfare Marine said. "Everything in this area is dead. If it ever *was* in use, they actively shut it down."

"This doesn't look much like a lab," Roslyn said.

"You haven't been in many corporate laboratories, have you?" Bolivar asked. "Most have an office section for the investors and accounting people. Even the researchers *have* offices, though they're usually much messier than this.

"Maybe they decided to plan for expansion?"

Roslyn grimaced behind her helmet.

"I hope not," she said. "These people are...not who I want expanding."

"Lights are at least on," Mooren replied. "Think they ever turn them off?"

"We are over two hundred meters below ground," Roslyn pointed out. "*I* wouldn't turn the damn lights off, and claustrophobia is contra-indicated in Navy officers."

The lead drones reached the end of the corridor, lights sweeping right and left as the Marines caught up.

"Left-hand rule?" Roslyn asked as she reached the T intersection. "Right looks like more offices, anyway."

She had mapping software running in her HUD that suggested the right-hand path would link up with the middle of the three corridors from the foyer area. That implied, to her at least, that those two paths flanked a large area of offices and boardrooms.

Some of the offices might even be in use—but they weren't looking for offices right now.

"I have power signatures suggesting an elevator to the left," Knight reported. "Seems like a plan to me."

"Keep the maps running," Mooren said. "I have the sinking feeling this place isn't going to be easy to find our way around."

"Are there any networks that might have a map we can access?" Roslyn asked.

"There's *a* network," Knight confirmed. "I can tell the damn thing exists, but I can't even get a wireless protocol off it. Military-style ghosting and encryption—and it's *not* Republic or Sorprendidan codes."

"Is it ours?" Roslyn said. "That would be a hell of a way to screw with everyone's heads."

"Checked that, too," the Marine replied. "I'm *guessing* custom software, but it's better than anything I've ever seen."

"We'll keep searching. There's people down here somewhere, unless they've already run for it."

And that felt...out of character. Everything about the facility so far suggested it was larger than Roslyn's worst-case scenarios.

Whoever was in charge had to have known the Navy and Marines coming for them was a chance. That meant there was a plan, and Roslyn wished she didn't have to find out what it was.

She was certain she wasn't going to like it.

The silence and emptiness of the complex only grew creepier as the Marine squad traveled deeper into the facility. After leaving the offices, they ended up in a storage section that was clearly along the south wall of the complex.

Nothing in the storage flagged as worth further investigation as they went along. The storage units were at least clearly in use, marked as containing all kinds of laboratory chemicals and similar working material for a lab...but there was still no one around.

"I'm marking side routes as we go, but I think this place is a maze," Roslyn concluded as they reached the end of the storage section and ran into a blank wall. "One dead end doesn't a labyrinth make, but...this place *is* weird."

"Agreed," Killough said grimly. "Head back to the last branch and see where it leads?"

"Not much else we can do unless we can crack the system or find a map," Mooren agreed. "Or find someone to interrogate."

"I have all *kinds* of questions to ask," Roslyn said. "Come on. Let's keep moving. There are answers somewhere in this godforsaken pit, I hope."

The branch off they headed back to was more of the same for a bit, then finally they hit a decontamination airlock. The system was entirely automated, to the point where it didn't even ask them for identification, but Roslyn hesitated.

"Send one fire team in first," she told Mooren. "That way, we can break them out if something goes wrong."

"On it," Andrews agreed. "It's just glass, after all."

Roslyn held her peace on that—transmutation Mages were quite capable of making a lot of very tough materials transparent—and watched the first three Marines go into the decon room.

The transparent barriers slammed shut on either side, scanners beeped, and several different systems activated at once.

"Knight?" Roslyn murmured.

"Antiseptic spray and several radiation purges," the Marine told her. "Not sure I'd want to be in there in regular scrubs, but everyone's armor should be fine."

After thirty seconds, the airlock cycled, releasing Andrews's fire team into the next area.

"Team by team," Roslyn ordered. "Let's be careful."

Three by three, her team made their way past the decontamination room into a more stereotypically medical portion of the underground complex. Walls had been painted sterile white. Doors were clear glass but heavily secured.

"Sir, you need to see this," Andrews announced, gesturing Roslyn forward to join them.

She joined the lead team next to a clear glass wall as they pointed into it. It took her a moment to register what she was looking at, and then a hard, cold shiver ran down her spine.

The room had four fully articulated beds designed to hold patients and adjust them for examination. Blinking arrays of computers and sensors walled the room—but what drew Roslyn's gaze were the iron-bar restraints positioned to hold patients against the beds.

As the Marines' lights filled the room, the beds became more clearly visible. All four had seen heavy use, with visible damage to the fabric where the occupants had struggled against the iron bars.

"Fuck me," Mooren whispered. "What the hell *is* this place?"

"Somewhere several hundred people came to die," Roslyn said grimly. "That's not news, even if it's horrifying to see the evidence of that."

"Yeah," Killough agreed, his voice very quiet. "Turn around, Commander."

She did, following his gaze to see what had drawn the MISS spy's attention. There was only one bed in the room on the other side of the hallway, but Roslyn recognized the equipment in it. She'd never seen it in person, but every Mage in the Protectorate had seen pictures of the brain-extraction equipment at the heart of Project Prometheus.

She just hadn't expected to see it *here*, even knowing that the lab was run by Mages from that project.

190

"Is that what I think it is?" Mooren asked.

"Yes," Roslyn said shortly. "I should have expected it, but I didn't. This place is a fucking nightmare."

"We knew that," Killough said. "We should keep moving. There isn't anyone here."

"Knight, can we get into those computers?" Roslyn asked, gesturing to the blinking machinery around the medical horror show.

"Let me see," the Marine replied. An exosuit gauntlet demonstrated that while the transparent material *wasn't* glass, it wasn't tough enough to stand up to the powered muscles of Marine battle armor. A drone zipped through the gap and clicked on to the computers.

A few seconds passed and Knight cursed.

"Different network," she told them. "Same encryption. I might leave the drone here and see if some of our software can break through over time."

"Do it. We need to keep moving," Roslyn ordered. "We're not going to *end* this horror show without finding the people behind it."

The Marines slowly got moving again, but everyone had seen the restraints and the damage. The beds had been *heavily* used. Roslyn suspected that if their targets had been any less fastidious, there would have been blood on the beds.

But that probably would have contaminated the experiments.

"Fuckers," she muttered.

"Sir?" Mooren asked.

"Just...these fuckers," Roslyn repeated. "We need them alive, Sergeant. But we can't lose your Marines, either. I trust your judgments, all of you."

"I know," the Marine Sergeant replied. "We are going to get them, sir. I promise."

"Sir, Sergeant..." Andrews's voice came through the channel again, but this time, they sounded actively ill. "You need... You need to see this."

At first glance, Roslyn thought that Andrews had just found another storage unit and wondered what it was doing in the sterile medical section. Then she recognized the side of the square sixty-centimeter-by-sixty-centimeter doors that lined the walls of the room in even rows.

"Open the fucking door, Corporal," Roslyn ordered.

Gauntleted fists smashed glass door and wall alike, clearing the path for everyone to step into the morgue. Roslyn looked around as she followed the Marines in, counting and estimating.

There were at least a hundred cadaver drawers in the room, and she suspected this wasn't the only one.

Worst, though, was the far wall. A section large enough for a dozen drawers instead held a single large door. Roslyn couldn't stop herself. She crossed the morgue and pulled the door open with a flash of power augmenting her muscles.

Even through her armor and hazmat helmet, she felt the heat wash up out of the open door. A conveyor belt started as she stared at the slanted surface leading away and down toward a secured hatch.

"Plasma flue from the reactor core," Andrews said quietly. "At least a thousand degrees. Instant incineration."

"Corpse disposal," Roslyn said. "When they learn everything they can from their victims, they burn them away so there's no evidence of what happened. They just...disappear. And then they die. And then they are incinerated."

Anger burned through her and she glared at the disposal conveyor belt. Her magic slammed the door shut and she turned back to face her team.

"This isn't working," she told them. "This place is too big, and we don't know enough about what we're looking for. I hate it, but we *have* to split up. Andrews, Knight, your fire teams are with me."

She stepped outside the morgue and looked around her.

"Mooren, take the rest and Killough. You sweep right," she ordered. "I'll sweep left. Use the drones as relays and keep in touch, but the priority is finding Ulla Lafrenz and Connor ad Aaron.

"Do *not* engage either unless you are certain you have complete surprise," she told them. "You know how to fight Mages, all of you, but leave them for me if you can.

"These people are the last vestige of the worst Magekind has produced in the last two hundred years," she continued. "We *will* bring them to justice. The people who died here will have justice."

It wasn't safe to split the squad, but sweeping the facility one corridor at a time was taking too damn long. Mooren didn't even object, gesturing for her Marines to form up around her.

"You heard the Commander, Knight, Andrews," she told her Corporals. "Go with her; watch her back." The Marine turned to look at Bolivar, the suit of armor looming over the Guardia officer.

"Not too late to get out of here, Captain Bolivar," she told him.

"I'm with Mage-Lieutenant Commander Chambers," Bolivar replied, glancing over at Roslyn. "This is my damn planet, and the people in that morgue are *my* people.

"I'm not going fucking anywhere until the bastards behind this are dead or in cuffs."

CHAPTER 33

SIX MARINES and a Guardia officer followed Roslyn deeper into the laboratory. They made less noise than the entire squad, but their armored boots still rang sharply in the silence of the underground complex.

"This place feels like a fucking tomb," Knight murmured. "But...I think the drones might have some activity ahead."

"Activity, Corporal?" Roslyn asked.

"Movement, active equipment, possibly people," the Marine confirmed. "Might be part of the lab that's in use right now?"

"Sounds promising," Roslyn said. "Everyone's got stunguns, right? We want these people alive."

"Can we torture them to death after?" someone asked quietly.

"I did *not* hear that," Roslyn snapped. "But if I *had*, the answer would be *no*. We are Her Majesty's people. Everything we do must be guided by Her desires and Her principles...and she'd be very, very angry with us for torturing people.

"We know it doesn't work for info, and the Protectorate does not go in for revenge. Am I clear?"

She understood the urge. If there was ever a time she wanted to go for revenge, this was it. But...no. She'd see the people behind this lab put on transparent public trial...and then shot.

That was *justice*, not revenge.

"We need them alive," she reiterated. "As many as we can get."

"Wilco, sir," Knight and Andrews chorused. From their body language, they *did* know who had spoken and there would be words the Navy officer couldn't hear.

"Let's move," Roslyn ordered, unslinging the stun carbine she had hung over her back. She didn't need the weapon, but she was far more likely to accidentally electrocute someone to death than the SmartDarts were.

"Twenty meters ahead," Knight murmured. "Looks like a temporary security checkpoint set up to lock down a segment of the—*ow*."

"Corporal?"

"Security checkpoint," the Marine confirmed. "Three Augments, one of them saw the drone and shot it."

"Move up and secure," Roslyn ordered. "Stun them if you can, but do what you have to."

Augments would be proofed against Nix, but Protectorate military-issue stunguns had SmartDart coding to deal with the cyborgs' defenses. The SmartDarts would take longer to take an Augment down, but that Augment would need *repairs* before they got back up.

The Marines passed Roslyn almost before she'd finished giving the order. She couldn't match the speed of their powered muscles, but she was still barely behind them. She heard gunfire crackle ahead and slid around a corner to take cover *behind* one of the exosuited Marines.

The Augments were fast and accurate, but that did them only so much good when they didn't have penetrator rifles. Their standard battle rifles were almost useless against the Marines, but the lab's protectors took what cover they could and threw lead downrange.

One was already twitching on the floor when Roslyn joined the fight, SmartDart pulses burning out the electrical hardware woven through their body. It was unquestionably cruel, but it was effective.

Almost as effective as Corporal Knight putting a tungsten penetrator dart through a second Augment's skull as the ex-Republic trooper popped up to take a shot. A spray of metal, bone and gore splattered the wall of the lab as the woman went down.

"Surrender," Roslyn barked.

"Fuck off and die!"

She shrugged and gestured. Using the man's voice as a guide, she yanked the Augment out from behind cover, suspending him in the air in shock as three stunguns opened fire.

The last Augment hit the ground as Roslyn released him, twitching like the first one.

"Andrews, cuff them and check their vitals," she ordered. "We'll need medevac for them both in short order, but let's make sure they don't die on us until then."

There were definite downsides to disabling integrated cyberware. The Augments *should* be fine...but Roslyn wasn't going to risk potential sources of intelligence on *should*.

"Knight, get the security door open," Roslyn continued, gesturing the cyberwarfare Marine forward. "Everyone else: cover her. No surprises."

"The only drones I have left are maintaining the link with Sergeant Mooren," Knight warned as she plugged wires from her armor into the panel next to the door. "No more warnings in advance."

"I'm still surprised at how many of them you all had stuck in your armor," Roslyn admitted, watching the door with her magic ready. "We've made it this far. We'll make it the rest of the way."

The drones were integral in building the map she had of the complex. It was *maybe* half-complete, with massive gaps, but she knew everywhere her people had been and everywhere Mooren's team had been.

She figured they had to be near to the center and close to the section supporting the fusion reactor. There couldn't be much more lab space left, but they were also in what had to be the most secure sections of the complex.

Nobody, even a bunch of rogue ex-Republic scientists, was going to leave the fusion reactor unprotected, after all.

Protected or not, the security door slid open under Knight's tender ministrations. The space beyond was another sterile empty corridor. Empty.

"Marines first," Andrews told Roslyn as their armored gauntlet appeared in front of her. "Something about this stinks."

"Something about this whole place stinks," she replied—but she didn't argue.

Andrews and their Marines swept forward, weapons at the ready as they moved.

"Clear; you can move up," the Corporal reported.

Everyone else followed and Roslyn shivered as she saw *another* set of well-used restraints—and another brain-extraction machine. There was only one set of "test subject" rooms, though, before she entered a space that she couldn't help but recognize.

Every Mage would know it, but a Jump Mage or a Rune Scribe would recognize an enchanting workshop instantly. The runes that propelled a starship through the stars were the most critical use of the silver polymer humanity used for magical constructs, but it was hardly the only one.

Roslyn herself had a third rune most Navy Mages didn't. Inlaid at the top of her right palm was the projector rune of a Marine Combat Mage, acquired after her sojourn as a Republic prisoner.

The lab in front of her could have easily fit a tank and allowed a team of scribes to work on it. The number of microscopes and what Roslyn guessed were micro-manipulator tools suggested the work was being done at a different scale...a scale that sent a chill running down her spine.

She didn't have time to do more than recognize the room before a door on the far side opened and a tall blonde woman dressed in a white lab coat stepped out, leveling a sardonic gaze on Roslyn and her Marines.

"If you lay down your weapons now," Mage-Surgeon Ulla Roxana Lafrenz told the people who'd come to arrest her, "I will make your deaths painless and spare this city the horror you risk unleashing."

Roslyn wasn't even sure which of her Marines tried to shoot Lafrenz. At least four stunguns fired at the Mage in near-unison.

The SmartDarts shattered on the shield the woman had raised before she'd even entered the room, and she flicked the fragments back toward the Marines with a dismissive gesture. The fragments hit with enough force to send at least one Marine crumpling backward, their armor penetrated—and a sparking broken capacitor buried in their flesh.

"Fall back," Roslyn ordered calmly, raising her own shield in time to intercept Lafrenz's next strike. Tiny darts of fire, both more precise and hotter than Roslyn herself could summon, hammered into the barrier.

She walked forward anyway, bringing her shield with her as her Marines thankfully followed her orders.

"Mage Ulla Lafrenz, by the laws of the Protectorate, the Charter of Mages, and even the damn law of the former Republic, you are guilty of more crimes than I can count," she told the other woman. "You are under arrest. Submit to Mage-cuffing or I will take you in by force."

Lafrenz laughed.

"Really, child? Do you think that's going to happen?"

"No," Roslyn admitted—and *she* hurled lightning across the room. Machinery and scanners shattered or overloaded as electricity arced across the air and she hammered into Lafrenz's shield with wave after wave of power.

She couldn't be sure, but she suspected there was a moment of concern in the other Mage's eyes. Despite that, Lafrenz's shield stayed up, and the Mage managed to take several steps forward against Roslyn's barrage.

"It will cost millions to replace that," Lafrenz noted. "Your incursion into this lab has been an unexpected complication, but believe me, child, we are more than ready for you. Did you really think one Mage would succeed here?"

The Marines were out of the room now, Roslyn recognized. Almost certainly at least one was set up with a penetrator rifle, waiting for a shot—but unless Lafrenz was less competent than expected, they weren't going to get it.

"I've had a *lot* of practice," Roslyn told the other woman in response to her question, sending lightning hurtling into the roof *above* the Prometheus Mage, trying to collapse debris onto her.

To her surprise, Lafrenz's shield extended above her head at an angle. The debris Roslyn pulled down hit the slanted armor of force and slid aside.

She made a mental note, adjusting her own armor slightly as she watched the effect. Lafrenz was surprisingly good at this for a research Mage.

As she was thinking that, Lafrenz launched her own next attack. For a second time, tiny superheated motes of fire flashed across the room—but this time they were *all* targeted on Roslyn.

The young Mage's shields weren't as efficient as Lafrenz's, but she channeled more power into her defenses as the older woman's magic hammered against her. Slowly, Roslyn walked forward.

Then she was moving faster, pushing through Lafrenz's attack like it didn't matter, and the other Mage took a step back. Then another—and then Lafrenz tore up the floor, trying to both fling Roslyn back and create a barrier between them.

Roslyn countered with a blade of force as large as she was, a variation of the antimissile spell she'd adapted on the fly at Hyacinth. The blade cut the debris away, clearing a path for Roslyn's advance.

Now Lafrenz looked worried. She was better at this than Roslyn. Better trained and more experienced—both of them could tell that—but she was *not* more powerful than Roslyn.

Roslyn was born of some of the direct bloodlines of the last children of Project Olympus. There were very few Mages in the galaxy who could match her one on one...and Ulla Lafrenz was *not* one of them.

"Surrender, Mage Lafrenz," Roslyn repeated. "Or I will take you in by force."

"Like your friends did Sam?" Lafrenz demanded. "The man the Protectorate *shot in the head?*"

"He didn't surrender," Roslyn said reasonably. She'd heard the entire story from Montgomery and figured that Samuel Finley had *definitely* deserved worse than he'd got.

"Fuck off and die," Lafrenz snapped, unconsciously echoing the Augment outside. Power flared around her, and a veritable tsunami of fire motes, accompanied by darts of pure force, hammered across the room.

What equipment had survived Roslyn's lightning bolts now shattered as the older Mage threw every scrap of power she had at the Navy officer. Scanners and tables melted. Gas canisters exploded. Debris tore across the room in a whirlwind of force that lasted for ten seconds. Fifteen. Twenty.

Then it collapsed and Ulla Lafrenz collapsed with it. Roslyn walked calmly forward, hiding as best she could the degree to which the other Mage's attack had drained her.

The Mage-cuffs—silver-rune-inlaid manacles—were in her hand, but she could see the blood on the floor around Lafrenz. She poked the other woman with her foot, then knelt down as Lafrenz twitched away.

The cuffs snapped onto the woman's wrists, but Lafrenz just chuckled bitterly.

"Too late, little girl," she whispered. "You've met the Orpheus weapon once, haven't you? I watched the news. That was version *thirteen*."

"What do you mean?" Roslyn demanded.

"You don't even know, do you?" Lafrenz laughed bitterly. "This was Project Orpheus, Finley's long-term plan. Everything we did with the Republic was to set up this place. We were going to rule *everything*.

"But it kept failing. Complex thirteen, though, had potential to be a *weapon*. You met it."

"The toxin," Roslyn said quietly.

"*Toxin*." Lafrenz coughed bitterly. "The most complex piece of nano-technology and magitech ever developed, and you call it a *toxin*. We can override the human brain with magic delivered by a nanite. Did you even know what you were *fighting*?"

"I need to know how to fix the damage it did," Roslyn told her. "I don't care how it works."

The Mage laughed and lifted her arm weakly, showing her wrist-comp.

"You should have cared," she replied. "Because I just activated a go-to-hell plan...and you and all of Nueva Portugal are going to hell."

"Complex thirteen wasn't self-replicating, which made it a tactical weapon at best. A failure both at the original goal and as a weapon."

Lafrenz coughed again, spitting blood up on the floor. Roslyn could recognize the signs of thaumic burnout. There was nothing she could do for Lafrenz—the amount of blood on the floor suggested that the other Mage was already blind.

The other woman had intentionally overloaded and killed herself to not be taken prisoner.

"But this was a research lab, and if I couldn't control all humanity, I could sure as hell find a way to damn them," the dying woman said. "Complex twenty-two is a self-replicating nanoplague. It will infect everyone. It will control their brains—and we never did work out how to give them *orders*.

"They just kill."

Lafrenz giggled.

"Seems appropriate, since you killed me," she told Roslyn. "Enjoy what you've unleashed, Navy bitch." She coughed up more blood, turning bloodily blinded eyes toward the younger woman.

"And when they catch you, I'll see you in he—" Lafrenz's words dissolved into choking coughs...and then silence as Roslyn stared down at her in horror.

CHAPTER 34

THE MARINES RETURNED in that silence, six of them circling around Roslyn with weapons trained on Lafrenz.

"Is she..." Knight trailed off, looking at the pool of blood.

"Dead?" Roslyn replied. "Yeah. Lethal thaumic burnout. She killed herself trying to kill me...but not before she triggered a go-to-hell plan. Corporal, I'm pretty sure she came from her office, that way."

Roslyn pointed toward the door Lafrenz had entered from.

"Find a computer. *Any* fucking computer. She says she released an updated version of the toxin. It's a self-replicating nanotech plague that affects people's minds with magic."

All seven of her companions were silent for several seconds.

"Is that even *possible*?" Bolivar asked. "This was an UnArcana World, I don't know much about magic..."

"I didn't think so," Roslyn replied. "But it would explain just about everything we saw in the victims in the quarantine zone. We need more data—how it works, what they were trying to do.

"She said the current versions of Orpheus were useful weapons but failures at the main goal. I need to know that main goal," she continued. "That's on you, Knight. Go."

She turned to the rest of the Marines and tapped into the command channel.

"Mooren, Killough," she barked. "The situation here has gone very weird and very bad. Report."

There was no answer.

"Knight, is the drone relay up?" she asked, then realized she'd already sent the cyberwarfare Marine ahead.

"We lost the tail end while you were fighting Lafrenz," Andrews told her, their voice grim. "No warning, no report from Mooren and the rest. Just...silence."

"*Fuck*." Roslyn looked at the map. She needed options. She couldn't leave her people down here to an unknown fate, but she also needed to address the Orpheus lab's GOTH plan.

"Bolivar, take a look at this," she instructed the Guardia officer. "Do you see the same probable linkage I do here?" She tapped a spot as she projected a hologram. There was a gap between what they had mapped, but it looked like there should be a route through.

"I do," he agreed. "What do you need?"

"Take Knight's Marines—the Corporal is going to stay here and get into the computers—and head for the surface," she instructed. "If Lafrenz is telling the truth, we just hit a scenario so far beyond our worst case, I didn't even consider it.

"I need you to get in contact with the Cardinal-Governor and with Captain Daalman," Roslyn continued. "The quarantine has to go full lockdown. No one leaves the city. No one leaves the peninsula."

She took a deep breath and met Bolivar's gaze as best she could through their mostly faceless hazmat helmets.

"No one leaves the planet, Victoriano," she told him, using his first name for the first time. "Full planetary lockdown and quarantine until we know more."

"I...see the need," he admitted. "But you don't have that authority..."

He trailed off as she pulled a parchment-wrapped datachip from a pocket on her armor.

"I bear a Warrant of the Voice of the Mage-Queen of Mars," Roslyn told him. "The chip will confirm my authority. *Full planetary lockdown*."

"I understand," he agreed, staring at the crowned-mountain seal of the Protectorate on the parchment. "What will you be doing?"

"Taking Andrews's Marines and finding the rest of the people I brought into this hellhole," Roslyn told him.

"We all need to move, *now*."

The threat of imminent apocalypse was surprisingly effective at getting even Martian Marines to find an extra scrap of speed. The fire teams split at Roslyn's instructions, two exosuits following Bolivar out toward the surface as three gathered around her.

That was going to leave Knight dealing with the computers alone, and that, Roslyn figured, would end badly.

"Andrews, leave one of your people with Knight," Roslyn ordered. "Then let's move."

"Pavel, you heard the LC," the Corporal ordered. "Klinger, let's go."

The indicated Marine saluted with an armored gauntlet and followed Knight into the offices. The other two fell in with Roslyn as she took off at a steady jog. There was a clear path that would take them to where Mooren had gone silent.

It might not be the fastest path, but the *last* thing she could afford now was to get lost. She could only afford the time to look for Mooren and Killough because she had sent Bolivar to the surface with her Warrant.

She hadn't expected to ever actually *need* the Voice of the Mage-Queen, but there could be no delays, no arguments. Depending on how Lafrenz's GOTH plan worked, the entire city could already be at a contamination risk—even the entire *planet*.

Roslyn knew, in her heart of hearts, that she might have just ordered the rest of the planet to cut Nueva Portugal off and let the city die. If that was what it took to prevent the Orpheus weapon from spreading, that was what they would do—and she would die with the city if it came to that.

"Here," Andrews said suddenly, interrupting her thoughts. "This was where we lost contact with Mooren's half of the squad."

It was a sterile corridor, like every other one they'd followed. Except that there were three wrecked drones on the floor, clearly taken out by precision gunfire.

"Clean shots, simultaneous," Andrews reported, checking the debris. "The team probably didn't even realize the drones had gone down for a half a minute, maybe more."

"They were headed that way," Klinger noted, gesturing along the hall. "I don't see any sign of battle other than the drones."

"Agreed. On me," Roslyn ordered. The two Marines flanked her as she followed the path.

A security checkpoint like the one her team had shot their way through was waiting around the next corner. The armored door there had been blown outward with explosives, clearly followed with fire from penetrator rifles...or so Roslyn judged by the shattered armor of the two dead Marines in the checkpoint.

"Mooren would have pushed up," she said quietly. "I don't hear fighting, so let's keep moving. We need to find anyone who's alive."

Or give up and run for the surface. Every dead Marine reduced the reasons for her being down there.

The rest of the Marines hadn't made it far. The space behind the security door appeared to be one of the main access points to the fusion reactor. The battle that had followed the destruction of the door had been ugly—and it did *not* look right to Roslyn.

Four dead Marines were scattered around the space. They'd taken down four times their number in Augments before they'd died, but at least two had been killed with magic.

"Mooren was good," she said quietly, "but she wasn't *this* good."

Sixteen Augments with the advantage of surprise and ambush, even a half-expected ambush like this, should have massacred the half-squad Roslyn had sent with Killough. Especially given that the area had been set up as a kill zone, with prebuilt covered firing positions and everything a defender could dream of.

There'd even been automated twenty-millimeter turrets and a laser, same as at the main entrance, to back up the defenders. *Those* had fallen to penetrator-rifle fire, but as Roslyn stepped forward, she could see that several of the Augments had been taken down by very different attacks.

"A Mage killed these Augments," she said slowly. "Check for survivors," she told her people. "Stun anyone you have to."

"Wait," a pained voice replied. "That's...uh, one step further than I need to deal with today."

Roslyn turned toward the voice. It was coming from the farthest strong point. Grimacing and summoning a shield of power, she walked over and tore the damaged bunker door open with her magic.

Somehow, she wasn't surprised to recognize the dark brown hair, neat mustache and warmly brown eyes of Connor ad Aaron waiting for her. The rogue Mage was in...awful shape. One of his legs had been torn off by weapons fire, and he was hanging on to a rough tourniquet with his left hand.

His entire right arm was a shattered wreck, and he looked up at her with a level look of despair.

"Only one Mage-Lieutenant Commander who was going to find me in this hole, was there?" he asked, looking at her insignia, then coughed. He shook his head as she stepped closer.

"Your fucker broke my ribs," ad Aaron told her. "Your Marines got my leg, but your Mage finished me off. And my men. Thought we had you pinned."

"I don't have sympathy for anyone working for Orpheus," Roslyn told him. "If I can't get you out alive, don't see a reason not to leave you here."

She wasn't sure just who "your Mage" was. There hadn't *been* a Mage in Mooren's team.

"You don't have it in you, Chambers," he replied, coughing up more blood. "And...I can be useful in the time I got left. Ulla activated the GOTH, didn't she?"

"So she said," Roslyn conceded stiffly. "What do you know?"

"Orpheus is nanite magitech, reversal of the runic structure of a Prometheus Interface on a microscopic scale," he told her, then laughed. That brought on more bloody coughing and he leaned back against the wall.

"That's *all* I really know," he admitted. "But I know the version in the GOTH plan is self-replicating and infectious...and I know where the GOTH plan put the dispersal units."

He shuffled a bit to sit up straighter, then stared down at the wrist-comp on his left arm hopelessly and sighed.

"Guess that'll be a problem, won't it?" he said with a sigh. "Comp, authentication Prydwen-twenty-six-Llandudno."

Roslyn *heard* him say the words, and she wasn't sure she could duplicate his pronunciation.

"Project file Go-To-Hell-Nueva-Portugal Sprayer Map, latest version," he instructed. "Then format, authentication llosgi'r sothach hwn."

"Fuck you, ad Aaron," Roslyn snapped—but the map of Nueva Portugal was now hanging in the air between them. Six green pyramid icons glittered on it, and she recorded it before it went away.

"You're too good for me," he told her, then coughed up more blood. "Don't know where you found the fucker who killed me. He knew...he was here for..."

More coughing. This time it didn't stop as the rogue Mage doubled over. He fell over, his working hand slipping away from the tourniquet.

Roslyn didn't have time to do anything before the leg started bleeding again, deep spurts of arterial blood...blood that ad Aaron didn't have much left of to lose.

He was dead before her magic replaced the tourniquet.

CHAPTER 35

"WHERE'S KILLOUGH?" Andrews asked, looking around the wreckage.

Roslyn rose, looking with distaste at the blood on her knees. Connor ad Aaron's blood. There weren't many people out there she'd have expected to be happier to see dead, but it was still disturbing to have his blood all over her.

"I don't know," she admitted, joining the Marines in sweeping the battlefield. "My math says this was all the Augments? Assuming they had a full platoon in the complex?"

"A bit more," the Marine Corporal told her. "Forty at least. There may still be more around."

"And they may have taken Killough," Roslyn said quietly. "But the time I can spend looking for seven people, I can't spend looking for one."

She only had two Marines with her, and she was carefully *not* trying to work out which of the half-dozen dead Marines in the battlefield was Mooren. She'd been leaning on the Sergeant for this entire mission, and losing her *hurt*.

"I have to get to the surface," she decided. "And I can't leave one of you looking for Killough on your own."

"*You* can't travel on your own," Andrews told her. "You're the commanding officer *and* a goddamn Voice."

Roslyn grimaced. She *really* hadn't wanted to use that Warrant.

"Only until this is over," she told the Marine. "Assuming we all live that long."

She gave the defenses around the power core another look and shook her head.

"We've wiped out most, if not all, of the Augments—but I don't know what Mage killed ad Aaron," she admitted. "Killough...is either dead, a prisoner or lost. I can't leave someone to look for him in any of those cases."

"I don't like leaving our dead behind either," Andrews told her, their voice grim. "Let alone a living agent. But we can't send you up to the surface on your own, either."

"Believe me, Corporal, I'm more capable of protecting myself than Killough is," Roslyn told the Marine, her decision suddenly made. "Voice or CO or whatever else I'm hauling, I'm a trained Mage, and I haven't met anyone on this planet yet who can threaten me."

There'd only been one person on the planet she'd been *personally* afraid of—and his blood was smeared across her armor's kneepads.

"You and Klinger stay here, keep up the search for Killough," she ordered. "We don't leave anyone behind." She shook her head. "Make sure no one tries to detonate the reactor or something similarly stupid while we're at it.

"Knight will get me the data from the lab. You make sure the lab is still *here* for her to do it and find our stray MISS agent. Understood?"

"You can't trave—"

"I can," Roslyn told them. "If I had slightly better data of where I was, I could *teleport* out of here, let alone anything else. I'll be fine. Killough *won't.*"

"Most likely, whatever Mage killed ad Aaron has him," Andrews warned.

"And you will under no circumstances engage a hostile Mage," she agreed. "But if that Mage killed ad Aaron, they're probably on our side." She shook her head. "Find them, too. But I'm going and you're staying and that's an order."

"Yes, sir," Corporal Andrews conceded. "Good luck, sir."

"Same to you, Marines," Roslyn told them. "I think we're all going to need it."

The trip back out through the lab complex was even creepier than the way in. She knew what the place had been now—everything she'd feared it was and more—and the deathly silence was stark and terrifying.

If nothing else, there *should* have been prisoners in the complex, and the lack left her with grim suspicions of other parts of Lafrenz's go-to-hell plan. Either Finley had trained his people to *be* psychopaths or he'd recruited psychopaths like him to begin with.

Either way, her conversations with Lafrenz and ad Aaron were going to join her nightmares. So was the entire damn lab complex.

She guessed as to where the connections would be to get her out of the underground facility and got it right—or, at least, figured she had when she made it to the decontamination room.

The sprays washed off ad Aaron's blood along with anything else she'd picked up in the bioweapon lab, while a radiation pulse swept her to kill off anything the antiseptics missed.

Roslyn froze in a moment of realization as the doors slid open in front of her. The entire central core of the facility was sealed and atmosphered to keep anything from *escaping*, but the same protections and securities would stop anything getting *in*.

The vast size of the laboratory complex suddenly seemed far too *small*, but there was space for thousands of people in the Orpheus lab. It had other dangers they'd sweep for, but it would be safe from the damn nanites.

She took off toward the exit tunnel at a full run. She didn't know if she'd be able to save *everybody*, but if she made the right use of her enemy's tools, she could save a *lot* of people.

CHAPTER 36

BOLIVAR AND THE MARINES she'd sent with him were standing by the vans in the treatment plant parking lot, looking...lost. The body language of their stunned horror came through the armor, and she knew it had to be as bad as she'd feared.

"Bolivar, report," she snapped. Only her Warrant gave her the authority to command local law enforcement, but since that cat was out of the bag, she might as well ride it.

"It's bad," he said quietly. "No one was sure what was going on before I reported, but we have riots starting in several sections of the city. They're expanding...exponentially."

"Like they're infectious," Roslyn agreed. "Where are we at?"

"The Army is solidifying the quarantine lines in the mountains. They're trying to pull Guardia in from the rest of the peninsula to lock in the city, but I don't give that more than a fifty-fifty chance of being in time," Bolivar admitted. "Your Captain has used your authority to impose a planetary quarantine and ordered all spacecraft to dock at the orbital. No further contact between orbit and surface; no one allowed to leave at all."

"Good. I'm calling upstairs," Roslyn told him, "but we need to start moving toward the school."

"The school?" Bolivar sounded confused.

"There are thousands of people near here who have not yet been exposed, and we're sitting on top of the largest biologically sealed safe zone on the planet," Roslyn said. "We have to start funneling people into the lab, and that school is the closest concentration of people—and kids."

"And the lab will keep them safe," he agreed. "Maybe. Fuck."

"It's a better chance than doing nothing," she told him. It was a *terrible* idea. But it was the only way she could see to keep the nearby children safe. "Get them moving while I call home."

The Guardia officer nodded and took off at a run. She couldn't give him much hope, but it was enough to break his paralysis.

If only someone could lift *Roslyn's* fears so easily.

"Marines, I'm going into conference; cover me," she ordered. The two exosuits shifted toward her wordlessly as she tapped commands on her wrist-comp and took a seat in the passenger seat of the van.

Her view of the world in front of her vanished as her helmet locked in to full conference mode. A moment later, the image of *Song of the Huntress*'s bridge appeared around her.

"Lieutenant Commander, you're alive," Mage-Captain Daalman greeted her. "And apparently promoted?"

"I was given a Warrant in case something like this happened, sir," Roslyn told her boss. "I was always hunting a rogue Prometheus lab. We just didn't expect *this*."

"I got the gist of it, I think, from the Guardia Captain, but what the *hell* is going on, Chambers?" Daalman demanded.

"The Mages working for the Republic set up a secret lab to work on nano-scale magitech based on the Prometheus Interface," Roslyn said, summarizing as quickly as she could. "They developed a weapon they called Orpheus, a magitech nanite that codes microscopic runes inside the human body to take control of the body away from the brain—an inversion of the Prometheus Interface.

"The version they put in the bomb was non-replicating. The version they're deploying now *is* self-replicating. It is infectious and I'm not sure of the vectors. I've got people in the lab working on getting into their data, but I *also* have the locations of the aerosol sprayers deploying the nanites.

"Transmitting now."

"Anyone I send down to the surface to deal with those has to go into full quarantine," Daalman said quietly. "No external air, no surface contact, but I still can't let them back aboard *Huntress*."

She paused.

"I'll ask for volunteers from the Marines. Those sprayers will be down in five minutes. Stay on this channel, Chambers."

Daalman disappeared and Roslyn had a view of the outside world for a few moments. She forced herself to breathe steadily, trying to calm her emotions as much as possible to allow her to work.

An entire city was at risk now. She wasn't so naïve as to think she was *responsible* for what Lafrenz had done, but she was still going to do *everything* she could to stop it.

When the conference mode resumed, Daalman wasn't alone. A man in the formal red robes of a Catholic Cardinal sitting behind a large stone desk filled half of her view now as the helmet split-screened a three-way conference.

"Cardinal Guerra," she greeted the planetary Governor. She'd only seen file footage of Fulvio Guerra, which had clearly either been taken longer ago than she'd thought or been doctored. Guerra was one of the oldest-looking human beings she'd ever seen, with deep lines carved into his face and thin but neatly cropped white hair.

"Envoy Chambers," Guerra greeted her, extending the traditional title of a Voice holding a Warrant. "You'll forgive me for being frustrated. We did not expect to be *surprised* by one of Her Majesty's Voices."

"The intent, Cardinal, was that I never use the Warrant and carry out the investigation of the Orpheus lab as a Navy officer on a classified basis," Roslyn told the old man. "That is no longer an option. Nor is keeping any of this secret."

"What are we facing, Envoy?"

"A self-replicating infectious nanoweapon," she said simply. "It takes over control of the nervous system of the victim and triggers a massively violent response." She sighed. "Evidence from the original quarantine zone suggests there's some level of programming that results in them not attacking each other, but the victims do not eat...sleep...anything.

"They will attack everyone they find until they either can no longer find victims, or the lack of normal bodily maintenance kills them," Roslyn concluded. "It is...possible that the Orpheus nanites may be able to sustain activity even in a dead host for some unknown period of time."

"Zombies."

The Cardinal's single word hung in the air like a dangling sword.

"In the original Haitian sense, unquestionably," she admitted. "But... like those original Haitian zombies, the infected are innocent. They haven't chosen any of this. They are as much victims as anyone."

"I understand." All three of them were silent.

"We have elevated the quarantine of the Nueva Portugal peninsula to the maximum level," Guerra told them. "That requires all interaction with potential infected to be handled by remote drone and a hundred-meter clear zone between the quarantine line and quarantinees... maintained by lethal force."

"I..." Roslyn swallowed against a suddenly dry mouth. "I'm sorry, Cardinal-Governor, but I cannot disagree with your logic. You have the full support of the Warrant I bear in these choices."

"Unfortunately, that doesn't change the other half of the quarantine, Governor," Daalman noted grimly. "No further launches from the surface will be permitted. I will do everything possible before shooting ships down, but I cannot risk Marines by boarding any vessels launching from the surface of Sorprendidas."

"Surely, if we can keep the infection contained to Nueva Portugal, that is not necessary," Guerra argued.

"We do not know enough about the nature of the Orpheus weapon yet to definitely say it can only spread with people," Roslyn told him. "It is entirely possible that it was designed to be airborne over significant distances and we will begin to see outbreaks outside the peninsula as time goes on."

"May the Holy Spirit protect us," the Cardinal whispered. "Very well, Envoy. The orders will be sent. No one has launched in the last hour, in any case, but we will secure all spaceports and launchpads.

"You have my word as a Cardinal of the Church."

"We will do what we must," Roslyn told them. "I *think* that the Orpheus lab itself should be safe against the weapon, and I will be organizing an evacuation to move as many people into it as possible.

"From there, we will see what we can learn and if we can find an answer...or even an off switch."

"This is a strategic-area-denial weapon," Daalman said. "I'd be surprised if there was any way to turn it off. Once they activated it, they likely intended it to damn the entire planet."

"Doom us, perhaps," Guerra replied, his tone firm. "But as the Envoy pointed out, the souls of the infected are innocent. We will do everything we can, but I assure you—even the victims of this horror are not damned.

"Its *creators*, on the other hand, will not enjoy their meetings with St. Peter."

"Quite likely, they've already met him," Roslyn murmured. "I need to get to work."

"Hold on one second, Commander," Daalman told her. "The Marines are hitting the first of your aerosol sprayers. A bit more intelligence might come in handy, don't you think?"

"I will wait," Guerra agreed. "God be praised that your people are here, Mage-Captain. I dread to think of what that lab might have managed, left unbothered."

Roslyn hoped she managed not to look too guilty in response to that. While the Orpheus lab wouldn't have done any *good* left alone, they also probably wouldn't have dusted an entire city with their weapon without her poking them.

"Sergeant Colburn reporting," a new voice interrupted. "We are at the location indicated in the map and we have located the target. It appears to have been built into the roof of a large office tower, but..."

There was silence for a moment and a video feed from the shuttle appeared on Roslyn's helmet screen. Several nozzles had clearly emerged from the roof of the tower, each at least a meter high and aimed over the side of the building.

"We can't be sure until we put boots on the ground, but they're not spraying anything," Colburn said grimly. "They might be out of supply."

"I can't ask you to put anyone down there, Sergeant," Daalman replied.

"You didn't, sir," Colburn conceded. "We are violating quarantine and will not be able to return to the ship. Sorry, sir."

The camera shivered moments before two exosuited Marines appeared in the camera feed. Powered gauntlets tore one of the sprayers out as the two began to dismantle the entire structure to find the feed tank.

"Looks like about a hundred-liter tank feeding this one, with separate feeds for each sprayer," Colburn passed on his people's report. "And they're dry. Best guess is this site pumped about six hundred liters of the nanites into the air.

"I don't know what that translates to in terms of doses beyond 'way too fucking many,'" the Marine concluded. "Sir. We've violated quarantine and cannot follow the original plan. New orders?"

Daalman sighed.

"Report to Lieutenant Commander Chambers at the main target site," she ordered. "She has a potential evac location, and you will provide air cover. You will *not* make contact with Chambers, as your vessel and armor are almost certainly contaminated."

"We know, sir," Colburn said quietly. "But someone had to do it."

"Now I need to make sure none of our *other* volunteers pull the same stupid stunt," Daalman told the Sergeant. "Good luck."

The channel to the Marines cut, and Daalman turned her attention back to Guerra and Roslyn.

"Looks like you have air support and some extra hands, if you're careful, Chambers," she told Roslyn. "Cardinal-Governor, we have work to do. We'll keep you in the loop."

"God bless you, my children," Guerra told you. "He knows His warriors. He will see you to safety."

"God helps those who help themselves," Roslyn replied quietly. "And right now, I need to go help a bunch of other people."

"And in that, you are His tool today," the Cardinal told her. "And He will bless and guide you, I promise."

CHAPTER 37

THE CONFERENCE VIEW finally dropped, and Roslyn pulled herself out of the van. A small stream of people was heading her way... Too small.

"Bolivar, I was expecting a few more people heading my way," she said over the radio. "What's going on?"

"I'm in the Guardia net and they're sending everyone they're finding your way," the Captain told her. "The school is proving...more difficult."

She sighed.

"Ping me your coordinates," she told him.

"Commander?" he questioned.

"Just do it," Roslyn ordered.

A moment later, his exact GPS position appeared on her helmet. She took a second to double-check her numbers on her wrist-comp, then nodded to herself...and *stepped*.

"What the *blazes*?" the middle-aged woman in the prim suit standing in front of Captain Bolivar exclaimed as Roslyn appeared. They were apparently gathered just outside the main entrance to the school, which had heavy shutters closed across it.

"I am Roslyn Chambers, Voice of the Mage-Queen of Mars," Roslyn told the woman she presumed was the school principal. "What's going on?"

"This *man* is trying to get me to evacuate the children from the safest place I have for them," the woman snapped. "I don't care if he's Guardia; the school is designed for any crisis."

"Your name, ma'am?" Roslyn asked, as gently as she could.

"Abhilasha Anika Yoxall," the dark-skinned woman replied. She was probably older than Roslyn had initially guessed, with gray streaked through her black hair. "I am the principal of this school and I am responsible for these children.

"The school was designed during the war; it doubles as an air raid bunker, and the barricades can hold against weapons fire," she continued. "My charges are safer here than anywhere else."

"Neither the Protectorate nor the Republic used bioweapons or nanotech weapons during the war," Roslyn told the principal. "Is your school's air system rated to filter out weapons-grade nanotech, Ms. Yoxall?"

Yoxall blinked, her face darkening as she glared at Bolivar.

"I don't know," she admitted.

"And it doesn't matter," Roslyn told her. "I am the Voice of the Mage-Queen of Mars, Ms. Yoxall. Do you know what that means?"

"I am a schoolteacher. I know what that means," Yoxall replied. "But these children—"

"Will be safer on the *right* side of a bioweapons filter than they will in your school as this city is under bio-attack," Roslyn said. "And this isn't discretionary, Ms. Yoxall. I will tear those doors open myself if it will get those children to safety—and if it comes to it, I will die to defend them.

"Now get them moving."

Something in Roslyn's tone—because she doubted her faceless armor was any more sympathetic than Bolivar's—convinced the woman. Yoxall tapped a command that lifted the barricades.

"Where are we taking them?" she finally asked.

"Adkins, show her the way," Roslyn ordered one of the Marines. "I have more Marines incoming. I need to coordinate."

She gestured for Bolivar to join her as the looming exosuit stepped up to the principal—and then went down on one knee to present a less intimidating figure.

Thank god for *smart* Marines.

"What's the Guardia doing?" she asked Bolivar quietly.

"Panicking," he admitted. "We barely train for bioweapons attack, let alone zombies, and we don't have the numbers for this. Out-city Guardia is *trying* to blockade the main roads, but people are panicked and running.

"And the Guardia isn't much better."

"I'm guessing subdividing the city to try to contain the infected zones isn't going to happen?" Roslyn asked.

"If we had ten times as many Guardia officers, maybe, but we're just cops, sir. There aren't that many of us. How much violent crime do you think this city *has*?"

"Not that much," Roslyn conceded. "So, what can you do?"

"Right now, I've got maybe a hundred Guardia officers on a tac-net around the park," he told her. "From the map you gave me, none of the sprayers are close to here—and those decon units in the lab should deal with any non-active infection."

"They should," Roslyn agreed. "You're sending people our way?"

"Exactly. Right now, this section of the city is quiet. People are having a hard time believing how bad it is elsewhere."

"*I'm* having a hard time believing it," Roslyn admitted. "I just can't believe anyone would build a weapon like this, let alone use it in this messy of a way."

"Some people are broken and can be helped," Bolivar told her. "I'm a cop; my job is to find those people and find them their help. Some people, though... Some people can't be helped."

"Usually, that's when we send in Marines," she said. "Speaking of, I have more coming. I need you to coordinate with the school, the Guardia, everyone local. Let's get some cables run down into the lab so we can communicate.

"We can't waste time on trying to hack their communications system. I need Knight to tell me how to turn off these damn nanites."

"Magic, maybe?" Bolivar asked. "I'll admit I know nothing about it."

Roslyn shook her head.

"It's not that easy, Captain. It's never that easy. You need to *know* what you're doing—I can kill a lot of people at once if I'm pushed, but I barely know enough about the human body to splint a broken bone with magic, let alone actually *fix* the bone."

"A man who knows nothing can hope, at least," Bolivar said quietly. "I'll see if we can source that cable."

A chirp in Roslyn's helmet told her the Marines were closer.

"Sergeant Colburn?" she asked.

"Yes, sir," the Marine replied. "I've got Lieutenant Evanson on the channel as well; he's flying the shuttle."

"How are you doing for fuel, Lieutenant?" Roslyn asked.

"Enough to get back to orbit again, so about twelve more hours in the air," Evanson said. "I'm in contact with the other shuttles as well. Despite the plan...well...we all got close to those sprayers, sir.

"There's no way we can trust our hulls not to be contaminated. I don't want to bring us too close to your area. We'd be bringing the damn weapon with us."

"I wish I could tell you going into orbit would kill it, but I have no data," Roslyn told them, considering how best to use them. "I need you to orbit the city and provide whatever coordination support you can to the Guardia. They're undermanned and terrified, but the sight of RMMC assault shuttles might help them find nerve, even keeping them high enough to avoid any infection risk."

"Understood, sir," Evanson replied. He paused and audibly swallowed. "What mapping we're getting from *Huntress* flags major movement of infected victims. Mobs, basically. Do we...engage?"

"Negative," Roslyn said. "For now, at least. Those people are as innocent as the ones we're trying to protect. I'm hoping to find an answer in the damn lab, and everyone who dies isn't someone we can help later."

"I really, *really* wish Nix worked on these poor people," Colburn admitted.

"Me too," she agreed. "And that is why the monsters who designed the Orpheus weapon made sure Nix *wouldn't*."

"Please tell me those fuckers are dead," the Marine said.

"They're dead," Roslyn confirmed. "Cost too many good people even *finding* them, but they're dead."

"Good to hear," the Sergeant told her. "Linking into the Guardia net now, sir. We'll see what we can do."

Roslyn sighed as she dropped the channel.

"I hope you find something, Sergeant," she whispered. "Because I'm not even sure what *I* can do."

CHAPTER 38

THERE WAS nothing calming or peaceful about a crowd of thousands of children under the age of ten. Their teachers were doing everything in their power to keep the kids moving, but there was only so much they *could* do—and many of the children were panicking.

Roslyn stood back from the slowly moving crowds, using the Guardia network and the overhead from *Huntress* to try to estimate the spread of the infection. So far, it looked like the park was safe, which meant the lab was *definitely* safe.

But the more people they got underground, the better.

"Abiodun, what does *Huntress* have aboard in terms of filter systems?" she asked the destroyer's logistics officer. "We should have some stuff for emergency epidemic aid, right?"

"I think so," Lieutenant Commander Jamshed Abiodun told her. "I'm not sure we have anything rated for weaponized nanotech. I mean...what kind of monster even builds that?"

"The kind that worked for Project Prometheus," Roslyn told him. "You have the map of the facility, right? I can forward it if you don't."

"A partial one, anyway," Abiodun confirmed. "I'm guessing that's all we've got?"

"Yeah. I'm thinking about that tunnel, though," she said. "It's most of a klick long and large enough for heavy vehicles. If we put a refugee camp in there, it isn't going to be *comfortable*, but if we seal the entrance with our filtration systems, that should let us put at least another couple thousand people somewhere safe."

For now was unspoken. Roslyn wasn't even sure how she was going to feed everyone they were stuffing into the Orpheus lab. But every person she got onto the other side of their filters was someone who *wasn't* at risk of being turned into a murderous killing machine.

"I'm checking the manifests now, and we've got the setups for two temporary class six biohazard containment facilities," the other Navy officer told her. "They're supposed to be set up as prefab buildings, but I *think* you can use the walls as a blockade and get the filters running."

"Even if we can't, they're not going to be any use sitting in *Huntress*'s storage holds," she said. "Can you get them down here?"

"They're designed for air drop. I'll have to check with the pilots we've got left, but I *think* we can get them into a hundred-meter target zone from thirty klicks up," he said. "If you can mark out that kind of zone, I can send them down."

He paused.

"We've got a few air-drop supply capsules designed for that," he noted. "I'm guessing a couple dozen thousand ration packs wouldn't go unused, either?"

Protectorate emergency ration packs were wonders of modern nutrition technology, providing the protein, nutrients and minimum hydration a human needed for a day in a reasonably tasty, if unappetizingly goopy, package.

"I can hope this won't last long enough for us to need more than that," she agreed. "So far as I can tell, our biohazard suits are safe, but once the nanites *reach* here, anyone outside won't be able to go in the safe zone.

"So, drop whatever you can, Jamshed," she said. "It might make all the difference."

"Already got people loading the shuttles," he promised. "Get us that drop zone and we'll get you the decon and filtration gear for the sites immediately. We'll sequence food and whatever else we can dig out of the holds until we run out of drop pods...or time."

"Thank you," Roslyn said. "It *will* save lives."

"What use is Her Majesty's Protectorate if we don't protect people, Chambers?" he asked. "We'll do what we can."

Organizing a clear safe zone for the drop pods to come down was a relief from watching the overall state of Nueva Portugal, but it only occupied a few minutes of Roslyn's time—and she had to delegate someone else to watch the slow descent of a city of two million souls into madness.

That someone was Victoriano Bolivar, and even through full coverage body armor, he seemed ill when Roslyn returned to him.

"We've got the biohazard gear and food supplies coming in," she reassured him. "We should be able to get it all set up before..."

He shook his head.

"Bolivar?"

"The spread is accelerating," he told her, his voice dead. "I don't even have Guardia contact in a third of the city anymore. We've lost control. What's left of the Guardia is falling back on us here, but...even that's a risk."

"I know," she said. "But we don't have anywhere else to send them."

"We don't have space for the uninfected," Bolivar reminded her. "And...we can't tell the difference until they snap. I just watched a precinct station of thirty officers go dark after *one* person they'd hauled in earlier as a drunk snapped.

"Everyone in the cell block was infected and started snapping as well...including the officers guarding them. It's a nightmare, Chambers. What do we *do*?"

"I don't know," Roslyn admitted. "We get as many people to safety as we can and protect them."

She brought up the map of the city and grimaced, glad no one could see her face behind the armor. As Bolivar had said, entire sections of the city—everything within ten kilometers, at least, of the aerosol sprayers—were now only showing data coming in from *Huntress* above.

There were still potentially uninfected people in those areas, but how were they supposed to find them?

"Assuming this version works like the previous version, anyone we can scan with bioscanners is going to dissolve the nanites," she said slowly. "That's the only protection we've got. We're going to have to start scanning everyone we send down soon."

"Now, I suggest," Bolivar told her. "It's the only tool we've got."

Roslyn gestured at the crowd still filtering through the park toward the Orpheus lab.

"Scanning them all is going to slow this down to the point where we'll lose *more*," she reminded him. "The decon chambers in the lab will kill it, theoretically. Andrews is supposed to be cycling everyone through those, whether they stay in the main lab or not."

"And what happens if this one is tougher, less designed to be subtle?" the Guardia officer asked.

There was a hopelessness to his tone that threatened to drag Roslyn down into despair with him, but she shook her head firmly.

"The last one survived being blown up," she pointed out. "This one only had to survive being sprayed into the air and scattered across the city. If anything, it's probably *more* vulnerable than the first one."

Neither of those really matched up with something that dissolved under the controlled radiation of a standard bioscan, but that was the evidence Roslyn had to work with. Everyone who might know more was *dead*.

Well, not everyone.

"We have to continue on as planned," she told Bolivar. "Once we've got a secondary filtration setup outside the secured nanotech lab, that gives us a chance to triage people and make sure they're clear of the nanites while separating our definitely clean population from the risk groups.

"For now, I want you to keep people moving and keep that drop zone clear. Let me know once our likely infectious zone gets within five kilometers of us."

"What are you going to do?" Bolivar asked. They'd both thought she was going to take most of that back from him.

"I'm going to be listening to everyone's reports...and talking to the Augments we captured alive."

CHAPTER 39

UNLIKE THE first time Roslyn had ventured into the Orpheus lab, this time she had full communications with everyone. Drones and relay stations and even physical cables had been laid to make that possible. They couldn't afford delays in communication, not as expanding mobs of Orpheus's victims were heading in their direction.

She wasn't sure how many people were infected or even how many were dead. The Orpheus nanotech appeared to leave other infected alone, but everyone and everything else was a target.

There was going to be a lot of heartbreak in Nueva Portugal when this was over—and that was assuming that Roslyn managed to *fix* things. Her only current hope for that lay with the handful of Augments they'd shot with SmartDarts.

Only one of them was conscious when she reached the cell they'd been stuffed in. A trio of nervous Guardia officers stood watch, but they recognized her and silently allowed her past.

The conscious Augment was carefully shuffling across the floor, as if every single motion required specific thought and analysis. With her cybernetics offline, that was probably true.

She still heard Roslyn approach and looked up, bright green eyes flashing in the dark as she saw her captor. A few commands opened the door to the cell and Roslyn gestured for the woman to join her.

"Let's have a chat," the Navy officer told the prisoner. "I'm hoping you can help me."

"I'm not seeing any real reason for me to bother," the Augment replied. "Runa Hase. Master Sergeant, Republic of Faith and Reason Augment Corps. KCD-One-Five-Nine-Z-D-Five."

Roslyn crooked a finger, lifting Hase off her feet and hauling her out of the cell with magic. Unable to resist the bonds of force, the Augment glared at her in silence until they were in the cell next door, which was just as bare.

Sighing, Roslyn used the same trick to pull two chairs and a table in from the guard station outside—to the surprise of the Guardia officers, from the sounds of it.

"Make sure the other cell is sealed," she told them loudly. "Just because people *look* like they're asleep doesn't mean they are."

She'd closed it behind her, but a double check never hurt.

With that settled, Roslyn turned her gaze on her prisoner, standing stiffly next to the seat.

"You may as well sit down, Ms. Hase," she told the Augment.

"Runa Hase, Master Sergeant, Republic—"

"The Republic was officially dissolved by act of the Republic Parliament nineteen months ago, as required by the Hyacinth Treaty," Roslyn reminded Hase. "You are not a soldier of any of the so-called Free Worlds—who would disown you in an *instant* to avoid conflict with the Protectorate."

Four of the former Republic worlds had voted against rejoining the Protectorate. Each had their own reasons, and they hadn't managed to create any kind of joint structure. Each of the Free Worlds stood alone—and their governments were *very* aware of the power imbalance between one world and the Protectorate's hundred-plus.

"Since the Republic no longer exists and you do not serve any government that would claim you, you are not a prisoner of war," Roslyn laid out calmly. "You are a *terrorist*, involved in the manufacture and deployment of a nanotech bioweapon.

"Even the Republic did not allow or condone the development of biological or nanotechnological weaponry, Ms. Hase," she reminded the Augment. "By the laws of the Republic, let alone the Protectorate, you are guilty of crimes against humanity. The evidence of this facility is more than sufficient to condemn everyone working in it."

"Runa Hase, Master Sergeant, KCD-One-Five-Nine-Z-D-Five," Hase reeled off, her eyes focused on the ceiling. She didn't seem to have any illusions about her ability to threaten Roslyn without her cybernetics, but she remained standing and unhelpful.

"Right. Take a *fucking* seat, Ms. Hase," Roslyn snapped.

She locked gazes with the green-eyed brunette across the room. Hase was pale, almost disturbingly pallid—presumably from living underground in the lab for extended periods.

After maybe fifteen seconds, Hase finally took a seat in the chair.

"The only reason we are having this conversation is because your boss apparently had a *fuck-everybody* plan that involved deploying an infectious version of the Orpheus weapon," Roslyn told the woman. "Right now, you're on the right side of the lab's biofilters, but that means you are using up space I can use for at least a dozen actually innocent people.

"It would be entirely reasonable, I think, to transfer you to holding cells on the surface."

"That would be a war crime," Hase hissed.

"Would it?" Roslyn asked. "Or would I be acting to protect the people I am *actually* supposed to defend? If I can preserve several dozen lives by risking a handful, is that a crime? You'd still be held under all normal protocols."

"And when the nanites take us, you're a murderer," the Augment told her.

"Or would I have murdered the dozens of people I can save if I turn those cells into dorms?" Roslyn said. "You know what I'm looking at up there, Ms. Hase. You know damn well I'm not staying down here myself. Not when there are kids I can stick in this bunker instead.

"So, when my hazmat armor runs out of air, I'll die," she said grimly. "On the surface, honoring my oath to protect people. Of course, with the Orpheus weapon, it'll take me a while and I might hurt other people before I finally fall down.

"Given that fate, Ms. Hase, I don't expect to have to face a court-martial for anything I do here." Roslyn conjured visible fire around her fists for a moment, reminding the Augment of what she was.

"There are lines I still don't think I'll cross, but *you* knowingly worked for the project that made this shit. I might bend a few more with you." She shrugged. "We both know torturing you for information is pointless, but if I summarily execute you and interview the next prisoner next to your corpse, I think that might make a point?"

Roslyn *probably* wouldn't do that. It was a violation of every code she'd sworn to uphold, everything she believed in. But she was *tempted* enough that she suspected she could make Hase believe it was a risk.

"I'm just a guard," Hase finally said quietly. "I don't know *anything* about the damn weapon."

"You can give us access codes for the base network," Roslyn said. "That gives us a starting point. I'm guessing you had training on countermeasures for the damn weapon, too?"

"Okay." Hase exhaled. "How bad is it?" she asked.

"We've quarantined the peninsula with a secondary quarantine around the planet," Roslyn admitted. "Best guess is around six or seven hundred thousand civilians infected or dead. We can't evacuate the rest of the city— we don't have the biohazard-secured lift capacity anywhere on the planet.

"So, at a minimum, we're looking at writing off the two million people in Nueva Portugal," she said coldly. "Less whoever I can shove in this bunker and feed until everyone on the surface is dead. It's about as bad as it could possibly be, Ms. Hase."

Hase nodded. Unless Roslyn was crazy, there were actual tears in the woman's eyes.

"Most of my codes are in my implants," she warned Roslyn. "I'll give you my backup login, but I'm not sure how much help that will be. As for emergency procedures... The decon rooms."

"The decon rooms?" Roslyn asked.

"That was all we were told," the Augment admitted. "If we had *any* reason to believe we'd been exposed, we were to immediately proceed to the nearest decontamination chamber and let it run.

"My understanding was that there was a purge function that would kill any unprotected nanites in the facility, but I don't know what it was," Hase continued. "I *do* know that the decontamination chambers have *something* that is specifically tailored to kill the nanites.

"Otherwise...I know they need silver, carbon and iron to self-replicate. Most of that they can find in humans, but we weren't permitted *any* silver in the facility. Jewelry, art, electronics, whatever. It all was checked for silver before it entered the main lab."

She looked down at the table.

"I don't know what else to give you," she admitted. "I was a loyal soldier of the Republic. But this... You *do* know there's a suicide charge in our implants, right? It's not supposed to be externally accessible...but ad Aaron could."

"I'd keep that in mind when you go in front of a judge," Roslyn told Hase. "*I* will make sure the judge knows you cooperated as best as you could."

She snorted bitterly.

"The value of that, of course, depends on me being alive to tell them."

Andrews was waiting for her when she left the cell, the Marine Corporal she'd left to search for Killough now drafted to help keep people organized.

"Did you find him?" was her first question anyway. She knew the answer—someone would have *told* her if they'd found Killough.

"No," they confirmed. "We didn't find Killough. We didn't find the Mage. We did successfully sweep up what we *think* are all the remaining Augments, but there's no evidence anyone else was here.

"It's like Killough just vanished after the fight with the security Mage. Except for..."

"Except for?" Roslyn asked, after the Marine trailed off.

"We did find Lafrenz's lab partner, another Mage," Andrews said. "Shot in the back of the head, three times. He never even realized he wasn't alone, I don't think. But...other than the bullets, no real sign of a shooter."

"That makes no sense, Corporal," Roslyn pointed out.

"Someone knew how to hide their tracks, even in a place like this. I don't know what they did, but they were a ghost." They shook their head. "Killough seemed good at his job, but this was magic. Literally. I think we had a Mage ghost in here somewhere, and I'm not entirely sure they were on our side. The doctor's console had been accessed."

"Hopefully, they were just as blocked as we have been," Roslyn said grimly. "I'll admit that I want to see most of this place's databases burned. I've passed access codes to Knight that will hopefully help us get in, but..."

"This place is a nightmare. It looks like they didn't have any prisoners at the moment, but at least one Augment was shooting scientists when we found him," Andrews admitted. "We've found twenty-two presumably non-Mage scientists in the complex. All are dead."

"Fuck."

"Yeah. Cleanup protocols. We interrupted enough that I think we still have databases, but...they really set this up to make sure no one could deal with what they unleashed in their GOTH plan."

"What I know, right now, is that they told the security detail that the decon chambers were guaranteed to remove the weapon," Roslyn said. "I want you to find whatever techs or engineers we have in the evacuees, pick a decon chamber and tear it apart.

"We'll cycle everybody through them before they go deeper, but we're also hoping our class six protocols hold up for the outer entrance. If there's something those chambers are doing that our class six protocols *aren't* doing, we need to know."

"Understood. Where will you be?" Andrews asked.

"On the surface. I'm the only Mage we have, which means I'm our first line of defense," Roslyn told him. "Keep Knight working on the databases. Find out what you can about anything this base has that we wouldn't expect—supposedly, there was an emergency purge that could kill all of the nanites in the facility.

"We've got a lot going on, but if we can find that, we might just have a chance."

Andrews exhaled a long sigh and nodded firmly.

"I'll get it done, sir, but I could use more Marines," they admitted.

"We can't risk it," Roslyn said. "Any Marines I bring in have definitely been exposed. Their armor and shuttles are keeping them safe, but we don't know how well the weapon will survive on the exterior of a sub-orbital craft.

"Or even in vacuum, for that matter. Despite its effects and patterns, it's not actually a biological weapon. Vacuum probably won't hurt it at all."

She shook her head.

"There's an answer in this place and several ways to find it, Corporal," she told Andrews. "I will do everything I can to make sure we live long enough to help."

"What happens if all of this fails, sir?" the Marine asked.

"I don't know," she admitted. "At that point, I'll probably be dead."

The problem, however, was that Roslyn Chambers was a Royal Martian Navy tactical officer. She knew what the answer to a major untreatable infection that had effectively wiped out a major population center was.

When all other options ran out, *Song of the Huntress* would use thermonuclear weapons to sanitize Nueva Portugal from orbit.

CHAPTER 40

IT WAS A STRANGE FEELING, walking up the Orpheus complex access tunnel while hundreds of people streamed the other way. They'd started with children from the school, but now it was everyone they could find.

They had to desperately hope that no one was making it into the underground structure who was infected. Roslyn had always hoped that the decontamination chambers in the complex would be able to handle the Orpheus weapon—they'd have been of little use to the complex if they hadn't—but confirmation was valuable.

The fear was the other end of the tunnel, where the wrecked door from the water treatment facility was being sealed off when she arrived. Multiple layers of prefabricated plastic panels were now set up, with a smaller stream of people passing out of the double-wide doors on this side.

After a moment, Roslyn confirmed people were coming through in batches of twenty—as many as the two class six decontamination chambers they'd brought down from *Huntress* could handle.

With the chambers operating alternately, twenty people entered the tunnel every thirty seconds—and Roslyn didn't see an easy way *out*. Whoever Bolivar had co-opted to assemble the quarantine array hadn't considered the chance anyone might be leaving.

That was...probably reasonable. Sighing, Roslyn pulled Bolivar's current coordinates and ran a calculation as she stepped to the side of the crowd heading deeper underground.

GLYNN STEWART

A few seconds later, she dropped from the air next to the Guardia officer, grunting as she absorbed the impact. Without knowing what was around Bolivar, she'd teleported high enough that she'd have landed on someone instead of appearing *in* them.

"Sir!" Bolivar greeted her. "The quarantine arrays are set up and the infection zone hasn't reached us yet."

"That's good news. How close are we?" Roslyn asked.

He grimaced.

"It's not good news," he told her. "We are now surrounded on all sides. Closest approach is seven kilometers on the north side. There are Marines hanging out above the closest group, and they're eyeballing a mob of about twenty thousand."

"Who's left inside that zone?" Roslyn asked. Nueva Portugal was a large city, with two million people spread across a zone sixty kilometers or so across. Even with the park, though, there should have been at least a few hundred thousand people within seven kilometers of the park.

"A lot of people," Bolivar admitted. "We've got almost ten thousand people underground, I think, but the decontamination slows us to forty a minute...and we don't know what the infection radius of someone carrying the weapon is."

"We need to decon everyone," Roslyn agreed. "Fuck. How many, Bolivar?"

"We've probably got another fifteen thousand gathered around the park now," he told her. "Maybe twenty. But there are a hundred and thirty thousand people living inside that radius of us, Commander Chambers."

"We can't even save them. We're ordering everyone who can to shelter in place. Seal their windows and doors as best they can. Most homes have enough air to last the occupants a day or two if they manage to get a proper seal."

"It's all we can do," Roslyn agreed. "And if the danger zone around an infected is low enough, it might be enough just for them to lay low."

"Maybe," he agreed. There was very little hope in his tone, though. Somehow, Bolivar kept going—but Roslyn could tell he was beyond hoping for more than saving everyone in front of him.

Roslyn *had* to hope for more. She wasn't sure what the answer was going to be yet, but she had a Royal Martian Navy destroyer and half a dozen fully trained Mages. Whether the answer was firepower or magic, she would find a way.

"Sir, this is Sergeant Colburn," the Marine reported in. "We're flying overwatch on your closest problem. What can we do for you, Commander?"

"Video relay to start, Sergeant," Roslyn told him. She was looking at an overall map, but red icons didn't tell her what she was really dealing with. She *needed* that view, that understanding of the nature of the problem.

"Understood. Linking through now."

The projection on her helmet HUD shifted. A square view from the assault shuttle's cameras lit up, and she zoomed in on the threat and shivered.

Even *mob* was the wrong word. It was more like a flood of human beings. The front and sides of the flood were smashing into doors, vehicles, anything that looked like it might give way. There was no attempt to use handles or anything like that. Just full-body smashing into accessways until they gave way.

"It's terrifying, Commander," Colburn said quietly. "We've been watching this for twenty minutes now, and I just feel sick. They're moving fast and I'm not sure how much is being left behind them."

"Me either, Sergeant," Roslyn replied. "I had to...see. It's too easy to just mark them as hostile on the map and carry on. Looking at them..."

"They're...rabid, mindless," Colburn told her. "But they're just... people."

"I know. All my plans are built on that, Sergeant, but I need more data."

She heard the Marine swallow.

"We are Her Majesty's Marines, sir," he said quietly. "Lieutenant Evanson can get you whatever you need."

"I don't need Evanson right now, I don't think," Roslyn replied. "Your people have sensor drones, yes?"

"Of course," he confirmed. "There's two loaded in the default combat loadout for the exosuits. We didn't have time to adjust from default."

"All right. I want you to start deploying the sensor drones into the crowd," Roslyn told him. "If the Orpheus weapon is in the air, there will be densities where the drones can detect it. In infection mode, it *can't* just dissolve when hit with radio waves.

"But even so, passive scanners only. I want the drones taking air samples and examining them for nanites." She grimaced. "I presume I don't need to tell you to destroy those drones well away from the shuttle?"

"I'm not sure I'd bring them back aboard if you *ordered* it, sir, without a damn good reason," Colburn admitted. "There might end up being accidental weapons discharges."

Marines were...sometimes a bit *too* honest.

"I didn't hear that," Roslyn said drily. "But believe me, Sergeant, if I do order you to bring one back aboard, there'll be a reason."

"What are we looking for, sir?" Colburn asked.

"I need to know the infection radius, Sergeant," she told him. "Right now, I have to assume that as soon as that mob reaches the park, everyone still above ground is effectively dead. But if it turns out that they're only infecting people within a few meters or just those they touch...the options change."

"I see, sir." Colburn paused. "I'll get my people on it. We'll have you your data as quickly as possible."

"Thank you, Sergeant."

"Anything I can do to save these people, Commander. At any cost."

Roslyn watched through the feed as the pigeon-sized drones plunged toward the mob. For a few seconds, even knowing the purpose, she thought they were going to crash *into* the mob, but then the engines turned on about ten meters up, sweeping across the top of the mob.

Mindless as the Orpheus infected were, they still noticed the drones. Colburn wasn't bothering to be subtle—if nothing else, he was in an assault shuttle that was only another hundred meters up.

Several people jumped into the air, trying and failing to reach the robotic aircraft before falling. At least one of those was promptly crushed under the chaotic movement of the mob of infected, forcing Roslyn to wince and close her eyes.

"We are orbiting at ten meters," one of the Marines reported. "Air samples are being picked up and analyzed. Passive opticals aren't picking up anything, but we are talking nanotech..."

There was a pause.

"Air samples are clean so far as we can tell," Colburn finally told Roslyn. "Ten meters *up* is probably equivalent to something like...a hundred meters horizontally for a nanite, though. We'll dump the air and lower the drones for another pass."

"Carry on, Sergeant," Roslyn replied. "I'm listening, but you know what you're doing, and I've got a few other irons in the fire."

The mob Colburn was orbiting was the closest to the park by a kilometer or so and moving quickly—but it wasn't the *only* chaotic mob of Orpheus infected. The only thing that had saved them so far was that the infected couldn't use vehicles of any kind. Even *fast* walking for a mob was only four or five kilometers an hour.

No matter what happened, Roslyn had an hour. That would only get another twenty-five hundred to three thousand people underground, though, and she wasn't sure how many people they *could* fit in the lab.

If they had ten thousand in there, they were probably already starting to fill the spaces outside the decon chambers.

"Drones are circling at five meters," Colburn's Marine reported. "Still nothing at this level on the exterior optics and we are taking air samples."

Roslyn figured there had to be *some* level of dispersal from the infected. As Colburn had noted, though, for every meter the nanites went up, they probably spread out ten.

But if five meters up was clear, that gave her a radius she *could* engage the infected at. She didn't *want* to kill them—but if push came to shove, the Guardia could probably hold the infected a hundred meters away.

They'd kill a *lot* of innocent people doing it, and Roslyn wasn't sure she'd be able to live with herself for giving the order...but it would save the lives of everyone in the park.

"Internal air examination shows nanites at roughly two-point-one parts per billion," Colburn said quietly. "I don't know if that's enough to infect—I'm going to guess *not*—but it does suggest a maximum limit."

"Understood. We don't really have another use for those drones right now, do we?" Roslyn asked.

"No, sir," Colburn agreed. "We're going to cycle them through at each meter as we go and see, well, how low we get."

The answer turned out to be "one hundred and eighty-two centimeters from the top of the crowd."

That was the height at which the Orpheus infected started to *successfully* yank drones out of the air and smash them on the ground.

"Okay, so they've wrecked fourteen drones," Colburn concluded after taunting the crowd for a minute. "But we now have data at one-point-eight meters from the infected."

"And?" Roslyn asked.

"At one-point-eight meters, we're up to about a hundred parts per million, which my counter-*bioweapon* training suggests is infectious," he told her. "Given the replicating abilities we know of for the nanites, I'd honestly say anything above *one* PPM is infectious. Which put our safe radius somewhere between three and four meters.

"I could send out new drones to confirm that, sir."

"Faced with a mass human wave attack by unarmed civilians, Sergeant, would you be prepared to guarantee they wouldn't get within fifty meters?" Roslyn asked instead.

Colburn gave a tired sigh.

"In this circumstance, sir, our biggest problem is ammunition. Most of our arsenal will *overpenetrate* against that kind of...target," he said carefully. "We tend to assume that we can neutralize unarmored opponents with Nix or SmartDarts.

"A human wave attack like the infected will launch... We only carry so many bullets, sir. And we can't risk bringing the Marines into the park, can we?"

"No," Roslyn agreed. "What we *can* do is set up a perimeter around the park. Blockade streets, funnel the infected. We have an hour, Sergeant. Even without bringing the shuttles within, let's say, two hundred meters of the refugees, can we secure the area?"

"The infected may well just go over any barrier we build," Colburn warned. "I've been watching them. We can't funnel them on a large scale; they will go over instead of around. On a stack of bodies, if necessary."

"But we can still hold a perimeter?"

"It's a three-kilometer-wide park," he noted. "Roughly square, so twelve kilometers of perimeter. If we bring all the Marines from Huntress and build the positions right...maybe.

"If nothing else, we can buy *time*. With exosuits for us and biohazard gear for Guardia volunteers, we can keep them a hundred meters from the civilians for a while. Maybe long enough."

"If you have an answer for how long is *enough*, Sergeant, you're ahead of me," Roslyn told him. "Pull the shuttles back to the edge of the park. Leave drones orbiting over that mob; it's our first threat."

She shivered.

"I don't want to order this, Sergeant," she said quietly, "but if the only way I can save fifty thousand of this city's people is to kill another fifty thousand...what choice do I have?"

"I don't know, sir," he admitted. "May I pray that we *find* that choice?"

"There's Marines in the lab working on it," Roslyn told him. "Pray away, Sergeant. If anyone can do the impossible, I trust in your Corps."

CHAPTER 41

"THERE HAS TO be another way."

Cardinal-Governor Guerra sounded exhausted. To be fair, Roslyn *felt* as bad as the planetary Governor sounded, and she stared past the image of Guerra's face on her helmet to the crowd of refugees filling the park.

The prospect of killing tens of thousands of his citizens was still unacceptable to him—a *damn* good thing, in Roslyn's opinion.

"I agree," she told him. "I've got everyone I can spare trying to access the databases of the Orpheus lab and people tearing down a decontamination chamber we aren't using to try to identify if it's doing anything differently.

"If we can establish that the standard class six biohazard decontamination protocols can neutralize the nanites, then we can at least begin considering evacuating the not-actively infected portion of the population," she continued. "Until we can establish that, though, the current quarantine has to remain in effect—and I'm not certain we'll find a way to disable the Orpheus weapon in the people it's already taken control of."

"What can I do?" Guerra asked. "I am praying as hard as I can, but God acts through people."

"We will forward everything we learn from the Orpheus facility," she promised. "You have the resources of a planetary government. I have a handful of Marines and whatever engineers and techs ended up in my evacuation zone.

"Also." She paused. There was *something*, but it was planning for a victory even she wasn't sure she'd see.

"What, Envoy Chambers?"

Roslyn shivered at that title. She'd be happy to *burn* that fucking Warrant when this was all over.

"We know that even if we do manage to deactivate the nanites, the victims are badly injured afterward," she told him. "The first version of the weapon we encountered was neutralized by standard bioscans, but the victims went into comas and lost autonomous system control.

"If we find *any* answer, we're going to be facing tens to hundreds of thousands of people requiring immediate major medical attention, and there aren't enough doctors in a city of two million to handle that."

"Sorprendidas has some of the finest medical seminaries in the Protectorate," Guerra told her. "We train priests from ten worlds to be doctors—and laymen from a dozen more. While we focus on the mental health and psychological well-being of God's children, we also train many thousands of surgeons and general practitioners.

"Give me time, and I will have an *army* of doctors ready to handle anyone you can save, Commander Chambers," he promised. "We will be ready when you need us. I presume your Captain Daalman has information on the symptoms and problems you've encountered?

"I hope—I pray—that we were already working on finding a treatment for this...post-Orpheus syndrome," the priest said calmly. "But I assure you, we *will* have one. If you can save them."

"I don't know if I can, Your Excellency," Roslyn admitted. "I have half a dozen chances to find a way, though. We have to have hope."

"No, my child," Guerra said quietly. "We have to have *faith*. In God, yes. But also in your Marines. In our fellow humans. I have faith in you."

"I'm not Catholic, Cardinal, and I served in the war," Roslyn told him. "I'm not sure how much faith I have in anything, let alone myself."

"No one is perfect, Envoy Chambers. I will have enough faith in you for us both, then. You *will* find an answer."

Roslyn swallowed, both touched and stunned by the quiet determination of the man in charge of Sorprendidas.

"I hope you're right," she said. "And I will do everything I can to *make* it right."

A new icon blinked on her screen and she forced a smile.

"And there is the next call on my schedule," she continued. "We'll keep your people informed of everything we find, but now I need to talk to Captain Daalman."

Mage-Captain Daalman somehow managed to look less tired than Roslyn or Guerra, but some of that had to be a façade. Roslyn knew the Mage-Captain had been following everything since Roslyn had first taken her Marines underground—and that felt like it had been weeks ago, even though it had been less than four hours.

"Where are we at, Chambers?" Daalman asked.

"Quarantined," she replied. "We're clear for six to seven kilometers out from the park on three sides of four, but the closest mob of infected is only seven kilometers from the entrance we're using.

"I have Marines trying to blockade the street entrances and add distance, but we don't know how well it will work. We *have* established that we can engage at ranges in excess of about sixty meters safely, but..."

"But the infected are just as much victims as everyone else," the Mage-Captain agreed with a sigh. "Any *good* news, Chambers?"

"We *know* the Orpheus decontamination chambers could kill the nanites—or so they told their own people, at least," Roslyn said. "That gives us a starting point. We're tearing one apart now to see if they're doing anything different.

"Otherwise..." She sighed. "I swear there's an answer in front of my face, sir, and I'm too damned in the middle of things to see it."

"That's about how it normally goes, but you're not a doctor, Chambers," her Captain said gently. "You're a tactical officer and the Voice of the Mage-Queen of Mars. Your job, right now, is to provide other people the authority to do what they have to do."

Roslyn exhaled.

"I don't think I like that job, sir," she admitted.

"Get used to it. That's also a description of being a starship captain," Daalman told her. "We've run out of drop pods for supplies, but if there's anything we can do to support you..."

"Knight is linked up to our cyber department on *Huntress*, right?" Roslyn asked.

"I authorized it, at least," the Mage-Captain agreed. "Where's your MISS agent? Shouldn't he be helping?"

"He vanished in the lab. No idea what happened to him and no *time*." Roslyn knew she was turning *time* into a curse word. "We didn't even manage to fully sweep the lab before we started pouring evacuees into it. We're clear *now*, but...

"Hell, I need to check that we sealed the accesses to the storm sewers," she admitted. "Too many moving pieces, sir."

"Can we help coordinate?" Daalman asked. "We're that step removed and above everything, but we have overhead visual and we can see everything going on. Kristofferson and I can help organize things—I'll have him check with Andrews on the storm sewers."

"That would help," she said with a sigh. "I... I'm running out of options that aren't 'kill a lot of innocent people,' sir."

"Well, what are their targeting priorities?" the Mage-Captain said.

Roslyn blinked.

"I don't think they have any," she replied. "From what Lafrenz said, they're basically just running on an order to kill everything that isn't Orpheus-infected."

"So, they're not actively hunting for your evac zone," Daalman pointed out. "If you lure them elsewhere, that buys time, right?"

"That's brilliant, sir," Roslyn said. "I... I can't believe I didn't think of it."

"You're face-down in the middle of it all, Commander," her boss told her. "I'll start picking people's brains up here and elsewhere on the surface. We'll see what we can come up with for clever ideas...but you're on the ground. A lot of it ends up on you."

Roslyn nodded, swallowing hard—and then it hit her.

Bioscans.

"Sir, I need to talk to my tactical team," she said. "I don't know if I've got a final answer, but a possibility just occurred to me."

Roslyn managed to get both of her Mage-Lieutenants and the ship's doctor on a single conference within a couple of minutes, a sign of the priority her Warrant and the situation were getting her.

"Commander Chambers, how are you feeling?" Dr. Judith Breda asked immediately.

Roslyn snorted.

"I'm going to have some new nightmares and PTSD symptoms when this is over, doc," she told the other woman. "But that's a 'Future Roslyn' problem. Kirtida, Semele."

She nodded to her two direct subordinates as their images appeared on her helmet screen. They couldn't see much, but hopefully they'd get the intent.

"What do you need us for, sir?" Kirtida Samuels asked, getting one second ahead of Semele Jordan asking the same question.

"I need you three to sit down with whichever Chief is most familiar with our new modular warheads for the Talon Ten ground-bombardment missiles," Roslyn told them. She could *see* the confusion in everyone's eyes—especially Dr. Breda's.

"I want to know if you can rig up a warhead to pulse the entire city with the radiation pulse of a standard bioscan."

The call was silent for several seconds.

"A standard bioscan involves a lot of different types of sensor and pulse, Commander," Breda told them. "It includes, over the course of a ten-second sequence, X-rays, ultrasound, magnetic imaging and several other EM radiation pulses."

She shook her head.

"I'm not sure much of that can be duplicated outside of the very specialized structure of a bioscanner," she noted. "We might be able to manage the radiation sequences, but to achieve it on that kind of geographic area, you're going to drastically increase a series of other medical risks."

"Doctor, if we can't disable the Orpheus weapon, those people are going to starve to death," Roslyn pointed out. "I will trade ten years off the average life expectancy of Nueva Portugal's people in exchange for saving them today. *That* decision I will gladly make."

"But why a bioscan?" Samuels asked.

"The nanites from the first Orpheus weapon we encountered dissolved in the bioscan, fast enough that we didn't even see them on the scan, right, Doctor?" Roslyn said.

"That's correct," Breda agreed. "There was very little on the bioscans of the living—or dead—victims of the Orpheus weapon to suggest they'd been infected with anything at all.

"Given the sturdiness of the delivery mechanism required to survive an explosion, that designed fragility surprised me," she admitted. "This is extremely sophisticated nanotech...with literal magic baked into the design.

"Even what little information Commander Chambers got from Dr. Lafrenz suggested a level of sophistication on both the nanotech and magitech sides of the equation beyond anything I am familiar with."

She shook her head.

"Even the science parts of this may as well be magic, I'm afraid. It is entirely possible that the nanites dissolve on exposure to the magnetic fields present in a bioscan unit, before we even commence the scan."

"We live in a nation that for two hundred years has relied on magic for almost everything," Roslyn said quietly. "And I think this might be the first thing I've ever seen that I would actually call *black magic*. Nothing about this *thing* isn't inherently evil."

"I don't believe anything is solely evil, Commander," Breda countered. "I can see potential for the use of nanites writing runes like this. Just not...the use they've made of it."

"Fair. But...can we do *something* to convince the nanites they're in a bioscanner?" Roslyn asked. "I know we can't do the magnetic fields, not across an entire city, but the X-rays?"

"If the doctor can get us the frequencies and energy levels the bio-scanners use, we might be able to rig up something," Jordan said. "I'll have to talk to Chief Westcott, but I *think* we can rig the EMP warheads to pulse at a lower energy level. It won't burn out the unit like the EMP does, so we should be able to get a sequence of a given radiation... maybe."

"It might not work, but I agree that it's worth a shot," Breda said. "We'll take a stab at it, Commander Chambers, and get back to you."

"I have a plan for buying us more time," Roslyn told them all. "Well, Captain Daalman had a plan. We're going to see if it works—but we're still talking hours to rig this up, people. Not days."

"We know," Jordan said quietly. "We'll do whatever we can, sir."

"I know," Roslyn replied. "I have faith."

And if she didn't, apparently Cardinal-Governor Guerra did.

CHAPTER 42

ROSLYN TOOK a few moments to assess where her people were with everything as she returned her attention to the surface. Barricades were going up across the streets connecting to the park, mostly being assembled by volunteers.

They had enough personal protective equipment to cover everyone who had gone out, but they still weren't sure they could *clean* the suits of the nanites. The people on the barricades weren't going to be able to go into the underground sanctuary—and unless Bolivar had done differently than Roslyn had told him, they knew that.

But there were far more people in the park than they'd ever be able to get underground. The only real hope for tens of thousands of people was to hold the rough line they were assembling around the park.

On the other hand, the longer she could keep the infected *away* from the line, the more secure it was going to be and the better chance she had to save *everyone*.

"Sergeant Colburn," she pinged the Marine. "Is there someone actually in charge of you Marines I should be talking to rather than just calling the latest noncom to answer my messages?"

The Marine laughed.

"Mage-Captain Daalman made *damn* sure our officers didn't pull any crazy stunts, sir," he told her. "Major Dickens and the Lieutenants are still in low orbit above the city, providing overwatch from the last pair of assault shuttles that didn't drop.

"I've been letting him know what you're telling us, but everyone figured we were a bit too busy to insert another person in the loop."

"Well, now I need *all* of the Marines, so let's loop them in," Roslyn replied. "Can you get me into the Marine command net? I need to talk to all of you."

"Give me five seconds," Colburn told her. Maybe half that later, a small chirp announced she had access to a new channel.

"Marines, this is Commander Chambers," she announced herself after flipping over. "Who have I got?"

"Captain Chiyembekezo Dickens," the Marine CO said instantly. "Lieutenants Firoz Kneib and Ainoa Figueroa. Sergeants Colburn, MacCrumb, O'Mooney, Toft, Day and Kaiser. Six of eight squads, Mage-Commander. One went in with you and Sergeant Mooren; one is still onboard *Huntress* with Sergeant Carl Horton.

"What do you need, Mage-Commander...Voice...whatever title you want."

"*Mage-Commander* will do, Captain Dickens," Roslyn said calmly. "I assume you're also in contact with Corporals Andrews and Knight?"

"I am," Dickens confirmed levelly. "I'm doing my best not to joggle your elbow, Mage-Commander. You're in the middle of all of this mess."

"I needed every Marine I hadn't already sent underground for the next step, so I figured I should talk to their commander," Roslyn admitted. "How many are down here? I'll admit I haven't kept as much track as I should."

"Five squads on the surface. Kaiser is up here, playing bodyguard to a trio of officers who should know better than to want what they want," Dickens told her. "You've got sixty Marines to hand, Mage-Commander, and fifteen more of us on high, plus twelve more on *Huntress* if things get *real* messy."

"They aren't already?" Roslyn asked. "I didn't know zombies were part of your training."

"As much as anything, Mage-Commander, my understanding is that we're hoping for solutions that aren't going to involve Marines and automatic weapons," the Captain said grimly. "When the answer comes down to Marines, a lot of people are going to die."

"Not yet," she said flatly. "And not ever, if I have my say."

"Good. What do you need of us now, then?"

"Bait," Roslyn told them with a chuckle. "Mage-Captain Daalman asked me what the mob's targeting priority was. My understanding is they don't have one—they're operating on a single order from the nanites that basically says *kill everything.*

"If we give them targets away from the park, they should chase. But even with hazmat gear, if I send regular folks in on foot..."

"They're going to get run down," Dickens agreed. "But there's no way in hell mind-controlled civilians are going to catch exosuited Marines."

"That's what I was hoping you were going to say, Major," Roslyn said. "There is a mob of twenty thousand of said mind-controlled civilians three kilometers from the perimeter we're drawing. I want them going every direction *but* south.

"Think you can do that?"

"Only one way to find out, Mage-Commander," Dickens told her. "Sergeants, you heard her. Think Marines can distract an army of zombies long enough to cure them?"

"Oorah!"

"Thought so." There was a grin in Dickens's voice that Roslyn could *hear,* even if she couldn't see him on this channel. "There's enough Guardia and civilian volunteers to keep building the perimeter if we pull the Marines out.

"Marines, report back to your shuttles. It's time to do what we do best: *maneuver.*"

Even with the rush and chaos and pressure on everyone, Roslyn was surprised by how quickly the Marines made it back onto their shuttles. She had access to the video feeds from the spacecraft and, after a moment, realized that the Marine command net gave her access to the video feeds from individual Marines.

That was dangerous. She still had a job to do in the park.

"How many people are we at?" she asked Bolivar, rejoining the Guardia officer at last.

"Hard to say," he admitted. "We're only registering and tracking people as we send them inside." He shrugged. "Sixty thousand still on the surface? Maybe more?"

She whistled softly in shock.

"We have to have cleared most of the area around us," she told him. "And...we should be able to keep them safe, even up here. For a while, anyway."

"All we can do," he whispered.

"No, it's not," Roslyn said fiercely. "We have incredibly smart people everywhere on this planet, digging into every scrap of data Knight gets out of those computers. We have the cyberwarfare team on *Huntress* backing up Knight on that hack and analysis. We have Andrews tearing apart the decon rooms, and I have people on *Huntress* trying to rig up warheads to duplicate whatever effect the Orpheus people built into the nanites as a fail-safe.

"There *is* an answer somewhere," she told him. "I do not—I can-not—believe that these people built a weapon like this without the ability to turn it off if they risked losing control.

"Everybody who knew how is dead, but we *will* find that key and we *will* save these people."

"Or we'll die with them," the Guardia officer replied. "I don't have any hope left, Chambers, I'm sorry. I'm keeping it up and afloat, but..."

"You're doing enough," she said. "But there *is* another side to this, Victoriano. We have to believe that."

"Or just keep working regardless," he half-whispered. "It doesn't matter if I'm going to die, Commander Chambers. It matters whether I get ten thousand people to safety or only five thousand because I gave up.

"I won't accept the latter. So, I'm going to keep working until the damn thing kills me. But don't expect me to have hope."

"Fine," she told him. "I'm heading to the northern perimeter. If our plan fails, they're going to get swarmed in about forty minutes. I might be able to make a difference—and I'm as available by coms there as here."

"I'll keep these people moving in," Bolivar promised. "Till the end. You have my word."

"I know. We'll all be here to the end, Captain. One way or another."

She just had to hope that they'd save more than ten thousand along the way.

CHAPTER 43

"MARINES DEPLOYING," Sergeant Day reported as his shuttle swept in on the east side of the mob. There was an audible thud through the command network as the Sergeant joined his people in jumping from a shuttle still five meters in the air.

"Distance is one hundred twenty meters from the eastern side of the target," Day continued over the command network.

Roslyn was still well short of even the inner perimeter, but she kept one eye on the feed from the Marines as she walked briskly north. Once she was clear of the inner perimeter, there was no turning back. That was the downside—they couldn't be sure that the armor of the people they were sending out wasn't contaminated with the nanites. The outer perimeter was fifty meters outside of the park, and the inner perimeter was two hundred meters *inside* the park.

Hopefully, that would be enough. The exosuits and hazmat suits *should* be enough to keep the perimeter defenders safe, but the suits would carry the Orpheus weapon themselves.

"We have no response from the mob," Sergeant Day reported. "They continue to maintain a southerly course with a few stragglers in any given direction."

"Based off what we're seeing elsewhere, it's almost Brownian motion," Dickens told the Sergeant. "They don't have a direction in mind, but they started moving south, so they'll keep moving south until interrupted."

The *big* problem, to Roslyn's mind, was the ever-shrinking circle marked by smaller groups of the infected. Their current focal point was only one of four groups of twenty thousand or more infected, but the other three were in completely different sections of the city.

But there were groups of five hundred to a thousand Orpheus infected everywhere in the city. Daalman's suggestion might help them break up the big mob, and if worse came to worst, Roslyn's people could *destroy* a single mob of twenty thousand.

A hundred mobs of a thousand infected each coming from a hundred different directions was an entirely different problem.

"Move in closer, Sergeant," Dickens ordered. The Marine was running this operation, with Roslyn as an eavesdropping observer. The orders were hers. The execution was theirs.

As the Marines moved in, she reached their inner perimeter. It wasn't much at the moment. A painted line on the ground and a nervous-looking collection of teenagers with megaphones.

"We can't let you back through if you go any farther," one of them told her. "Hazmat suit carries the bug."

"I know," she replied. "I'm Commander Chambers. Everyone going over the line should know, so thank you. Hopefully...you won't have much to do."

The boy chuckled nervously.

"They say you're the Mage-Queen's Voice?" he asked. "That means you're a powerful Mage, right? You're gonna save us?"

"Yes, yes and I damn well hope so," Roslyn told him, glancing at the others. "But the rules we made say I don't come back across this line either. Understand? It doesn't matter who is coming from out there; you warn them back and call for support."

"We know," another of the teens agreed. "Good luck!"

"Thank you," Roslyn told them.

She meant it. Faith. Luck. Whatever they wanted to call it, she and her people needed every scrap of it they could find.

"Range is eighty meters; we have no response," Day reported. "I think the suits might be stopping them from registering us as targets."

"No clever ideas, Sergeant," Dickens snapped before Roslyn could. "You're *probably* safe at that range, but if you take off your helmet, I am relieving you on the fucking spot. *Am I clear?*"

"Didn't consider it for a second, sir," Day said virtuously.

Like Dickens, Roslyn figured he was lying.

"Continuing to move in. Seventy meters…"

The gap between the two perimeters was deathly silent as Roslyn walked the quarter-kilometer. They'd know soon enough whether the mob could be distracted.

"Range is fifty meters," the Sergeant reported. "Should we take air samples to test for infection risk?"

"Not a bad idea," Roslyn interjected. "Assuming they give you the time. They went for drones above them, after all. Even in exosuits, you should be pissing them off by now."

"Taking samples." Day paused. "Under one PPM, sirs. Fifty meters should still be safe."

"All right. If you have any suggestions for getting their attention without getting closer, I'd appreciate them," Roslyn said. "I don't want you to risk it if we can avoid it."

"I figure we just make a lot of noise," Day replied. "Loudspeaker mode active."

Roslyn closed her eyes in half-exhaustion, half-amusement as the Marine Sergeant paused to consider his words.

"Hey, you smelly zombies," he bellowed. "We're from the government and we're here to help you!"

There was another pause, then Day chuckled ruefully.

"Yep, that worked. Time to move, Marines! If any of them get within thirty meters of you, you're buying the beer!"

The icons for Day's squad told Roslyn the Sergeant and his people were already moving—and dozens of the infected were surging after him.

"I'm not sure we're pulling away enough," she murmured after a moment. The momentum of the mob was still south, even as plenty of infected surged after Sergeant Day and his Marines.

"Each round is an experiment," Dickens admitted. "Now we've got a response, Sergeant Toft is going in on the west side to see what *she* can pull away.

"Piece by piece, Commander, we're going to distract them from the northern perimeter."

That was ahead of Roslyn now, a line of trucks and foxhole-grenade cement filling the between two office towers. This *particular* barricade was the one directly in the mob's path.

The one that would see twenty thousand innocent-but-rabid victims of the Orpheus weapon swarm it if the Marines failed.

"I'm playing backstop, Major," Roslyn said quietly. "But I can't handle twenty thousand of them."

"I know, Mage-Commander. We'll do everything we can."

Roslyn had never met Sergeant Milly Toft, but she watched through the woman's helmet cameras as the shuttle dipped down toward the crowd.

"Drop point is fifty meters, and then you get the hell out of Dodge, Lieutenant. You read me?" she asked in a soft Australian accent. "No games."

"No games," the pilot agreed. "Beyond abandoning you fifty meters from *that*."

"*That* is the objective, Lieutenant. I make the range one hundred meters. Marines, are you ready to play bait?"

There wasn't even enough time for a cheer before the shuttle ramp popped open and the first Marines went barrelling out. Exosuits could handle drops of up to ten meters while absorbing the impact for the user, and that was the height Toft went out the side of the spacecraft at.

Roslyn winced in sympathy. She'd never made an exosuit cold drop, but her understanding was that while ten meters was doable, it wasn't comfortable.

"We're down," Toft reported. "Twelve Marines in the wind; watching a whole bunch of people just... Well, I don't know if I have a word for what these people are doing."

Toft's helmet cams gave Roslyn one of the better views of the Orpheus victims she'd had so far. They were moving in a crowd, but it clearly wasn't a planned or organized thing. Individual infected were bashing themselves against everything to hand, and every one of them that she could see had visible injuries and torn clothing.

The heat of the afternoon sun in Nueva Portugal and a lack of hydration was probably going to hurt the victims as much as anything else, but the chaotic mess was bone-chilling to see.

"Still ignoring us. Well, not quite," Toft noted. "I've got a few eyeballs on us and a couple of people heading our way. Moving in to see what else we can draw."

Roslyn swallowed the urge to order Toft to run. The Marines were playing a very specific game, and the half-dozen or so infected now approaching them aggressively were *not* the prize they needed.

"All right, this isn't going to work," Toft said after a moment. "I am *not* going to test if our exosuits stand up to the weapon while the infected are trying to tear them open. Marines! Form a line."

The rough skirmish line on Roslyn's helmet displays tightened into a parade formation in a heartbeat. There was still twenty meters from the nearest infected, but Roslyn suspected that wasn't enough.

If nothing else, those Marines' exosuits were now coated with infectious levels of the Orpheus weapon. So long as the seals held and they didn't come near anyone else, that was fine...but now Toft's Marines *definitely* couldn't enter the inner perimeter.

"Marines..." Toft said grimly. "Over their heads, volley fire on my command. Fire!"

Roslyn heard the sound of a dozen heavy weapons through the Marine command net and shivered. What goes up must come down—the rounds were high-velocity, but they weren't going to reach orbit.

Somewhere, those bullets would fall back down. For now, the sound of unsuppressed exosuit weapons echoed across the gathered mob of infected—and hundreds of heads turned.

"Yep, that worked," Toft said calmly, as if she was considering a chess strategy instead of a charging horde of rabid humans. "Let's move, Marines!"

Her exosuited soldiers obeyed with enthusiasm, rabbiting away from the gathering storm.

Roslyn watched them long enough to be sure that they were clear, then turned her attention back to the mob. Toft's efforts had been more effective than Day's, but the vast majority of the infected were still heading her way.

"Next up, Captain Dickens," she said quietly.

"I know," the Marine CO replied. "Sergeant Colburn is swinging in from the north, and I've got O'Mooney and MacCrumb swinging in from each side. We'll see what three distractions at once buys you.

"Give us five minutes to set it up."

"The core mob is maybe forty-five minutes from the outer perimeter," Roslyn warned. "We only have so much time."

"I know. And I know what the options become if we *don't* distract them," Dickens said softly. "But we need the time."

"Understood. I'm checking in on the outer perimeter now," she told him. "Keep me informed."

CHAPTER 44

ROSLYN MUTED her command channel and called her magic to allow her to "hop" fifteen feet up onto the top of the barricade. The Guardia officer standing with a pair of binoculars started and dropped the tool.

She wasn't in position to catch them and watched the electronics-enhanced optics shatter on the roof of the big transport truck at the middle of the blockade.

"Sorry," she told him, then recognized the name on his Guardia-issue armor. "Lieutenant Oliveira?"

"Yes, sir," the Guardia officer replied. "Commander Chambers! Are you here to help?"

"That's the plan, Lieutenant," she said. "Though the Marines are doing everything they can to make sure you and I don't have to do anything. Report."

Even in hazmat armor and a full mask, Oliveira was vibrating like a happy puppy to see her. The apparent hope her presence alone brought was almost scary to Roslyn.

"We managed to get in touch with a bunch of truck drivers who were still mobile and uninfected," he told her. "They use a different communication network than everyone else, but once we were in touch, we had the key components for the outer perimeter.

"This is the furthest south of our barricades on the north end. We're making an attempt to funnel them here. Most of the rest of the area across this district has taller buildings we've incorporated into blockades we don't think can be breached, but here…"

Olivera gestured around them. The blockade there was drawn between a two-story strip mall on the east side of the road and a story-and-a-half light industrial complex on the west.

"We don't have the buildings to work with here," he concluded. "So, we've blocked the road with the transport trucks and used up the foxhole grenades the Navy provided, but we're pretty sure we're not going to be able to keep them from at least *trying* to come over the barricade here."

"That was the plan," Roslyn agreed, looking out at the wide road and parking lot directly north of the barricade. It made for a perfect killing field for the machine guns she could see positioned across the top of the trucks and foam-crete bulwarks.

"Personnel?" she asked.

"Me and three other Guardia," Oliveira told her. "Twenty-six civilian volunteers. We have twelve eight-millimeter light machine guns from the Guardia armory and four twelve-millimeter multi-barrels from the supplies the Navy dropped."

As Sergeant Colburn had pointed out, none of the Marines' lethal weapons were designed to deal with unarmored opponents. The four-barrelled twelve-millimeter automatic weapons they used for squad support were designed to go through armor like what Roslyn and Oliveira were wearing.

"Ammunition?" The Marines had said that was their biggest fear.

"Fifteen hundred rounds per gun." Oliveira shivered. "If we run out of that, I've got a dozen shotguns and maybe a hundred shells for each of them as a reserve."

"Nonlethals?" They'd tried all of those already, but it was still worth having them on hand.

"Guardia armories have functionally infinite supplies of stunguns and SmartDarts," the Lieutenant told her. "We have a SmartDart *fabricator* at each key armory. I've got thirty stunguns here… Habit, I guess."

"Not a bad habit, Lieutenant," Roslyn said. "I figure there's enough Nix on the Marine assault shuttles to make at least one more pass with the gas. Maybe if we hit them with *enough* Nix, it will take them down."

It was extremely unlikely at this point, but she saw no reason not to try.

"How bad is it, sir?" Oliveira asked, his helmet close to hers and his voice quiet so none of the volunteers could hear him.

"We've got eighteen thousand people heading this way, and they're as innocent as anyone else," Roslyn said quietly. "We've got plans to distract them and pull them away, to buy time for us to find the answer in the bioweapon lab files, but...if they make it here, you'll have to use those machine guns."

"I know." The Guardia officer swallowed and turned to look north again. "We're ready," he said, but his tone was weak.

"The Marines have a plan," she assured him. "*I* have a plan. And there's an answer in that damn lab, I'm sure of it."

"Chambers," Dickens's voice interrupted. "Marines are ready for round two. Sergeant Day has broken contact and is coordinating for round three with Sergeant Kaiser."

Distance was time and time was hope. That was the only calculation Roslyn could make right then, and it was the calculation that mattered.

The Marines needed to buy her distance, and she watched as three more shuttles swept toward the infected crowd in a perfectly synchronized operation, engines and loudspeakers screaming as they passed over the mob of infected.

Marines plummeted out the back of each shuttle, twelve each to the west, east and north of the infected, hooting and hollering as they hit the ground. At the same moment, Roslyn saw that the loudspeakers went silent.

But the exosuit speakers were loud enough that she could hear from three kilometers away. Not in detail, but the cacophony the Marines were creating was definitely audible—and unlike Toft's pass, they were now close enough to Roslyn for her to hear the gunfire as the Marines fired over the mob's head.

"Oh, yeah," someone, presumably one of the Sergeants on the ground, said brightly. "We have *definitely* got their attention."

"So I'm seeing," Dickens replied. "*Move* your asses, Marines. If you get infected, you become part of the problem, not the solution. So, *move.*"

Despite the Captain's tone and words, the Marines were already moving. The icons were splitting up as Roslyn watched, the Marines dividing into half-squads to split the Orpheus victims up even further—and continuing to taunt and jeer at the rabid civilians chasing them.

This time, the mob fractured like a dropped glass, and Roslyn exhaled a deep sigh of relief. There were now thousands chasing each Marine section—which could be better, but at least they weren't continuing to lunge south.

"Keep moving," Dickens said, his voice grim. "Corporal Laurent, break contact. Break contact *now.*"

Roslyn's attention followed the Marine Captain's and she swallowed. One of the Marine fire teams had discovered the disadvantage of planning based on overhead. An alley they'd assumed was clear from the air was blocked on the ground, and the Marines were trying to physically move the small truck barring their way.

They didn't have time.

"We are pushing through," a woman's voice said, exhaling sharply as she was struck. "Barrier is moving at last, but they are on us. Armor is... holding."

Roslyn didn't have access to do more than hear Corporal Laurent's report. She could get it, but she wasn't sure she *wanted* to.

"We are through," Laurent reported. "They are with us still. Trying to accelerate to break free. Horatio, no, stop! Stop!"

The channel was silent for at least a minute before Corporal Laurent's voice returned.

"Contact broken. Not sure...what happened. Private First Class Horatio Estevez's armor seals failed and his left vambraces broke off. He..."

Laurent swallowed audibly.

"Private Estevez is KIA, sir," she said in a small voice. "I do not believe we can retrieve his body without using lethal force."

"The suit has tracking, Corporal," Dickens told her, his voice gentle. "We'll come back for him. For now, break contact and hunker down. You got too close. We can't retrieve you."

"Understood, sir. Will stand by for further orders."

The entire command net Roslyn was listening to was silent, and then her coms chirped as Dickens switched her to a private channel.

"I read you as still having about eight thousand heading your way," he told her. "That stunt should work again, but I think the triple whammy was key. Toft is still engaged, and rushing her is likely to result in more Marines sharing Estevez's fate."

"What's your plan, Captain?" she asked.

"I've got a free shuttle," he told her. "We're dropping from orbit now to rendezvous with Sergeant Day and Sergeant Kaiser. We'll make one more pass, Commander Chambers...then I'm afraid it's down to the shuttles."

"What can the shuttles do?" Roslyn demanded.

"They carry antipersonnel cluster bombs," Dickens said flatly. "The shuttles can't distract the infected, Commander Chambers, but they *can* destroy whatever's left of that mob."

"That's the last option, Captain."

"I agree. But once we make this pass, Mage-Commander, we are *out* of other options short of your perimeter."

"Not entirely, Captain Dickens," she told him. "Make your pass. Whatever's left...I'll deal with."

She muted the Marine and stepped to the edge of the barricade.

"Oliveira," she called the Guardia officer. "Do we have any vehicles outside the perimeter?"

Roslyn had used Oliveira's ID badge to boot up a Guardia power bike and was driving north when the Marines made their final pass. She still had the scan data on the main mob on her HUD as she traveled, making sure she didn't get lost in an unfamiliar city—but she could also hear the shuttles with their loudspeakers and the Marine exosuit speakers as Dickens led his people into action.

"Report," she told the Marine, unmuting the channel now that she was moving under her own power.

"We're on the ground, which I might need your Warrant to protect me from the Captain's wrath over," Dickens told her cheerfully. "Same triple whammy as last time; there are a *lot* of angry mind-controlled people chasing us.

"There's still some left for you, but I think we've managed to pull at least three-quarters of that mob apart and scattered around the city. It's not a perfect answer, but we bought you some time."

"Thank you, Captain," Roslyn said. "How many are left still heading for the perimeter?"

"Scans from my shuttle say two, maybe three thousand," Dickens told her. "We can break that up with cluster bombs or cannon...potentially even without killing too many of them."

"One last chance first, Captain," she told him. "We have a Mage on the ground, even if we're holding most of the crew in orbit.

"Let's see what I can do."

"There are still *thousands* of them, Mage-Lieutenant Commander," Dickens said quietly. "You're just one Mage."

"I am spectacularly aware of my limits, Captain Dickens, but also of our mission. I have a vehicle and I'm moving to intercept. I want your shuttles ready to drop Nix on my command."

"We know it won't do anything," he objected.

"We know standard dosages won't do anything. So, I want your shuttles to plaster the target area with *every* canister of Nix they have."

The problem with self-neutralizing neural paralyzers, though, was that Nix literally could *not* get above its target dosage. Still...it was worth a shot.

"Understood. Tactical shuttle command is yours. I'm linking in Lieutenant Herbert as your contact. Nix, missiles, guns, cluster bombs... whatever we've got that you need, he'll drop on your command."

"Thank you, Captain, Lieutenant Evanson," Roslyn said as a chirp announced Herbert was on the channel. "Run safely, Captain?"

"Believe me, that's the plan. Do...what you can and what you have to, Commander Chambers," Dickens told her. "We'll see you on the other side."

CHAPTER 45

IT WAS ONE THING to look at scans, data, even *video* of a mob.

It was quite another to park a power bike in the middle of the street and watch twenty-five hundred people surge toward you in a single body.

"Lieutenant Herbert," Roslyn said quietly. "Nix *now.*"

The shuttles dropped from the sky in sequence like stooping pigeons. Each plummeted downward and then across the crowd of Orpheus infected, plain steel canisters crashing into the ground in carefully selected positions.

Roslyn couldn't see the clear gas, but she knew she *should* see the effects. There should have been dozens of people falling over—*hundreds.* Normally, there was enough Nix out there to put down the original twenty-thousand-strong crowd.

And it was doing nothing. She hadn't really expected anything different, but it had been worth a shot.

"We are standing by with cluster munitions or whatever else you need, Commander," Lieutenant Herbert said in her ear. She and Roslyn knew each other's tones at least a little bit by now—and Roslyn knew the younger woman was nervous.

It was extremely unlikely that Herbert had deployed cluster munitions against *anybody*, ever, let alone against an unarmored mob like this. Even Roslyn wasn't sure how bad it would be.

But she could also hear the determination in Lieutenant Herbert's voice. If Roslyn gave the order, the Marines would do their jobs. They would take the blood guilt of the next few minutes on themselves so that the volunteers at the barricade didn't have to.

Because that was part of what Marines *did*.

Before that happened, though, Roslyn was going to do everything she could to prevent that. She'd already watched someone burn out their life with magic today. If she had to do the same, what was one life against over two thousand?

"Range is one hundred twenty meters," Herbert murmured in her ear. "Do you *have* a plan, sir?"

"That's rude to ask, isn't it, Lieutenant?" Roslyn replied. She started walking forward. "If I was relying on anyone else, they'd be justified in asking for a plan...but I'm not."

Part of her wished she'd paid more attention in her limited classes on transmutation. If she turned all of the silver in the area into lead, for example, that would neutralize the runes. It didn't strike her as a particularly *likely* answer, and it was beyond her abilities anyway.

Her training had been *very* focused. She was a Navy Mage: trained as both a Jump Mage and a Combat Mage. She could teleport herself a long way and she could fight.

And today, Roslyn Chambers wasn't planning on running.

"Range is ninety meters," the pilot told her. "I'm just going to keep updating you until you give me orders, sir."

She didn't say anything in response. There was no point. Roslyn exhaled through the hazmat helmet, wishing she could take the thing off. Claustrophobia wasn't helping her regain the power she'd already expended today.

Lafrenz had lost, but holding off the strike she'd killed herself with had taken almost everything Roslyn had. She'd barely restored enough power for a single fight, and what she was about to do was more than that.

Fortunately—or unfortunately, she supposed—the Navy had long before developed a solution for that.

Exalt was a mix of drugs and thaumaturgically modified chemicals designed for exactly her current condition. The primary ingredient was a powerful amphetamine, and even the Mages who'd put it together weren't sure why some of the other ingredients worked as they did. A dose would give Roslyn a full "recharge" and keep her going for an hour.

The comedown from that would *suck*...but if she took more doses, the comedown could kill her.

The syringe she took out of her medpack *glowed*. The metal tip fit neatly into the port on the hazmat suit designed for the purpose, and Roslyn winced as the hazmat suit's own needle stabbed into her shoulder.

Inhaling deeply, she looked up at the slowly surging crowd and slammed the plunger down.

Her exhaustion faded. Her feeling of depleted power also faded, and a new surge of hope and energy filled her as she withdrew and discarded the needle. Baring her teeth, she straightened and faced the oncoming mob.

"Range is *thirty* meters," Herbert told her. "You are now in the infection zone."

"I know. That's enough, Lieutenant. I'll see you on the other side," Roslyn told the pilot, echoing Dickens's words as she summoned her power.

Nothing Roslyn could do would keep *everyone* from dying. They were past that already—just the movement of the mob was probably crushing people to death every so often—but she would be *damned* if she'd order the deaths of thousands of innocents.

"Time to see if you're as clever as I think you are," she told a dead woman—and then summoned lightning.

The Orpheus weapon had been designed to keep its victims functioning after a Nix attack or a SmartDart hit. Roslyn wasn't a nanotech scientist, but she *was* a warship officer. She'd studied the trade-offs between protection and firepower for military ships across history.

Every bit of protection and survivability the Orpheus nanites had came at the cost of weight and capability—and the Protectorate built their nonlethal weaponry to *very* specific standards. Nix and SmartDarts had maximum effects based off the target's size.

SmartDarts even networked with each other and could do a rough estimate of the target's cardiovascular health to make sure they didn't kill them. There were records of police officers using their stun-guns as impromptu defibrillators when medical equipment was lacking—*successfully*.

That meant that Lafrenz and her team had known the *exact* maximum voltage and amperage that the Protectorate's nonlethal weaponry would apply. Roslyn had no such control over her own less-than-lethal electric shock spells.

She tried to keep the wave of electrically charged air she threw into the teeth of the crowd beneath lethal levels, but it was only ever a guess. For an area effect like this, she was ionizing an entire mass of air, making every motion a source of shock and charge.

Roslyn's power swept over the lead infected in a wave of sparks and burnt ozone—and they fell. She couldn't spare the attention to cheer as she kept the cloud moving, burning through the charge of power Exalt gave her as she swept her storm through the mob.

There was no way *everyone* was going to live—a twenty-fifth-century pacemaker could take a lot, but this shock was beyond it—but it was a *lot* better than cluster bombs.

Exhaustion finally tore the spell from her grip, and Roslyn stared across a thoroughfare that had been full of charging zombies a minute earlier. The only motion was twitching, and for a painful second, she thought she'd killed *everyone*.

"I have thermal scans on the target," Lieutenant Herbert told her quietly. "They're still with us, sir. I don't know how long they'll be down for, but they're still with us. At least ninety-five to ninety-seven percent."

Roslyn could have lived without that clarification as she stumbled. She pulled a second dose of Exalt from the suit medpack. Even that one would be a *terrible* idea—but she had three.

She'd survive the third until she came down, if it came to that.

"Movement?" she asked Herbert.

"Negative," the pilot replied, her tone hushed. "Shock only puts someone down for a few minutes at best. The hell?"

"I'm investigating," Roslyn replied. "Cover me."

The shuttle dipped into view, settling onto the roof of a nearby building with its cannon trained on the crowd as Roslyn walked forward to the edge of the crowd.

Her suit warned her that ozone levels were high. The air was breathable but not entirely safe. That would change quickly enough, but Roslyn wasn't taking chances.

"Do you have a drone you can send in for an air sample?" she asked Herbert, kneeling by the closest person.

"Good idea. On its way, sir."

Roslyn's focus was on the youth next to her. He was maybe sixteen years old, dressed in an old-fashioned school uniform of blazer, shirt and tie in white and burnt orange. His pulse was ragged but present at her touch, and she could see him breathing.

"Vitals are weak but steady on first exam. Victim is unconscious and unresponsive," Roslyn said, as much for the record as anyone on the channel, as she worked her way down a checklist. "Minor surface injuries and abrasions from the mob. Some burns from the stun spell."

Still unresponsive. The entire *crowd* was unresponsive.

"I'm taking a blood sample," she decided aloud. There was a syringe in the medpack for that, and she swapped the Exalt for it. Something weird was going on.

Roslyn was by no means a qualified nurse, but she could manage a blood sample and a rough bandage on an unconscious subject.

"Do we have any way to analyze this on the surface?" she asked the command network. "Lieutenant Herbert?"

"I think Dr. Breda should be able to run the analysis remotely through the gear in the shuttle. I'm going to come in and land behind you; you can come aboard and load it in."

"That's not safe, Lieutenant," Roslyn snapped.

"Safer than you might think," Herbert replied. "There's no nanites in the air, sir. They didn't survive your zap."

Roslyn looked at the vial of blood in her hand...and then down at the unconscious youth she'd taken it from...and then at the over two thousand people she'd zapped down who'd *stayed* down.

"We need this blood sample analyzed *now*," she said firmly. "Bring the shuttle in, Lieutenant."

CHAPTER 46

"IT'S...NOT CLEAN, per se," Dr. Breda told her five minutes later. "But the nanite population *appears* to be below replication concentrations. I'm going off pure visual analysis here, Lieutenant Commander."

"Of course," Roslyn conceded. "Anything further we figure would dissolve what's left, yes?"

"Exactly. Now...the people you shocked, are *any* of them waking up?" the doctor asked.

"No," Roslyn said grimly. "I think we're having the same post-Orpheus syndrome that we had before. Mass comas. *Fuck.*"

"With what I'm hearing about the Cardinal-Governor's relief force, we can handle that," Breda told her. "What we can't handle is a violent and infectious populace. I'm still hoping for an answer in their files for dealing with the comas.

"Even if they didn't care about their test subjects, they had to at least have *tested* for how to handle recovery from the weapon," the doctor continued. "Basic sense, let alone medical ethics."

"I'm not sure Mage Lafrenz was aware of anything I'd call *medical ethics,*" Roslyn pointed out. "But...we're sure this is below replication levels?"

"If it wasn't, Commander, you'd be seeing people get back up under the weapon's control," Breda said grimly. Data flowed across the screen in front of Roslyn, spectrographics, zoom, video...the Mage understood about a quarter of it. "I need to use the unit to run deeper tests. Can you get more samples? At least three different individuals."

"Hey, Herbert," Roslyn said to the pilot. "Do we have a hazmat suit for you?"

"Would you believe me if I said no?" Herbert said. "On my way. I'm not good at blood draws, though."

"Neither am I. What kind of tests are you running, doc?" Roslyn asked.

"This unit is capable of a standard bioscan," Breda told her. "I'm moving the sample into it remotely and running the scan. I then want to run visuals on unscanned samples for comparison, *and* I want to see how different individuals have reacted.

"If nothing else, *I'm* the only person authorized to recalibrate the stunguns issued to our people," the doctor concluded. "I want to know *damn* well this worked before I do. The situation is already atrocious. Let's try not to make it worse."

"Agreed. Come on, Lieutenant. Let's go play vampire."

For all of her forced cheer, the street full of unconscious bodies chilled Roslyn. *She'd* done this. Arguably, she'd done *all* of this—everything in Nueva Portugal could easily be considered her fault, and she'd be surprised if she didn't end up in front of a court-martial, Warrant or no Warrant—but shocking twenty-five-hundred-plus people into unconsciousness had *definitely* been her.

But they were alive, and they *weren't* tearing into her evacuation zone.

"Chambers, this is Dickens," the Marine CO greeted her calmly. "We've pretty thoroughly broken up the mob, but the overall circle is drawing closer. I think we've got a steady plan and can slow things down, but..."

"But you're playing matador for a bunch of people we don't really want to hurt," Roslyn replied, carefully slapping a bandage on another subject. "We *may* have an answer."

"I think that might be the best news I've heard all day. I see a bunch of disabled contacts on my tactical; what's the sitrep?"

"Zapped down with a mass stun spell," Roslyn told him. "And they're *staying* down. Response appears to be similar to the prior victims that underwent bioscan. Comatose."

"Fuck." The Marine was silent for a second. "But they're alive?"

"They're alive. Dr. Breda is examining blood samples and plotting stungun recalibrations," she told him. "But...my spell cleaned the air around them as well. Not sure stunguns would do the same."

"Likely not," the Marine said. "And it's not like I have lightning cannon to hand anywhere—but if there's actually something the Mages can *do*, Daalman will bring the rest of you down."

Roslyn snorted.

"You mean *lead* the rest of the Mages down herself," she said. "Yes. And if that's the answer, I'll be right there with her."

The six Mages from *Huntress*'s crew could probably handle ten thousand or so of the infected at a time. It wouldn't be a *fast* solution, but...it might just work.

"I'll keep you informed, Captain," she told him. "Keep *me* informed of the situation of the evac zone. I get the feeling that circle is still going to shrink."

"Unfortunately," he agreed. "I think we've doubled the time you've got, so I hope that's enough."

"Here's the samples, Dr. Breda," Roslyn told the other woman, sliding samples into the analysis unit one at a time. "One from the same teenager, one from a mid-thirties-ish woman, one from a forty-ish male."

"Working remotely like this sucks," Breda noted. The analysis unit had a pair of remote-operated arms in the middle of a two-meter-tall cylinder with various tools. It was, by design, next to a full bioscan unit that doubled as a surgical bed.

It wasn't so much a portable medical analysis unit as it was a remote surgery unit, but the tools had been included anyway. Just in case they were needed for that remote surgery, Roslyn supposed.

"If it gives me the answers I need, I'll make it up to you however you need, Doctor," Roslyn promised.

Breda snorted.

"I've got *part* of an answer," she told the Mage. "Give me a moment to look at the new samples."

The arms grabbed each sample in turn, taking a tinier amount of each and putting it under a microscope sending images up to the destroyer's proper medical lab.

"Okay. So, all three samples are averaging four-point-two parts per *billion*, plus minus five percent," Breda told them. "Replication level, based on what we're seeing, is around four *hundred* parts per billion.

"I ran some...destructive testing on the first blood sample while you were collecting more," she continued. "The nanites are quite resistant to electric shock, but that resistance falls off rapidly above the designed maximum charge application of SmartDarts.

"It appears to be the magnetic-field aspects of the bioscan that cause the self-destruct," Breda noted. "I suspect the combination of electrical and electromagnetic fields created by your electrical storm was a perfect counter to their defenses."

"So, magic is the answer," Roslyn said quietly. "I can live with that. We can bring in more Mages if we need to. The Link is good for that."

"I'm forwarding everything I have back to Mars via the Link as soon as we're done here," the doctor agreed. "Hopefully, they'll see something I don't. Like a way to blanket the entire city in a Mage's electrical storm."

"Nothing is coming to mind," Roslyn admitted. "I'm going to check in with the people tearing apart the base. Maybe they've found an answer—but at least we know how to knock down the crowd."

She paused, then swallowed.

"How long can we leave these people without further medical attention?" she asked.

Breda was silent for at least five seconds.

"My preference would be under ten minutes," she admitted. "If... If we don't have a choice, as we don't, I project long-term degradation of their health outcomes within twelve hours. Twenty-four before anyone starts dying...most likely."

"We can't move them," Roslyn said quietly. "We don't have the hands; we don't have anywhere to put them."

"Knock out *everyone* and the Governor can send in his people. Hell... if we're sure we can secure your park, we might be able to send in extra doctors there," Breda suggested. "I'll have to talk to the Captain."

"We might be at that point, *if* we bring the Mages down," Roslyn agreed. "I'll talk to everyone..."

She shook her head. She didn't *want* that to be her call...but it probably was.

"Send your data to Mars," she ordered. "I'm going to have Jordan pull together a conference of you, me, the Captain and the Cardinal-Governor. And while she's doing that, I'm going to see if my friends underground have any clever ideas."

Because Roslyn was up to *one* clever idea—and while that was a hell of an improvement, there was no way they could secure the city in twenty-four hours. Now she knew she could win...which meant it was time to work out how to save *more* lives.

"We're just finishing up scratching our heads here," Corporal Andrews told Roslyn after she linked to the Marine. "The decon chambers look normal enough, but we think we found the oddity."

"Magnets?" Roslyn suggested.

There was a long silence on the channel, and then Andrews sent her their helmet feed.

"Basically," they agreed. "How did you guess?"

The video showed a series of solenoids. It took Roslyn a moment to realize they were mounted on a moving bar that looked like it belonged in a car wash.

"This wasn't even part of the normal decon suite," they continued. "This bar of electromagnets was *above* the usual array of gear in the ceiling. We almost missed it." They sighed. "We *did* miss the matching bar under the floor until we went looking for it.

"From what I can tell, it sweeps the entire space with an electromagnetic field. How it does that without fucking the electronics in things like our exosuits, I'm not sure, but it didn't trigger any warning signs when we took the suits through."

"Probably calibrated not to damage cybernetics," Roslyn told them. "And designed to mimic the magnetic scans of a bioscanner—which they intentionally made the nanites vulnerable to so that we couldn't work out what the hell they were doing to people."

"That fits with what I'm seeing here, sir," Andrews agreed. "I'm sorry it took so long. We didn't realize the magnets were there until we went back a second time, thinking there *had* to be something."

"It's better than nothing, Corporal. Do we have any software data on what sequence or anything those electromagnets would be using?" she asked. "They would have it calibrated *exactly* for what we need."

"I think we can pull that from the decontamination chamber's hardware without needing access to the overall systems," Andrews agreed. "Might take a few minutes."

"That's fine, I need to talk to Knight...and then to the Mage-Captain and Cardinal-Governor," Roslyn told them. "We've found a way for Mages to deal with this shit. Now I just need a *better* answer."

Andrews snorted.

"If we have *an* answer, that's better than we were doing when you left," they pointed out.

"Agreed. Forward that software, once you have it, to Dr. Breda and Mage-Lieutenant Jordan," Roslyn ordered. "Thank you, Corporal."

She had switched over to Knight before Andrews responded.

"Corporal Knight, report," she ordered. "Please tell me you've got something. We did get you a login."

"You got a surface-level user login from your prisoner," Knight pointed out. "From that, we had to work out how to get more user logins so we didn't lock ourselves. Then we needed to create higher-security logins, and *then* we needed to find the hidden encrypted files and *then* create logins to access those files—"

"And where in that list are you?" Roslyn said.

"Finding the encrypted files," the Corporal admitted. "We've built ourselves a decent array of access logins now, but we still don't have full admin control or access to anything of Orpheus clearance—that seems to have been restricted to Lafrenz and the researchers.

"We've got some basic medical data on their test subjects and a lot of information on how this place was built, but I don't think we have any answers for you," she confessed. "I'm sorry, sir; this isn't a fast process."

"I know," Roslyn conceded. "You're linked with *Huntress*?"

"That's the only reason we've made it so far," the cyberwarfare Marine agreed. "Give us a week, sir, and we'll have everything in this database spread out for you. But I don't know if I can get you anything soon."

"Okay," Roslyn said. "You said *medical data for the test subjects*, right?"

"Yeah."

"Forward that to Dr. Breda if you haven't already," she told the Marine. "We have *a* way to disable the Orpheus victims, but they all go into a coma we can't fix yet. There might be an answer to that in the medical data—so, let's hand it to all of the damn doctors we can find."

"Will do," Knight confirmed. "Sir...I hate to admit it, but the spy would be better at this. What happened to Killough?"

"I don't know," she admitted. "I *think* he may have run afoul of a third Mage, one who abandoned the facility. We'll find him, Corporal, but I don't think we're going to do so in time to help with this."

"I'll see what I can extract for the medical data beyond what we've seen," Knight promised. "Fuck...that was what we came down here for in the first place, wasn't it?"

"Yeah. And now instead of having two thousand people suffering from post-Orpheus syndrome, we're going to have something like a *hundred* thousand," Roslyn told the other woman. "So, that data might be the most critical thing on the planet."

"Right. No pressure."

"If it was easy, I wouldn't have asked a Marine to do it."

CHAPTER 47

"**MAGE-CAPTAIN,** Cardinal-Governor, Mage-Lieutenant. Surgeon-Lieutenant."

After the first three titles she greeted the members of the meeting with, Roslyn felt that Dr. Breda also needed the hyphen. Her full rank of Surgeon-Lieutenant wasn't used very often—it was rare, in fact, for a medical officer on a warship to use *any* title other than *Doctor*—but it was hers.

"Thank you all for joining me. I believe we have an answer," Roslyn told them all.

Daalman and Guerra both straightened, looking directly at her. Jordan was supposed to be Roslyn's "face" for this meeting, but the Captain and Governor appeared to be choosing to look at Roslyn's helmet plate instead.

"I am listening, Envoy Chambers," Guerra told her. "I hope, I pray, that your answer does not involve the mass death of my electorate?"

"It does not," Roslyn confirmed. "It is not, I must warn everyone, a perfect solution in any sense. Some of the Orpheus victims *will* still die. It's not going to be a fast solution, and it's going to require more Mages than we have to fully resolve the situation."

"We have five more Mages aboard *Song of the Huntress*," Daalman pointed out instantly. "I can request reinforcements via the Link. I am not certain of the number of *Mages* we can get here quickly, but my understanding is that there are at least four Link-equipped RMN warships within three days' jump. Another four without Links—and for every day we can wait, those numbers will at least double."

"I hear hope, officers," Guerra said. "Please. Do not dash this old man's hopes. Tell me."

"We used Marines as a distraction to split one of the major crowds of infected apart," Roslyn told them. "You should have received at least some updates on that. We believe we've successfully bought several hours to provide relief to the refugees we've moved into the park.

"However, a component of the crowd, estimated at approximately twenty-five hundred infected, was still heading for the park. To avoid the use of lethal weapons, I engaged them with magic."

"I know the only way you could have done that, Lieutenant Commander," Daalman said quietly. "When are you coming down?"

"Soon," Roslyn admitted. "So, we should probably hurry this up."

"Captain?" Guerra asked.

"The Mage-Lieutenant Commander used combat drugs to restore her magic after draining her reserves," Daalman laid out bluntly. "She is going to crash completely sometime in the next twenty minutes."

"I see. Thank you, Lieutenant Commander," Guerra told Roslyn. "Continue, please."

"Navy Mages are trained in several methods of less-than-lethal engagement," Roslyn said quietly. "We use the phrasing specifically—with stunguns and Nix, we can almost guarantee full nonlethal engagement. With less-than-lethal magic, we cannot.

"Since the Orpheus weapon was designed to survive both stunguns and Nix, this was to our advantage. I electrocuted the mob and disabled them. This is normally a short-term effect, relying on pain and uncooperative muscles to disable a target for more than a few minutes.

"In this case...it appears to have disabled enough of the nanites to knock the infected out and send them into post-Orpheus syndrome, the coma we've encountered in other victims," Roslyn concluded. "The victims were below the replication threshold of the nanites, as was the air content.

"Sufficient electric shocks appear to disable the nanites," she told them. "Analysis of the decontamination chambers in the Orpheus complex shows that they used electromagnetic fields similar to those in a bioscanner to destroy any nanites present.

"Between the shock and the EM wave of our area less-than-lethal stun spells, infected crowds will go down and *stay* down, without an infectious presence. We are, of course, vulnerable to the arrival of new infected to the target area who will restore the nanite levels."

She exhaled a long, determined sigh.

"I believe that our six Mages should suffice to provide a clear safe zone around the park and the Orpheus complex itself," she told them. "That would permit us to evacuate the citizens in the park and set up a hospital there to handle the post-Orpheus patients.

"It will not be a fast process to clear the city, not without significantly more Mages, but we can begin the process of securing and evacuating civilians," Roslyn continued. "We now know the sequence of EM fields used by the decontamination chambers and should be able to duplicate it aboard shuttles.

"My biggest fear at this point is that we will lose some of the people we disable without rapid medical care."

"And that we need to secure the entire city," Guerra said quietly. "I have doctors, nurses, medical personnel and field hospitals—all ready to go. But there are hundreds of thousands of victims. With six Mages... how long to clear them all?"

"Weeks," Daalman said grimly, before Roslyn could answer. "Even with reinforcements arriving, most of our Mages cannot duplicate Commander Chambers's spell to her scale. She is a powerful Mage."

Roslyn couldn't help but wish that Jane Alexander was nearby. She'd watched the Rune Wright Crown Princess of Mars demolish a fleet from the cockpit of a shuttle—that fleet had been *far* too close, but it was still a demonstration of the power of the Rune Wrights that ruled Mars.

Either of the Alexanders could likely have swept the entire city.

"Forgive an old man his foolish questions," Guerra said after a moment's thought. "But I understand that you were working on electromagnetic-radiation weaponry to try to secure the city before. Knowing what we know now, could those weapons be used to duplicate this effect?"

Roslyn froze.

"No," she said slowly. "The warheads available to us do not create electrical shocks or electromagnetic fields in the same way that the systems and spells we're talking about do."

"But?" Daalman asked.

"I think that the nanite we are seeing in the final infection is more vulnerable than the deployment version," Roslyn said. "We've seen the deployment version exploded, blasted out of aerosol sprayers, generally treated like a stable munition.

"But the actual infection can be shocked out with *enough* electricity."

"An EMP creates localized electric fields," Jordan said quietly, the junior tactical officer the person most directly responsible for the weapons. "It wouldn't be as effective as the area spell."

"It wouldn't destroy enough of the nanites to get them beneath replication thresholds," Breda objected. "For an active victim, we're likely looking at upward of five hundred PPM of the nanites in the blood, with the replication threshold being a thousandth of that.

"Without the localized, directed pulse of the spell Commander Chambers used, you'd be looking at...maybe a fifty-percent kill rate?"

"So, we hit them ten times," Roslyn said flatly. "Or twelve, to make damn sure. We sweep the entire city with sequenced electromagnetic pulses."

"That will destroy all but our most hardened gear," Daalman warned. "Exosuits, shuttles, the city's infrastructure... We'll *create* a new humanitarian disaster."

"I have the resources of an entire world standing by," the Governor said flatly. "We can restore power, repair shuttles, rebuild power lines— but we cannot rebuild *my people.*

"*Will it work?*"

Roslyn and Breda shared a long look. Neither of them was *certain*, but...

Breda nodded.

"At the very least, we'll probably get every airborne nanite and buy ourselves time for the rest," she concluded.

"We're talking about bombarding a Protectorate world," Daalman noted. "I have that authority, but..."

"You have my permission—my *order*, if that can be done," Guerra told him.

"And that of the Voice of the Mage-Queen of Mars," Roslyn added. "I think... I think it's the way we'll save the most people, sir. As the Governor said: we can fix the city if we save the people."

"What about the Orpheus lab?" Dr. Breda asked. "Our best hope for treating the aftereffects of this nightmare is still the databases there."

"It's buried deep and it's well shielded," Roslyn told her. "We couldn't detect it from the surface, and they have a *fusion power plant* down there. The lab will be fine. Even our military equipment is going to be in trouble on the surface, but...we can replace shuttles and so forth. People are harder to duplicate."

"So be it," Mage-Captain Daalman said firmly. "Mage-Lieutenant Jordan?"

"Sir?"

"Pull together the tactical Chiefs. I need a firing plan in fifteen minutes—and my tactical officer is on the planet."

And, as both Roslyn and Daalman knew perfectly well, about to fall over.

CHAPTER 48

THE EXALT CRASH HIT exactly on schedule, hammering Roslyn with a bone-crushing exhaustion that overwhelmed every corner of her body. Despite that, she managed not to stagger as she walked out of the shuttle—now guaranteed sanitized, thanks to an electroshock anti-intrusion system—into the middle of the evacuation zone.

Bolivar was waiting at the edge of the cleared landing zone, and he saluted as she approached.

"I heard we might have a solution, sir?" he asked.

"We've got two," she told him—but she couldn't keep the exhaustion out of her voice. "Mages can neutralize them nonlethally, and we *think* we might be able to disable *all* of the nanites.

"But it's going to disable everything *else* in the city. You should have got a heads-up from *Huntress?*" Roslyn *hoped* the Guardia had received an update from *Huntress*. She certainly didn't have the energy to walk Bolivar through everything that needed to be shut down for safety. Or to warn the Marines that their armor was about to get shut down—but they, too, should have received an update from *Huntress*.

"We did," he confirmed. "Multiple high-power electromagnetic pulses? That's...going to be bad, sir, but if it works..."

"Everything we have says it should," she said. "And I need to sit down."

"Are you all right?" Bolivar asked.

"She took a Mage combat drug to deal with the crowd of infected that nearly reached the park," Lieutenant Herbert explained before Roslyn could attempt to make up a story. "The aftereffects are harsh, I'm told."

"Come with me," Bolivar told them, offering Roslyn his arm to lean on. She gratefully accepted the gesture, supporting herself on the Guardia officer as they made their way to a section of the park with chairs.

Bolivar helped Roslyn seat herself, an apparently half-unconscious gentlemanly gesture that contrasted with the armor both of them were wearing. The folding chair creaked under the weight of Roslyn's gear, but it held her up.

She looked up at the darkening sky and realized it was twilight. Less than a day. Everything that had happened since she'd entered the Orpheus lab had taken less than a day.

"It'll be soon," she told Bolivar quietly. "The perimeters are secure?"

"Your Marines have been leading them on a merry dance," the Guardia officer said, bringing up the same holographic map she'd been staring at all afternoon. "Closest infected are at least fifteen hundred meters from the line. I don't know how long that will last if this doesn't work."

"Long enough for *Huntress*'s Mages to get down afterward," she promised. "We have a backup plan."

"That's appreciated," he told her. "I'm afraid, Mage-Commander. This is my city. These are my people. I have...hope now, I suppose. But there are so many people injured, lost, afraid. Who's going to help them?"

"The Cardinal-Governor has doctors, nurses, soldiers...the entire Planetary Army and every medical practitioner he could beg, bribe or blackmail into coming. They'll be here twenty minutes after we're clear."

"And if we're not clear?"

"There will be more Navy ships and more Navy Mages on their way," she said. "It's not over yet, Victoriano, but we know the dance steps now."

"Chambers, this is Daalman," the Mage-Captain interrupted via the channel. "This is the last chance I'm going to get to say anything before we blow up the sky, so this is your heads-up.

"Firing sequence commences in sixty seconds. We have two shuttles still up here that will be dropping immediately once the firing sequence completes. *You*, Mage-Commander, are going straight back to the ship and into the medbay.

"I do *not* trust Exalt. I understand why you needed it, but I still don't trust that shit."

Roslyn chuckled. Daalman was far from alone in that sentiment. Every Navy Mage and Marine Combat Mage had access to the drug. From what she understood, less than ten percent had *ever* used it—and that was after the Martian military had fought a war.

"Understood, sir. We'll stand by for the light show. Any idea when we'll have confirmation when it works?"

"When I get down there, one way or another," Daalman said. "And, Chambers?"

"Sir?" Roslyn was too tired to object to the Mage-Captain coming down herself if the zombie plague *wasn't* resolved. She was too tired for much of *anything* at this point.

"You did good."

The chair was uncomfortable, but it was still a struggle for Roslyn to stay awake. But she managed it until a blinking icon on her HUD informed her the firing sequence had started.

"Look to the sky, Captain Bolivar," she told the Guardia man next to her. "It's going to be a hell of a light show." She paused. "We have told people *without* auto-darkening optics not to look up, right?"

"Yes," Bolivar confirmed, looking upward himself. "Everyone knows. I'm not sure I believe in salvation by nuclear weapons, but I'll take whatever God sends me today."

For a few seconds after they both looked up, there was nothing. Then Roslyn's faceplate darkened as the sky flashed bright white, the first EMP bomb detonating directly above the quarantine zone.

Everything shut down. The heads-up display on her helmet vanished without much fuss, though the faceplate remained dark, making it hard to see in the twilight around her.

Roslyn sighed—and the second sequence of bombs detonated as she finished the exhalation. Multiple flashes lit the entire sky above Nueva Portugal in brilliant flares of multicolored light as nine EMP bombs went off simultaneously.

She hadn't seen the firing program, but she could guess. They would overlay the pulses to cover the entire city, but the first detonation had been a test to let them estimate the coverage.

The next Talon Ten detonated all ten of its warheads simultaneously, a crash of light and thunder that descended on the park like a falling god. Seconds after that, *another* ten EMP warheads went off.

"How many?" Bolivar asked loudly, clearly feeling at least a little deafened.

"Nine more," Roslyn said. "Twelve in total. Enough that we should be *definitely* below replication levels across the entire damn peninsula."

Another round of bombs lit up the sky as the Guardia officer parsed that. He leaned back and looked over at her.

"It's impressive, if nothing else," he told her.

"Worst-case scenario is that we only temporarily disable the infected," Roslyn said. "Even that opens options."

More explosions lit the sky and Bolivar nodded in silence. There was a steady staccato rhythm. Every ten seconds, a Talon Ten fell from the sky and ten electromagnetic pulses tore across Nueva Portugal.

With a twenty-two-second flight time and the wait for the result of the first salvo, it took just over three minutes from Roslyn's system telling her the sequence had started to the last explosion dissipating in the sky.

She sighed.

"That's twelve," she concluded, reaching up to remove the helmet from her hazmat gear. She breathed fresh, unfiltered air for the first time in hours. Her hair was a mess, she had pressure bruises from the helmet, and she wouldn't know if she'd won for several minutes yet.

She never remembered dropping the helmet as exhaustion finally overwhelmed her.

CHAPTER 49

ROSLYN WOKE UP in the medbay. There was a distinct sterile nature to a military medical facility that made that instantly clear—and then she spotted Dr. Breda poking at the console next to her bed.

"Hey, doc," Roslyn whispered. "I'm..." She exhaled. "I'm hoping I'm okay?"

"You're fine," Breda told her, the chubby redhead stepping over to her. "It was just easier to keep you here after we ran the tests to make sure you weren't in post-Orpheus mode.

"We were worried when you didn't wake up at any point while the Captain was bringing you aboard."

Roslyn coughed.

"How long was I out?"

"Fourteen hours," the doctor told her. "You'd run yourself ragged *before* you took the Exalt. Your body had to recover from that kind of debt."

She shook her head.

"So far as I can tell, you never had any of the Orpheus weapon in your system, by the way," the doctor noted. "That's *not* true of everyone they're examining in the evac zone you put together. Several were definitely cleared by the decon units you were running.

"Damn. That could have been bad," Roslyn murmured. "I need a report."

"You need to stay right where you are," Breda told her. "Like the Captain, I don't trust Exalt, and I want to run more tests on you now that you're awake."

"Doctor, the city, my people...my mission."

"The pulse worked," Breda told her. "Samples from recovered former infected show maximum levels around half a percent of that needed for replication. The city is clear.

"There may still be some of the original delivery units floating through the air elsewhere, but Sorprendidas now knows how to handle a localized outbreak," the doctor noted. "There are tens of thousands of local personnel swarming all over Nueva Portugal. The situation is under control, Roslyn.

"You did it."

"We did it," Roslyn replied, letting herself relax back into the bed. "I swear, the only thing I did was set the damn thing off."

"It's not my place to argue with you on that, but I think the Captain will have some *very* pithy commentary—probably quoting from the report she's putting together recommending you for every medal she can think of."

"If I hadn't gone poking around, they never would have set the sprayers off."

Breda sighed, pulled up a chair and brought herself down to the level of Roslyn's resting head.

"You and I are going to have some formal sessions over this, I'm sure," she noted. "But I'm going to remind you of one basic principle: you are not responsible for what your enemy does. Lafrenz had to be brought to justice—if you hadn't gone after her now, she might have ended up deploying this weapon on *her* terms somewhere we wouldn't have had her own systems to tear apart for treatment methods.

"Now *internalize* that," Breda told her. "And then say *ahh*."

Back in a proper uniform instead of combat armor, Roslyn returned to her office to see what information she could find. There were no formal reports yet, but she could pull a lot of data.

Her original Marines were now back aboard *Huntress*, a joint cyber-warfare team from her own electronic-warfare section and the planetary government having taken over from Knight. Three Marines had been replaced by at least three dozen specialist hackers.

They might get the data faster. They might not. But Knight deserved the rest.

Her evacuation zone was now one of six treatment-and-processing zones, the greenspace of the park given up for a massive temporary hospital with twenty thousand beds. The regular hospitals had been taken over as well, but what little formal data she had suggested that they had over two hundred and fifty thousand people being treated for post-Orpheus syndrome.

There were no breakthroughs yet, but the systems were in place to keep them alive until there *were*.

The next thing she checked was Bolivar's status. He showed as available, and she hoped that he'd managed to get some sleep at some point—but she called him anyway.

"Captain Victoriano Bolivar, Nueva Portugal Guardia," he answered crisply—and then recognized her face. "Mage-Commander Chambers! You're all right."

"I'm fine. Are *you* all right?" she asked.

"I did not fall off a chair unconscious, Chambers," he pointed out drily. "I handed command of the park over to a very nervous Planetary Army Brigadier General and then fell over in a more *planned* fashion for ten hours."

"I was worried you hadn't slept," she admitted. "Are you up to date on what's going on in the city?"

"As much as anyone," he said. "You want the rundown?"

"Yeah. I feel responsible."

"You didn't do this, Commander. Lafrenz did this," he told her firmly. "But, yeah, I can give you the high-level.

"Current estimate is that we ended up with about three hundred thousand infected," he noted. "We're not entirely certain how many died, but we've got two hundred and sixty-three thousand beds filled with comatose Orpheus victims and another twenty-five thousand people who apparently hadn't progressed far enough to go comatose when the nanites were destroyed."

"We're busy processing everyone we can through bioscanners to clear out the last remaining nanites and help us ID people who, at best, aren't entirely cogent yet," he said grimly. "We haven't even started to ID the bodies.

"We have Army troops on collection detail with freezer trucks. What's left of the Guardia are knocking on doors and checking on people, but it's a slow process." He grimaced. "We have retrieved over thirty thousand bodies so far."

A weight sank into Roslyn's stomach. Thirty thousand dead. Intellectually, she understood what everyone was saying about it not being her fault, but that *hurt*.

"Speaking of identification, I need you to see if you can find someone," she said. "His name is Angus Killough. I'm forwarding you what I can of his file, but he was instrumental in us getting as far as we did."

"Who is he?" Bolivar asked.

"Even at this point, some stuff is still classified, Victoriano," she said with a small smile. "I don't know what happened to him, and I'm hoping your wellness checks will help find him."

"I'll see what I can do. Quietly," he promised. "The city is...no longer a thing of chaos, but it will be time before we fully have a grasp on what happened. Our people are going to have a mental block on this mess for a *long* time."

"I'm sorry."

"Wasn't your fault," Bolivar repeated. "And, as I understand it, you arranged the next best thing to justice we're going to get."

"Yeah," Roslyn admitted. "Lafrenz is *not* going to stand trial. She's dead."

"And God will judge her," the Sorprendidan man told her. "I'll make sure my people keep you in the loop, Mage-Commander. We will almost certainly talk again, but if we don't...thank you, Roslyn.

"It was an honor to work with you. You did all we could have asked and more. *Thank you*," he repeated.

"I did my job, Captain. Just like you."

"And sometimes, that's more than anyone could possibly ask," Bolivar said. "You saved us."

"A lot of people working together saved Nueva Portugal," Roslyn told him. "I'm just glad we managed it at all!"

"Sir?"

Roslyn looked up from her desk after ending the call with Bolivar. A junior petty officer stood in the doorway. He was probably roughly her own age, but he looked nervous, being in her office.

"Yes, Petty Officer...?"

"Petty Officer Second Class Giraldo Coumans, sir," he said with a crisp salute. "We have a Link communication request for you from Mars. You're to report to the secure communications center."

Coumans looked nervous, clearly concerned about passing on orders to a superior officer. He was just the messenger, though—and Roslyn could guess who the order actually came from.

"Understood, Petty Officer Coumans. Thank you. Do you know who the request is from?"

"The Prince-Regent, sir," the noncom managed to squeak out.

As Roslyn had expected. Time to face the music for the use of the Warrant.

CHAPTER 50

THE SECURE COMMUNICATIONS chamber was set up as a standard conference room, with a Navy-issue standard table connected to a full wallscreen connected to the Link FTL communicator. Cut off from every other part of the ship, it was theoretically immune to eavesdropping of any kind.

Roslyn took her seat gingerly and tapped a command to close the room and accept the call. The wallscreen lit up, fading from metal into the crowned-mountain seal of the Protectorate—and then a moment later into the image of a slim middle-aged woman.

"Ah, Mage-Lieutenant Commander Roslyn Chambers?" she asked. "I'm Moxi Waller, the Prince-Regent's secretary and personal assistant. Please hold on while I connect the Prince-Regent and the Mage-Queen."

The screen dissolved back into the crowned mountain before Roslyn could even question the involvement of the Mage-Queen. She stared blankly at the seal for several seconds before it faded into a split-screen view.

Damien Montgomery was on the right side of the screen, his gloved hands resting on the big wooden desk in his office, the room she'd last seen him in. There were no babies or kittens in the room this time, but the Prince-Regent looked pleased with himself.

Her Majesty, Kiera Alexander, Mage-Queen of Mars, occupied the left half of the screen. The petite redheaded monarch was wearing the last thing Roslyn had ever expected to see her Queen in: a dress. It was a slim-fitting white sheath dress that stretched well below the camera view, and the young Mage-Queen *also* wore a relieved expression.

"*Thank you*," Alexander stage-whispered. "I'm afraid I've been pulled away from the reception for the arrival of the new Legatan Senator. What a shame."

"Eva Abatangelo will be an important part of the new Senate," Montgomery said gently. "The election *should* have been a year ago, but... better late than never."

"I like Eva," Alexander countered. "I *don't* like her head of staff, and the party was being barely tolerable. Besides, this is actually important."

"It is. Chambers, are you all right?" Montgomery asked Roslyn. "The last report we had from Mage-Captain Daalman said you were injured?"

"Unconscious, not injured, I hope," Roslyn corrected. "I took a dose of Exalt to protect the safe zone we'd established. I crashed afterward, exactly as expected." She grimaced. "I don't plan on repeating the experience."

"I've never taken it," Montgomery admitted. "But I'm told it's not a pleasant experience."

"Given the feeling of power from using the stuff, I imagine that's intentional," Roslyn admitted. Though it could also link to the fact that the medication was extremely dangerous—potentially *lethal*—for non-Mages.

"Captain Daalman told us the situation was mostly resolved thanks to you," Alexander noted. "I want your observations and assessment of the situation. Both as it unfolded and the final result.

"You did, after all, bear my Voice through all of this," the young Queen said calmly and firmly.

"I had hoped not to use it," Roslyn said quietly. "But the situation rapidly fell out of my control. I've never encountered anything like the Orpheus weapon before."

"No one in the Protectorate ever has," Montgomery reminded her. "It represents a fusion of magic and technology that worries me. I had hoped that we could use the developments in magitech that Finley worked on to benefit humanity, not create new ways to violate and hurt people."

"Finley appears to have sourced some monsters for his service," Roslyn agreed. She took a deep breath and considered the situation.

"I think it's best to start at the beginning and go through as much as I can," she told them. "Our operation began when we located the apartment rented by Angus Killough and scouted it out..."

The entire debrief took over an hour, and Roslyn felt completely wrung out when she finished.

"The sequenced EMPs worked," she told them. "We believe we have neutralized all active quantities of the Orpheus weapon on the surface of Sorprendidas. There are likely samples still stored in the lab that we will locate once the cyberwarfare team cracks open their security."

"Then you will give your final order as Voice to those teams," Alexander said quietly. "Any samples of the Orpheus weapon are to be held safely until we have confirmed we can treat this post-Orpheus syndrome, and then completely destroyed.

"I want nothing left of this monstrosity Ulla Lafrenz created," the Mage-Queen told them. "We have no need of such a weapon, and I have no desire to see it in the hands of anyone who would threaten the Protectorate."

"We don't have many enemies left," Montgomery noted, "but the capacity to manufacture the Orpheus weapon would turn a small terrorist movement into a planetary-scale threat."

"I will make certain it is all destroyed," Roslyn promised.

"Good. There are more resources on their way to Sorprendidas as we speak," the Prince-Regent told her. "Not just the warships Mage-Captain Daalman already summoned but humanitarian aid and industrial-support ships.

"It will take time to rebuild Nueva Portugal. Sorprendidas could do it alone, but—"

"No planet in my Protectorate is alone," Alexander finished for her Regent. "The tone of the Cardinal-Governor's request for assistance was such that I do not know if he truly believed he would get it.

"He will. And more. Nueva Portugal will be rebuilt at the expense of the Protectorate," the Queen concluded. "That will be made formal in the next few days, but you are welcome to share that with Governor Guerra as my representative.

"As for yourself, Mage-Lieutenant Commander Chambers, you have been our Voice well and faithfully. Your mission appears done, and so your Warrant ends," Alexander said formally. "I am beyond grateful for your service. Thousands live who might have died if I had sent another—or not sent a Voice at all.

"What reward would a faithful servant ask of the Mountain?"

Roslyn stared at the wallscreen in utter surprise.

"My Queen, I..." She swallowed. "I did nothing for a reward. This was my duty as an officer of the Royal Martian Navy, as a bearer of the Warrant you gave me...as a Mage and as a human being. I did nothing I would not expect of another."

"Your expectations of your fellow officers and Mages, Lieutenant Commander, may be rather high," Montgomery said drily. "Though they do align with mine."

"If you do not wish it, I won't force adulation and award upon you," Alexander told Roslyn—but there was a mischievous smile on the young monarch's face.

"I did my duty, nothing more," Roslyn said.

"You know the reward for a job well done is another job, yes?" Montgomery asked. "Your Warrant will expire once you have given the orders for the disposition of the Orpheus weapon, but your service will not be forgotten."

"I have a very short list of officers I know and trust, Lieutenant Commander," the Mage-Queen of Mars said calmly. "It grows by the day, but you are on it, and believe me when I say you will likely regret that one day."

Alexander smiled.

"For now, I believe we have exhausted you enough. Thank you, Roslyn Chambers, for honoring my Protectorate as I could expect far too few to do."

CHAPTER 51

THE NAVAL COMPONENT of the cyberwarfare team working away in the Orpheus lab reported to Roslyn, which meant she was the one interrupted when Chief Trevis called up to the ship.

Of course, what Trevis interrupted was Roslyn operating as air traffic controller, supporting the Sorprendidans' efforts in Nueva Portugal. The destroyer's sensors were notably better than those available to Sorprendidas's people, so they were providing data and backup hands to the locals.

It was the work of moments to pass her current workload over to Mage-Lieutenant Samuels, the officer of the watch.

"Chief," she greeted Trevis as she opened the video call. "I've been watching for your call. Any updates?"

"Yes, sir," the noncom said crisply. "We've found the medical files on post-Orpheus syndrome. With your permission, I'll forward them to the locals immediately."

"Granted. Get those files over right *now*," she ordered. "Hell, hang up on me if you need to."

Trevis chuckled.

"I'd already passed them to the local cyber team for packaging and distribution," he admitted. "They did a lot of the grunt work, but it was our people at the point. The software, the gear, everything here was the Republic's best.

"Better, even. I did some training sessions on what was supposed to be the Intelligence Directorate's last generation of hardware and software," he noted. "This stuff was better."

"And you're through?" she asked.

"Yeah, but..."

He trailed off, shrugging helplessly.

"That doesn't sound positive, Chief," Roslyn said quietly.

"We had a crack in the armor from the access logins you got from the security guard," Trevis told her. "It still took us a while to get control of the system, and even then, there were high-security sections we didn't have control of.

"Once inside those sections, we were expecting to collide with more security and more encrypted files," the noncom concluded. "Except...we didn't."

"I don't understand," Roslyn said.

"The files on post-Orpheus syndrome were right there, with the equivalent of a giant flashing neon sign pointing to them," Trevis told her. "Someone had decrypted them and put them behind the security barriers in the first place we'd look.

"Everything else is gone."

She blinked, taking a moment to be sure she understood what the Chief was saying.

"The files were deleted?" she asked.

"Copied, deleted, hashed and destroyed," Trevis confirmed. "We have the post-Orpheus syndrome treatment records and experiments and the general records on the prisoners. Our less-secured files gave us a lot of logistical detail on the laboratory, but everything on the Orpheus weapon and the Orpheus Project itself were behind the high-security barriers.

"All of that is gone."

Roslyn sighed grimly. They'd known someone had accessed Lafrenz's computers, but they hadn't had time to do that much.

"When?" she asked.

"It's hard to say," the noncom told her. "Definitely after we penetrated the facility, but...it honestly could have been anytime before we breached the final security layers. We'll dig more, see if we can find anything, but I'm not hopeful.

"The cleanup job was *very* thorough. The only reason we have the POS treatment data is because the person doing this *wanted* us to have it."

"Do we have enough to help?" she asked.

"I only took a surface skim of the data myself, but it looked like Lafrenz had a detailed treatment plan, not just experimental data. I'm no doctor, sir, but I think it's exactly what they need to help those people.

"I think it's more than we dared hope we had, even."

But the actual data on the weapon was gone. Worse, the data on the Orpheus *Project* and the people behind it was gone.

"Are you certain the data was copied before it was destroyed?" Roslyn asked. "Someone took this with them?"

"One hundred percent," Trevis confirmed. "They were good, but we have full hardware access. I can tell that several petabytes of data were transferred out of the system from the console we suspect was used."

"Damn." She shook her head. "That's not what I was hoping to hear, Chief. Any *other* bad news?"

"There was a fail-safe magnetic burn system installed on the sample-storage facility," Trevis told her. "We couldn't even *find* the damn storage until we broke the final security layer, but someone activated the fail-safe.

"From the video I'm getting of the storage unit, they had samples of forty-six different iterations of the nanite. All have been destroyed."

"I can live with that, to be honest," Roslyn admitted. "Our orders were to destroy any existing samples once we were certain we could treat the victims anyway."

"Can't argue with the logic, sir," Trevis said. "The test-subject records are bad enough."

"We'll want to make sure the Guardia gets those, too," she told him. "We can at least give the poor victims' families some closure."

"I will, sir," he promised. "What now, sir?"

"Finish up down there," Roslyn ordered. "Make sure you've cleaned out their main databases and that there aren't any personal wrist-comps or datapads floating around. My understanding is that our tour of duty isn't being adjusted, so we'll be here for a while.

"If we've got what we need to help the victims, the rush is over. Take the time to do it right."

Guerra, Daalman and Kristofferson looked disappointed but...unsurprised.

"I was expecting these meshuggener to have set something up to destroy their data," the XO said once Roslyn had completed her report.

Huntress's three officers were in Daalman's office, with the Cardinal-Governor's image taking up an entire wall as the old priest listened to them.

"That someone has copied it is disturbing," Guerra noted. "God will judge the people who built the weapon—Commander Chambers has seen to that—but I will admit I had prayed it would not leave my world.

"I fear we are now too late to guarantee that."

"Unfortunately, Your Excellency, you are correct," Roslyn told him. "With the level of chaos in Nueva Portugal and the wide options for exiting the Project Orpheus facility, we have no way of identifying who left the base with the data.

"While there has been limited traffic off of Sorprendidas since then, there is no way we can do anything to prevent the data leaving the planet."

"Are we certain of that?" Guerra asked. "It seems that such a threat would justify significant searches of outgoing shuttles and vessels."

"It wouldn't help," Daalman admitted. "Between your local resources and the RMN ships arriving tomorrow and later, we could search every single ship leaving Sorprendidas. But we could *dismantle* them and still never find the data on a ship carrying it.

"Hiding a data storage device is simply too easy. I'm tempted to make the effort regardless, Your Excellency, but I can see no value in it."

"God willing, it has fallen into the hands of someone who will destroy it," Guerra said. "We believe they are also the one who made the post-Orpheus treatment plan easily found?"

"We only have evidence of one person penetrating the facility other than us," Roslyn agreed. "They were definitely a Mage and definitely hostile to both Orpheus and us. But they also clearly felt a moral responsibility to make sure that data was in our hands.

"A moral responsibility I do not believe anyone from Project Orpheus would feel."

"They are demons, lost to the sight of God," Guerra ground out. "I pray that His wisdom guides the Navy to them sooner rather than later."

"We will be watching," Daalman promised. "The data and its thieves will not escape forever."

"So I pray." Guerra sighed. "In all this disaster, your ship and your people—especially Commander Chambers—have been present and willing to help.

"Thank you."

Unspoken was that the Cardinal-Governor probably didn't think he'd have received the same level of help from the Republican Interstellar Navy—if the RIN had even *had* a ship in Sorprendidas.

Even with the Promethean Interfaces and their murdered Mage brains, the RIN had never had enough ships to worry about local security.

"That is the mission we were sent here to carry out," Daalman told the Governor. "We are tasked with honoring Her Majesty's Protectorate. You are under the protection of Mars. That means something more and greater than merely being part of a nation. It means that we—that *someone* from Mars—*will be here* when you need it.

"That is Her Majesty's oath, the promise that underlines everything that defines the nation we serve, Governor Guerra," the Mage-Captain said. "Whatever you need, if we can provide it, we will."

"Thank you, Mage-Captain." Guerra shook his head. "A few weeks ago, even, I would have regarded those as fancy words meant to soothe the raised hackles of former secessionists. Today... Today I recognize them as God's own truth.

"And I thank you."

The wallscreen dimmed to darkness and Daalman exhaled a long sigh.

"I would love to believe that Project Orpheus was just this one lab," he said quietly. "But the Red List exists and tells me that there are another *dozen* Mages out there like Lafrenz."

"We're going to have an ugly few years," Kristofferson agreed. "But, as you told the Governor, Her Majesty will *not* leave those meshuggener be. We will hunt them down and we will make our people safe."

"From your lips to whoever's listening," Roslyn murmured. She wasn't very religious, though the exposure to the Sorprendidans' faith had been interesting.

"Indeed. But speaking of Her Majesty," Daalman said, "I have one more duty from her to discharge before we finish up this meeting. Chambers?"

"Sir?" Roslyn said, straightening her back and facing her commanding officer.

"Everything you did here was technically under your orders from Her Majesty as a Voice," the Mage-Captain pointed out. "While you unquestionably rose above and beyond your duties as tactical officer of this ship, you operated entirely inside orders you had received."

"I did my duty, sir. Nothing more," Roslyn agreed, as calmly as she could.

"So I'm advised you told the *Mage-Queen,*" Daalman said with a chuckle. "Fortunately, neither she nor I nor the emergency promotion board she ordered convened agrees with you there."

The Mage-Captain slid a velvet jeweler's box across the table.

"This was a sufficient nightmare that I don't know if there are going to be awards or medals out of it," she told the younger woman. "But Her Majesty had some clear opinion that *some* recognition was due—and my own reports agreed with her.

"Open it," Daalman ordered.

Roslyn obeyed. The golden pin inside wasn't significantly different from the one she already wore at her collar. Many civilians might not even notice that the middle bar was thicker—but any Navy officer or spacer would.

It wasn't the insignia of a Royal Martian Navy Lieutenant Commander. It was the insignia of a *full* Commander.

"Sir, I..."

"Will not be even in the youngest ten officers ever promoted to Commander," Daalman told her bluntly. "Somewhere around number seventeen, in fact—there were a *lot* of battlefield promotions going around at the start of the war."

Roslyn had received a battlefield commission at the same time, so that made sense. A lot of ships had fled from the overwhelming Republic surprise attack under the command of junior officers.

"It is the considered and weighted opinion of a board of eight senior officers that your actions on Sorprendidas were in the highest and best standards of the Protectorate of Mars and the Royal Martian Navy."

Daalman snorted.

"Five out of eight officers on that board admitted that *they* would probably have given up and used lethal force on a massive scale to secure the city. I think that they may be doing themselves an injustice, but that you chose another course remains to your credit.

"A quarter-million people are alive today because of you. They are receiving medical treatment that will allow them to return to their lives at least physically restored. While they will all require immense mental-health assistance over the years to come, it is thanks to *your* determination that they were as innocent as everyone else that they are alive to receive that help."

Daalman smiled thinly and delicately pushed the box a few centimeters closer to Roslyn.

"Take the damn insignia, Commander Chambers. You're still going to be my tactical officer, and we have work to do."

CHAPTER 52

"I HEAR congratulations are in order."

Roslyn couldn't keep herself from touching the new insignia on her collar as Bolivar spoke, then shook her head at the Guardia officer.

"I think it's more on the order of the 'the reward for a job well done is another job,'" she told him. "I hear they're considering *you* for Commissioner."

"Maybe," Bolivar said. "There are half a dozen Captains who distinguished themselves after Commissioner Petrovich died." He paused. "Most of us didn't even know he was dead. Communication in the Guardia was pretty rough there, even before you EMPed the city into the Stone Age."

"Everything's up and running now, though?" she asked.

"Full networks, full databases, the Guardia is back online and running," he agreed. "That's part of why I made contact."

"How's the treatment going?" Roslyn said.

"Better than expected," Bolivar told her. "We've got the first ten thousand out of the hospitals already. They're still going to need to be monitored for weeks at least, but they're walking and talking and remember who they are.

"Can't ask for more after everything that happened."

"Thank god," she said. "I can't imagine the nightmare they've been through, though. It was bad enough from our side."

"The doctors are setting up long-term psych treatment plans for, well, the entire city," Bolivar told her. "We're in control, but it's still a mess.

Power is expected to be back up everywhere tomorrow, but we're not even entirely sure we've found all the bodies yet."

She grimaced.

"Forgive me, but I'm glad I'm up here running air control instead of doing that," she admitted.

"That's fair," he said. He shook his head. "I've got a few requests on that front, but first...I did manage to find the guy you were looking for. Sort of."

"You found Killough?" Roslyn asked. "Thank God."

She'd thought he'd been taken by whatever ninja/Mage/hacker had stolen the Orpheus files.

"Like I said, sort of," Bolivar replied. "I guess...his family is almost lucky this mess happened. We normally only keep John Doe bodies on ice for about four weeks before they go in a pauper's grave."

Roslyn's train of thought derailed.

"He's dead?" she asked slowly. Angus Killough was dead. That...*hurt*, even against the scale of the crisis in Nueva Portugal. She hadn't had the people to go after him. He'd clearly been of *some* value to his kidnapper...

Then the timeline caught up with her.

"What do you mean, he's been dead for *four weeks*?" she demanded.

"I was wondering about that myself, since you weren't here then," Bolivar admitted. A file photo appeared on the screen next to the attractive Guardia officer. "John Doe One-Three-Five-Six," he reeled off. "Pulled from the beach thirty-seven days, a bit over five weeks, ago.

"No evidence of trauma; autopsy suggested death by drowning. It looked like he'd been thrown off a boat with some kind of weights around his ankles."

The Guardia officer coughed delicately.

"That call was made by the fact that his ankles and feet are missing," he admitted.

Roslyn was looking at the photo. It...was not the Angus Killough she'd met.

A few commands brought up the MISS file on the agent. The photo matched the dead man, a chubby, heavyset man of middle age. A few more commands brought up the man she'd been working with.

The stranger *looked* like Angus Killough...but an Angus Killough that had lost weight. She'd assumed that was exactly what had happened—he'd been missing for over six weeks, after all.

"Fuck," she said softly. "Bolivar...the civilian we went into the Orpheus lab with was supposedly Angus Killough, a Martian Interstellar Security Service agent."

The channel was silent, and Bolivar looked at his screen again.

"You gave us a DNA profile, everything," he told her. "There's no question. John Doe One-Three-Five-Six *is* Angus Killough. We can keep the body on ice and return it to his family—or to MISS, I suppose—but he's definitely been dead for at least...forty days. Maybe more."

"I'm not doubting you, Victoriano," Roslyn said. "It's just...if this is Angus Killough, who the hell did I lead into the Orpheus lab?"

CHAPTER 53

THE LAST SECURITY HATCH shredded under the force of three fully trained Combat Mages. Black-exosuited Nemesis troopers surged through ahead of Mage Kent Riley, penetrator rifles firing as they engaged the holdout Augments aboard the space station.

"Remember," he said calmly. "We need Dr. Carpenter alive."

"Room is secure, sir," a trooper reported.

There were no names here. Kent Riley had adopted that from his mentor, the man *he'd* eventually known as Winton. Roslyn Chambers had known him as Angus Killough—and he did *not* miss the facial prosthetics for that disguise, though the young Mage had impressed him.

Among people who knew *what* he was, even his closest people only knew him as "Kay." Everyone else knew him as Nemesis One, the only leader the organization had left now.

Those who even knew that much. With Winton's death, they were doing everything they could to make sure the Protectorate thought Nemesis had died with their founder.

Kent walked into the room, flanked by two other ex–Royal Martian Marine Combat Mages. One of his black-armored troopers was being treated for a gunshot wound that had gone through the exosuit, but all of his people had survived the breach.

None of the Augments had been so lucky.

GLYNN STEWART

In the middle of the space station command center was the man those Augments had died trying to protect.

"Dr. Damir Carpenter," Kent said calmly. "Project head of the Orpheus Project."

"I have no idea what you're talking about," Carpenter said, glancing nervously at the rifles pointed at him. The penetrator rifles could go through exosuit armor. What they'd do if they hit the unarmored scientist was *indescribable*.

"You were the mind behind the Orpheus nanotech system," Kent told Carpenter. "Initial concepts were developed here, on this station, and then forwarded to a secret lab on Sorprendidas when you realized you needed more test subjects than you'd be able to source in an uninhabited star system."

"This is a private corporate research facility, registered with the Protectorate out of Legatus," Dr. Carpenter insisted. "This is an act of piracy and murder!"

"All of that is true, yes," Kent said cheerfully. "But it does not change that your operation—and the corporation that is the registered owner of this station—is funded by money Samuel Finley defrauded the Republic of before its fall.

"You could play all the games you want about authority and legal proof and suchlike if I was with the Martians, but I'm not," he told Carpenter. His own exosuit loomed over the suit-clad doctor.

"My people are already placing thermonuclear demolition charges throughout this station while others are stripping your databases of anything useful. They've already told me that the files here are a disappointment.

"The Sorprendidas lab made it further than you did. The test subjects were important, I guess, for all that their acquisition doomed you."

"Who *are* you?" Carpenter asked.

"I am the man charged to see that humanity survives the inevitable," Kent told the scientist. "And everything that has been done on this station and on Sorprendidas alike is an atrocity I would love to execute you out of hand for; do you understand me, Dr. Carpenter?"

"We lost contact with Sorprendidas," Carpenter said grimly.

"Yes, six months ago, when one of my agents destroyed the covert Link facility you were operating," Kent agreed. "The Protectorate finished the job after that. I'm afraid your wife is dead, Dr. Carpenter. Mage Lafrenz was killed resisting arrest when the Navy came for her."

"Bastards," Carpenter cursed.

"You are not one to talk," Nemesis's leader snapped. "Your life now hangs on one very simple question, Dr. Carpenter.

"If I can provide you with Rune Scribes to work on the matrix, and all of Lafrenz's notes and experimental data, can you complete the Orpheus nanotech?"

"The Orpheus weapon is—"

"I don't give a fuck about the weapon," Kent cut him off. "It's horrific and frankly impractical. I am charged with the task of preserving humanity, Doctor. A planetary-denial weapon that only works on humans is useless to me.

"No, Dr. Carpenter, you only get to live if you can complete the *original* Orpheus System. Can you or can you not complete the mind-control nanotech?"

ABOUT THE AUTHOR

GLYNN STEWART is the author of Starship's Mage, a bestselling science fiction and fantasy series where faster-than-light travel is possible–but only because of magic. His other works include science fiction series Duchy of Terra, Castle Federation and Vigilante, as well as the urban fantasy series ONSET and Changeling Blood.

Writing managed to liberate Glynn from a bleak future as an accountant. With his personality and hope for a high-tech future intact, he lives in Kitchener, Ontario with his partner, their cats, and an unstoppable writing habit.

CREDITS

The following people were involved in making this book:
Copyeditor: Richard Shealy
Proofreader: M Parker Editing
Cover art: Jeff Brown Graphics
Layout and typesetting: Red Cape Production, Berlin
Faolan's Pen Publishing team: Jack, Kate, and Robin.

OTHER BOOKS
BY GLYNN STEWART

For release announcements join the
mailing list or visit **GlynnStewart.com**

STARSHIP'S MAGE
Starship's Mage
Hand of Mars
Voice of Mars
Alien Arcana
Judgment of Mars
UnArcana Stars
Sword of Mars
Mountain of Mars
The Service of Mars
A Darker Magic
Mage-Commander
Beyond the Eyes of Mars (upcoming)

Starship's Mage: Red Falcon
Interstellar Mage
Mage-Provocateur
Agents of Mars

Pulsar Race: A Starship's Mage Universe Novella

DUCHY OF TERRA
The Terran Privateer
Duchess of Terra
Terra and Imperium
Darkness Beyond
Shield of Terra
Imperium Defiant
Relics of Eternity
Shadows of the Fall
Eyes of Tomorrow

SCATTERED STARS

Scattered Stars: Conviction
Conviction
Deception
Equilibrium
Fortitude
Huntress (upcoming)
Scattered Stars: Evasion
Evasion (upcoming)

PEACEKEEPERS OF SOL

Raven's Peace
The Peacekeeper Initiative
Raven's Course
Drifter's Folly
Remnant Faction (upcoming)

EXILE

Exile
Refuge
Crusade
Ashen Stars: An Exile Novella

CASTLE FEDERATION

Space Carrier Avalon
Stellar Fox
Battle Group Avalon
Q-Ship Chameleon
Rimward Stars
Operation Medusa
A Question of Faith: A Castle Federation Novella

SCIENCE FICTION STAND ALONE NOVELLA

Excalibur Lost

Made in the USA
Las Vegas, NV
13 August 2024